Undeniable

FRANCIS RAY

Undeniable

ARABESQUE®

UNDENIABLE

An Arabesque novel

Arabesque/July 2007

ISBN-13: 978-0-373-83069-5
ISBN-10:   0-373-83069-6

First published by Kensington Publishing Corp.

www.kimanipress.com

Printed in U.S.A.

To my daughter, Carolyn Michelle Ray,
the delight of my life.

Special appreciation to Reggie Miller, Office Engineer,
Con-Real, Inc., and Mc Radford Jr., whose broad base
of knowledge always amazes his baby sister.
Thanks, fellows, for your never-ending patience.

Chapter 1

"I can't go."

"Well, I certainly can't leave Little Rock and go to Stanton, Texas, with this busted leg," came the terse reply from the couch.

Logan Prescott's defiant black gaze met that of his partner, Charles Dawson, before making a sweeping glance of the white cast covering Charles's left leg from mid-thigh to within a hair's breadth of his toes. Logan muttered an expletive under his breath. You'd think a fifty-three-year-old man who ran a multimillion-dollar construction company would know better than to attempt intermediate slopes his first time skiing.

Charles didn't even have the excuse of trying to make

points with a woman. He and his wife had been happily married for over fifteen years. No, Charles's excuse was that if he still had enough coordination to walk a twelve-inch-wide steel beam thirty stories up in their construction business, he could handle the ski slopes.

And despite his broken leg, he firmly maintained that if another skier hadn't cut in front of him and jarred his concentration, he wouldn't have hit the tree. Six feet tall, two hundred and thirty pounds, and built like a linebacker, Charles was a man who seldom changed his mind or backed away from an argument. But, neither was Logan.

Logan bit back another expletive. This time Charles was going to lose. After the hell Logan went through in Stanton eight years ago, he had made a vow never to set foot in the small East Texas town again.

Dark brown calloused fingers brushed across short black hair. "Gage can take care of things in Stanton," Logan said finally. "I need to finish the job in Springtown."

"Gage is the best foreman we've ever had, but he's just that…a foreman. The city manager and mayor of Stanton are expecting to see one of the owners of Bridgeway Construction Company," Charles explained, as he tried unsuccessfully to maneuver a brown, blunt-tipped finger beneath the layers of plaster to scratch.

"When I met with them a month ago and it looked like we were going to win the bid to build Stanton's city hall complex, I assured them that I would be there the first couple of days once the announcement was made in case anyone had any questions. Since I can't go, you'll have to."

Logan prowled the length of the white leather couch Charles reclined on, his booted feet soundless on the thick peach-colored carpet. The tranquil setting of the lake and woods beyond the immense plate-glass window did nothing to ease his irritation. "The Orion office complex in Little Rock—"

"Is a month ahead of schedule. If problems arise that the project manager can't handle, Gage can be there in an hour." Charles's brown eyes narrowed as he watched the angry strides of the man he had called friend for eight years and partner for six. "You're that afraid of seeing *her?*"

Logan stopped in mid-stride and spun around. A moment of unease swept through him, but none of the turbulent emotion he felt showed in his face. "What are you talking about?"

"You know. The *her* you've been running from since you left Stanton. The *her* you don't seem able to forget," Charles answered bluntly.

Logan's six-foot-three body of conditioned muscles clenched. His piercing black eyes narrowed. "You don't know what you're talking about."

"Yes, I do. Over the years you've told me more than once that Ida Mae Jones is your oldest friend. Yet you've never visited her in Stanton. I waited for you to go back once you decided to go along with her idea of renovating a condemned mansion and turning it into a shopping complex. Knowing how cautious you are about investing your money, I was stunned when you kept making excuses not to go see the place.

"When she declared she wanted your partnership more than your financial backing in one of the stores and you still didn't budge, I knew something wasn't right," Charles continued. "You confirmed my suspicions when you insisted I oversee the renovations on the Victorian mansion instead of doing it yourself."

"I trust you," Logan pointed out.

"That never stopped you from asking questions about a project before. You're fair, but demanding. You expect the best from yourself and everyone involved with Bridgeway and you've never settled for less. Yet, you acted as if the Victorian House didn't exist. So," Charles replied with a smile, "my guess is there's a woman involved. One particular woman you can't forget." Charles nodded toward Logan's clenched fists. "If you lay one finger on me, Helen is going to rearrange that handsome face of yours."

Logan's dark brow arched. Charles's wife was the gentlest, sweetest woman he knew. He started to snort, then recalled Helen's fierceness when it came to protecting her husband and their two kids. In the thirty minutes Logan had been at their lake home, she had checked on Charles at least twice. That kind of loyalty and love from a woman was priceless.

Once Logan thought he had finally gotten that lucky to find such a woman. A woman he would cherish and love for a lifetime. On a hot summer morning eight years ago he had been proved wrong…in spades.

"I'm not running from anyone," Logan said tightly.

"You must have hit your head on something when you took that tumble. You should have had it X-rayed along with your leg."

Charles shook his graying head and sent Logan a look of understanding. "Go back and face her, man. She probably has seven children and is as wide as I am," he offered, resting his folded hands on his wide girth in apparent satisfaction that he had spoken a truth.

A picture of a slim, beautiful girl with laughing, light brown eyes and cocoa-colored skin flashed in front of Logan. Hard-won discipline thrust the image from his mind. "I never said there was a woman."

"You didn't have to. Even the hardest working men I know like to take time now and then for a little relaxation. In the first two months I knew you in Oklahoma, you never accepted one invitation for a beer or a friendly card game. You just kept working harder than any two men and stayed to yourself. You were always the first to arrive at the job site and the last to leave; the first to offer to work overtime. I didn't know if you were trying to make brownie points, or be a millionaire, or you had woman problems."

Unconsciously, Logan's hands clenched again. Before today Logan had always admired his partner's intuition. Now Charles was getting too close to memories Logan had ruthlessly sought to bury. He didn't like to remember he was ever that stupid or that vulnerable.

Charles looked at Logan with knowing eyes, glanced

at the doorway and lowered his voice to a barely audible whisper. "You had me wondering which woman until you blew up that night at Bessie's club. It was a good thing Bessie was a close friend of mine."

Logan remembered the night in Oklahoma City with crystal clarity. He had gone with his construction crew to the small blues club because he had finally and irrevocably been shown that all his hopes and prayers for the woman he loved to change her mind and contact him had been for nothing. A polished, snotty lawyer had made sure Logan understood his client wanted nothing more to do with him. Apparently her future didn't include a man with dirt beneath his fingernails. Needing to dull the memory of the lawyer's visit, Logan had finally tagged along with the men.

Two hours later he had been ruthlessly working his way through a bottle of Jack Daniels in search of oblivion when a woman reeking of cheap perfume and stale sweat had invited herself to his table and to his whiskey. Feeling none too kindly toward women in general since he was trying to forget one in particular, he told the woman to go heavier on the bathwater and lighter on the perfume before she tried to mooch off someone else in the future.

The next thing he knew, some man with tree trunks for arms and dinner plates for hands had him by the collar roaring that he had insulted his sister. Laying hands on Logan was the wrong thing to do to a man who had been pushed to his limit. Logan's balled fist slammed into the man's bulbous nose. The fight was on. By the time it was over, the club was a wreck, the man who had attacked Logan was out cold, and the police were working their way through shattered glass, broken chairs and overturned tables.

Weaving unsteadily on his feet amid the shambles of the room, Logan closed his eyes and shook his head to clear the alcoholic haze. The sound of a rough male voice telling him to face the wall snapped his eyelids upward. Two policemen were less than ten feet away. One stepped forward to make Logan do as requested, the other began citing the Miranda Act.

Charles had rushed forward with Bessie Brown, the club's singer/owner. Although the robust woman's brown eyes were glittering like the jagged edge of a broken beer bottle, she backed up Charles's story that Logan had only defended himself. At Charles's urging, she agreed not to press charges if Logan paid for half the damages.

Logan was given a stern warning instead of a ride in a patrol car. He hadn't minded paying Bessie because he was partially to blame. Not like the other time when he had been faced with jail and he had been completely innocent.

"I still think I ought to arrest him."

"I still don't care what you think, Sheriff. And since I'm the one with the license to practice medicine, you'll have to go by what I say," Dr. Perry said, glancing again at the resident putting the last strip of tape on the bandage covering Logan Prescott's entire chest.

Sheriff Stone gave the peak of his sweat-rimmed straw hat a firm yank before settling his hand once again near his service revolver. The holster was unsnapped. "Johnson and the men at the construction site said Prescott here caused Mr. Malone's heart attack."

Dr. Perry sent the sheriff a slanting glance. "I thought Johnson was a construction foreman. When did *he* go to medical school?"

"Dammit, Doc, I ain't got no time for your tongue," the sheriff snapped. "You know Malone carries a lot of weight in this community. I don't want it said I didn't do my duty simply because he's black."

The sheriff and his anger were ignored as Dr. Perry stepped closer to the exam table on which Logan sat, then pressed gnarled, experienced fingers over the dressing. "How does this feel, son?"

"Better," Logan said, as he watched the scowling face of the sheriff out of the corner of his eye. More than once they had had a run in, but so far, Logan had yet to spend a night in Stone's jail—a fact the sheriff was obviously trying to rectify.

"What were you and Mr. Malone arguing about?" Sheriff Stone asked.

Logan's expression became shuttered. "Working conditions."

"My Aunt Fanny," Stone hissed and moved closer. "Now, you listen and you listen good. I've had about enough of your uppity, sullen ways. Just because your parents left you a house on a little bit of property doesn't mean you're any better than anyone else in town. You know, Malone hires a lot of men in his construction business, men who have to feed their families. You threaten a man's family and you've stepped into a hornets' nest. I have over fifty of Malone's men wanting a piece of your hide so I advise you to tell the truth. If you don't want them on your head, you—"

"Ned, stop bothering my patient," the doctor ordered and placed his narrow frame between Logan and the muscular sheriff. "Just because Logan likes to keep to himself is no reason to be so judgmental. Besides, those men you're so anxious to pacify probably didn't vote for you in the last election anyway." The doctor winked at Logan, his gray eyes dancing with devilment.

The sheriff flushed a dull red beneath his suntanned face. "Now, Doc, you ain't got no call to say something like that."

"Calm down, Ned. I was just having a little fun. You can't blame me. After all, you did drag me away from the patient you're trying to accuse Logan of harming in some way. I've told you over and over Logan was not the cause of Mr. Malone's heart attack, yet you keep insisting he was. Contrary to popular belief, heart attacks do not happen suddenly."

"I told you Johnson said Prescott attacked Mr. Malone for no cause and before anyone could stop the fight, Mr. Malone grabbed his chest and keeled over," the sheriff reminded him. "Prescott probably scared Mr. Malone half to death."

Dr. Perry faced the sheriff. "J. T. Malone doesn't frighten that easily and you know it. Besides, you can't scare a person into having a heart attack. I've examined thousands of patients in my forty years practicing medicine and hundreds of them had been in fights. I'm telling you for the last time that after examining Mr. Malone, who is forty years older and fifty pounds heavier than Logan, he hasn't been in a fight with anyone."

"What about the bruises on Malone's face?" Sheriff Stone persisted.

Dr. Perry's sigh was long suffering. He glanced over his shoulder at the silent Logan. "I wish he'd have shown this much tenacity when someone stole my hubcaps last week." He continued as the sheriff started to sputter, "Calm down before you wake up your ulcer. Malone had *one* bruise on the left side of his head. If you'll remember the ambulance attendants said Mr. Malone was semiconscious and slumped beside an unconscious Logan in the work trailer when they arrived.

"Malone probably sustained his minor head injury when he fell during his heart attack and hit his head. By the way, he didn't give Logan his four cracked ribs, but I'm guessing since the two were so close together, Logan probably tried to keep Mr. Malone from falling but couldn't because of his own injuries. The pain of such a large man falling on Logan is the reason *he* was passed out."

Both men looked at Logan. His face an unreadable mask, he asked, "Will Mr. Malone be all right?"

The doctor laid a comforting hand on Logan's bare, muscular shoulder. "He's conscious, but he's still not out of the woods. We'll just have to wait and see how he progresses for the next twenty-four hours. I'd better be getting back upstairs. If I were you, Sheriff, I'd be asking your witness about Logan's ribs." Dr. Perry pushed the exam door open, then he was gone.

The door hadn't swung shut before the sheriff's snarling face was within inches of Logan's. "You may not have caused Mr. Malone's heart attack, but something is going on and I don't like it. A man who doesn't smile and keeps to himself like you do can't be trusted. I want you out of town before the sun sets. Even if I had the inclination, I don't have enough deputies to protect you if anything happens to Mr. Malone. You listening?"

"Yeah," Logan said, then began to ease his torn, dirty shirt back on. He gritted his teeth against the searing pain the smallest movement caused, but at least he no longer felt as if he were going to throw up or pass out again. He knew the sheriff still watched, but the lawman had ceased to matter as far as Logan was concerned. Rachel Malone occupied all of his thoughts. He had to see her. Nothing else mattered until then, not even the pain ripping him apart.

He inched his way off the exam table and onto the footstool, then stepped onto the floor. A wave of nausea and pain swept through him. With teeth clenched and eyes closed, he fought to stay upright. He had to see Rae and make her understand it wasn't his fault.

When he opened his eyes, the sheriff was gone. With slow, excruciating movements he began trying to tuck his shirt into his jeans. The door swung open.

Logan braced himself for the lawman. Instead it was the doctor who had bandaged him. He held a white slip of paper in his outstretched hand.

"Get this prescription filled before you go home. You're going to need it when the shot I gave you wears off."

"Thanks, Doctor." Logan took the paper, shoved it into his shirt pocket, finished stuffing his shirt in, then cautiously explored his bruised face. It felt raw and misshapen, but his teeth were all there and everything seemed to work. At least he hoped the eye swollen shut still worked.

Johnson and his two buddies had enjoyed working Logan over while his arms were held. J. T. Malone wanted to make sure Logan received his message: the next time he went near his daughter, he wouldn't walk away. Rage, long suppressed, splintered through Logan that there was nothing he could do to avenge himself for the time being.

Telling the sheriff would only make Logan's dire situation worse. The three men who attacked him probably had a plausible lie ready about trying to protect Malone from a crazy employee. They'd get a pat on the back from the police, profound thanks from the community for saving the life of one of its leading citizens and Logan would find himself behind bars. Logan swore to himself, the cowardly trio weren't going to get away with beating him up—each one was going to pay.

"Mr. Prescott?"

With difficulty, Logan brought his anger under control and faced the doctor. "Yes?"

"You'll need to be checked in three or four days—sooner, if breathing becomes more difficult."

Logan frowned. He didn't see how breathing could hurt any worse, but from the serious expression on the young resident's face, he wasn't joking. "Okay, and thanks again," he mumbled, and left the room.

The red glow of the exit light beckoned at the far end of the hall. Logan turned in the opposite direction, toward the elevators. In less than two minutes he was weaving his way down the long off-white corridor leading to the intensive care unit of Stanton Memorial Hospital. He tried to think of anything except the last two times he had walked the same hallway. Each time he had lost someone whose love he desperately wanted, yet never gained. He had survived being unwanted by his parents, he wasn't sure survival was possible without Rae's love.

Turning the corner, he saw her. She wore the same yellow sleeveless dress he had seen her in two hours earlier. Her slim arms were clamped around her waist as she leaned against the wall. Her usually well-groomed long, black hair was in a wild tangle around her beautiful face. A face pinched with fear. He'd give anything to undo this morning, but his parents had taught him early that wishing didn't change one damn thing.

"Rae."

Her head jerked up. In her expressive brown eyes was none of the admiring sparkle he had seen earlier that day. Instead, her gaze traveled slowly over his battered face, his torn, dirty clothes. She tucked her lower lip between her teeth and shut her eyes. Pain greater than he had felt earlier sliced through Logan. Rae couldn't believe those lies about him, could she? The short time apart couldn't have changed the love they felt for one another.

Before this moment, he thought he had been on his own too long to explain or answer to anyone, but the panicky feeling that he was losing Rachel compelled him to do so. "I didn't start the fight with your father. I thought he was sweating and short of breath because he was so angry. By the time I figured out what was happening he was about to pass out." Logan's arm circled his waist. "I tried to keep him from falling, but I couldn't."

Her eyes opened and they were filled with such anguish that for a moment he wished she had kept them closed. "This is not what I wanted. Everything is turned upside down. D-Daddy in ICU. You…" Her shaky voice trailed off. Her entire body trembled. Restless hands continued their relentless sweep up and down her bare arms as if she were chilled not just of the flesh, but of the soul. Tears crested in her eyes, then rolled down her cheek. "I didn't mean for this to happen."

With his hand pressed against the wall to keep him from falling, Logan realized that in all of her eighteen years, Rae had never been touched by the real world. As the indulged only daughter of one of the most influential and wealthiest black families in East Texas, she had been shielded from the harsh realities of life and raised to believe she had only to ask to receive. She admitted that dating Logan was the first time she had done something she knew her parents wouldn't approve of.

Logan realized she'd really believed that in time she would be able to persuade her parents to accept a construction worker with only a high-school education as their son-in-law. After all, she had told him over and over, they had never denied her anything she'd really wanted. Logan had known better.

The Malones were too socially conscious to welcome a welder into their family. He had often wondered how Rae could have grown up so down-to-earth. She saw the person, not where you lived, not who your people were, not how much money you had in the bank. What she didn't understand was that all those things were important to her parents and more so if their daughter was involved.

He should have made her see that this was one time she wasn't going to get her way. Most of all, he shouldn't have given into her pleas to meet secretly. But he hadn't wanted to face the very real possibility of never seeing her again. Now, it looked as if it would inevitably happen.

"Welcome to the real world, Rae."

"Is that all you have to say?"

Logan felt eighty years old instead of twenty-two. "What do you want me to say?"

Before she could answer, the door behind her opened and Rachel's mother emerged with a distinguished-looking older couple Logan recognized as the Malones' pastor and his wife. One glimpse at Logan and Martha Malone burst into tears. Rushing to her mother, Rachel gathered the smaller woman protectively in her arms. Over her mother's head, Rachel's worried gaze locked with Logan's.

Reverend Rodgers cleared his throat. "Son, maybe it would be better if you left."

"I have a right to be here." Logan never took his eyes from Rachel's. "Tell him."

Martha Malone's grip on her daughter tightened as she lifted her pinched, tearstained face. "Leave my baby alone. You've caused enough trouble."

"Mrs. Malone, I'm sorry for what happened, but I have a right to be here. Rae is—"

"No!" The simultaneous shout came from Rachel and her mother.

"What's going on here?"

Logan heard Sheriff Stone's demanding voice and ignored it. His sole attention was focused on Rachel. Something inside his chest tightened when Rachel's gaze skittered away as if afraid of being caught looking at him.

"Is Prescott bothering you, Mrs. Malone?"

"Just make him go away," Martha whispered, her head of stylishly cut black hair barely reaching her daughter's shoulder.

The sheriff took a step toward Logan. "You heard Mrs. Malone. Move on."

Logan didn't move. His gaze still on Rachel, he tried

to compel her to speak up. She could stop all this with three little words: *he's my husband.* The lengthening silence was broken by the sound of a gun holster being unsnapped.

"I'm not going to ask you again," Sheriff Stone warned.

A strangled cry erupted from Rachel. She tried to disentangle herself from her mother, but Martha held on. "Mr. Prescott, we appreciate your concern, but you don't have to stay," Rachel said, the words tumbling out, her eyes wide with fear and desperation.

Logan remained where he stood. His gaze flicked to the sheriff's hand as it shifted toward the butt of his .357 Magnum, then back to Rachel. Logan knew Stone was floor-showing, trying to act the hero for one of the town's leading citizens. However, the sheriff wasn't stupid enough to pull a gun in a hospital without real provocation. And Logan hadn't given him any.

With a supple twist of her body, Rachel broke free. Ignoring her mother's pleading cry to stop, Rachel continued until she stood between Logan and the sheriff. Relief washed over Logan; he hadn't lost her. He started toward her, but her next words froze him in place.

"Please leave." Anger replaced the fear in her face. "You're only making things worse for everyone."

Then she did something he would have never imagined. She turned her back on him, reclasped her mother's hand, and thanked the sheriff for his help. To them, Logan had ceased to exist.

Stunned, he turned and started for the elevator. Yesterday, in front of a minister, Rae had sworn to stand by his side for a lifetime. Today she didn't want him anywhere near her.

Outside, he took a taxi back to the construction site to get his old truck. Thankfully, the crew had gone home and the place was deserted.

Once home, he turned on the TV, the radio, then eased into an overstuffed chair and tried to think of anything, but the last twenty-four hours. Ten minutes later his fingernails were digging into the cushioned fabric.

He couldn't stop thinking about Rae turning her back on him. It was too much of a reminder that his parents had done the same thing. They had made it clear from his earliest memories that he wasn't to be included in the special closeness they shared.

Logan was an unplanned inconvenience they cared for, but they never hugged him, never truly loved him. No matter how hard he tried to win their affection if not their love, he never succeeded. He had thought his uncaring parents had taught him to feel every conceivable emotion when your love is thrown back in your face. He was wrong. Even at their most callous moments, he hadn't felt as if someone was ripping out his soul.

Rae had hurt him in ways he had never imagined possible. Once again he had been shown he wasn't capable of inspiring loyalty and love. Pushing from the chair, he raised the volume to the radio knowing as he did so, the memories and the truth were waiting.

As the day progressed, Logan did little except battle with the past, take his pain medication and call the hospital and check on Mr. Malone. The man had wrecked Logan's life, but he was Rae's father and Logan couldn't help but care what happened to him.

Watching the lengthening shadows creep across the worn, cracked linoleum floor only served to remind Logan of how different his life was from Rae's. However, those differences hadn't seemed insurmountable until this morning.

Yet, despite what had happened at the hospital, something inside him refused to believe he had lost Rae forever. She had been upset and worried about her father. But once she had time to think things over, to remember how much they loved one another, she would call.

Logan shifted in the chair. He wasn't good at waiting, but at least it had given him a chance to think. He finally understood Rae getting him to leave the hospital saved him from spending a night in jail. He refused to listen to the little voice that whispered she also saved herself from admitting she married the man her father thought beneath her. Logan eased out of his chair and walked over to touch the gauzy blue window curtain Rae had put up the week before.

The memory of their first meeting settled over him like a warm blanket. Despite his working for her father, he and Rae had never more than nodded until three months ago when he stopped to help her with a flat tire on her car. The attraction he had been trying to deny for a high school senior and the boss's daughter, flared up like a blowtorch. Rae looking at him as if he were the answer to a fantasy she didn't know she had, didn't help. He managed to fix the tire without losing control, then twisted and turned all night thinking about her.

The next day she showed up at his house with lunch as a thank-you. She didn't bat a beautiful lash at his weathered house and its mismatched furniture. She just saw him. That kind of total concentration from a woman he was attracted to was hard to ignore. He had tried to scare her into leaving with stories of dangerous strangers and she had given him a wry smile and hugged him. A hug filled with complete trust. He didn't have the willpower to push her away. And he never looked back...until now.

His fist clenched. She had to call. He could not, would not lose her. They'd work things through, After her father was out of the hospital, they'd head for Oklahoma City, as planned.

Logan had already rented an apartment near the university where Rae's parents had enrolled her for the fall term. She didn't know it, but he planned to pay her tuition himself. If she had enough faith and trust to marry him, he'd work his fingers to the bone at his new job. But he didn't intend to remain a welder all his life. He was going to own his own company. When that happened, every material thing Rachel had gone without because of her marriage to him, he planned to give back tenfold. Their life together was going to be wonderful.

But in the morning there was no phone call. He had swallowed his pride and gone to the hospital. One look at Rae's anxious face and stiff posture, he had known she hadn't changed her mind. Seeing Johnson, the man who helped beat up Logan, whisper something in her ear, then touch her hand affectionately, had made Logan sick to his stomach. The next instant, Rachel nodded and walked into ICU. Johnson, a grin on his face, swaggered toward Logan.

Knowing if Johnson said one word, he'd lose what little control he had left, Logan had turned and walked away. Two hours later, his battered truck had roared past the city limits of Stanton. His eyes stung and his nose felt funny. His allergies hadn't acted up since he was a kid. Maybe it was a good idea he was going to Oklahoma's drier climate.

Glancing at his wrist to note the time, he saw instead a circular patch of lighter skin. A frown touched his brow, then his face settled into a scowl. He remembered taking the watch off the other night at the honeymoon suite in Houston because the mesh band had kept catching in Rae's hair.

Trying to stop the events of what had happened afterward was like trying to halt an avalanche. He saw flashes of her brown eyes dazed with desire, felt the yielding of her soft body beneath his, tasted her mouth, and knew the passion of her body rising to meet his.

If she had loved him enough he could have gone through anything, but she hadn't. The bottom line was that he wasn't good enough in the eyes of her parents, and she didn't love him enough to walk away from them. It hurt. It hurt like hell.

"Damn! Damn! Damn!" Logan bit out, pounding the steering wheel with his fist as the word hissed through clenched teeth. He welcomed the pain the jarring motion caused because at least for a little while he didn't have to remember Rae's betrayal. But soon his emotional pain mingled with his physical pain until he was no longer sure where one stopped and the other began.

His steel-toed work boot pressed on the gas pedal and the speedometer needle rocked farther to the right. The truck whizzed past the oldest speed trap in the area, a billboard for beer, and for once Logan neither noticed nor cared.

"You going or not?" Charles asked, breaking into Logan's thoughts. There was a note of challenge in his gravelly voice.

Logan evaded the question and asked one of his own. "Why wasn't I told about this bid?"

Hurt flashed in Charles's eyes. "You were busy in New Orleans with what's-her-name, and, if you'll remember, you left explicit instructions that you didn't want to be disturbed."

"That was last year," Logan yelled, refusing to let go of his unreasonable anger.

"Excuse me!" Charles flared, just as angry. "I'll leave a memo on your desk the next time I blow my nose! What the hell is the matter with you? You go through women like water through a sieve; why is this one making you act like a horse's behind?"

"I married this one," Logan ground out harshly, and watched the shock of his words spread across his partner's face.

Logan had always intended to keep that particular failure to himself. Not because he still loved Rachel, but because he didn't like to think of how his abrupt leaving had made him look guilty or of the satisfaction his disappearance had given some people.

Half the town probably thought him a coward while the other half thought he was too full of himself. They didn't know that by then he had built a protective shell around himself. No one cared about him so he wasn't going to care about anyone else. Pain and anger, not guilt or fear, had driven him from Stanton. It had shaken him to hell and back to think he could have been that wrong about the woman he loved.

"Logan," Charles said softly. "I didn't beg you to go to Kuwait with me and hound you to be my partner because I liked the color of your eyes. From the moment I saw you struggling to make a day despite your cracked ribs, despite Briggs refusing to give you light duty until you healed, I saw a man with enough determination for ten men. I've never once been sorry. If my two boys grow up to be half the man you are, I'll die happy."

Logan's anger died a quick death. That kind of praise from a man he respected and admired was difficult to ignore. Charles and Helen's teenage sons were outstanding kids. "You never did fight fair. The morning after the night at Bessie's, you started in on me about Kuwait and before I knew it, my signature was on a two-year contract. The only consolation was hearing Helen give you a piece of her mind for not discussing things with her first."

Charles shook his head in remembrance. "I didn't want to leave her and the boys either, but I knew I'd never make enough money to start my own business working in the States, and I was right. We've made Bridgeway the largest black-owned construction company in Arkansas," Charles pointed out. "I'm also right about this. No one likes to face bad memories, especially ones apparently as deep as yours. Yet, I'm asking you to go back because I don't think there's anything this side of heaven that can best you."

Logan rubbed the back of his neck and felt his resistance weaken a little more. Charlès certainly wasn't playing fair. But the bottom line was that Bridgeway was just as much Logan's responsibility as it was Charles's. "I'll go."

A smile creased Charles's face. "I know you wouldn't let me or the company down. By the way, we may have beat out a local company for the bid to build the city hall complex. If we do, the mayor and the city manager think he's not going to be too happy when the official announcement is made next week."

Every nerve in Logan's body went on alert. "What is the name of the company?"

"Malone Construction Company."

Logan's mouth flattened into a hard, ruthless line. "Fine."

Charles nodded. "Maybe it's best that you're going since there may be some professional fences to mend."

"What are you talking about?" Logan asked.

"In our move to expand into Texas, we've beat out Malone twice before. I learned a few days ago that the company is going through a money crunch," Charles explained. "We both said when we started Bridgeway if we couldn't take another black man up the ladder with us, at least we wouldn't knock him off. Looks like we may have knocked Malone off."

Logan's smile was feral. "I think I'm going to enjoy this trip after all. I may even go in a few days early." *It was payback time.*

Chapter 2

Adjusting the wide-brimmed sunshades over her eyes, Rachel Malone stepped from the half-ton truck onto the brick-layered street of Stanton, Texas. The intense dry heat of the sweltering June afternoon closed around her. She barely noticed. Her cocoa-colored face set in mutinous lines, she shoved the truck keys into the front pocket of her faded jeans and started for the Victorian mansion across the street.

On the immaculately kept lawn of the Victorian House, two grown peacocks, their tails unfurled in fans shimmering with iridescent colors, strolled beneath hundred-year-old oak trees. Both appeared oblivious to the people staring through the five-foot black iron fence, and to the clock striking three in the courthouse tower on the town square a block away.

Rachel wasn't. Every day she raced against a clock, and lately the clock was winning. Her pace increased, her long legs carrying her swiftly up the wooden steps of the once condemned Victorian mansion that had been turned into a shopper's paradise.

The multicultural shops carried an impressive selection of merchandise. From African wood carvings to Mexican pottery to Navajo rugs, it could all be purchased under one roof. Rachel was looking for none of these. *Whispers* was her destination.

The sooner she visited the upscale boutique and tried on the evening gown her mother insisted Rachel buy for an upcoming party, the sooner Rachel could get back to the construction site. Obviously, her lack of dating and her preference for denim over silk had caused her mother to think her only child needed assistance in finding a husband. However, the only men Rachel was interested in were the ones employed by Malone Construction.

A musical chime announced Rachel's entrance. Cool air greeted her. Absently she pushed her tortoiseshell shades atop her head. Immediately her eyes were drawn to the casual elegance of the shop. The room was spacious and interspersed with towering live tropical plants. Gleaming chrome picked up the late-afternoon sun and reflected the rays. Honey-toned, piney hardwood floors glistened beneath her booted feet. It was quite a contrast to the layers of dust Rachel had glimpsed that morning on her own floors.

Not seeing a saleslady, she turned to search for one. A low, throaty rumble of male laughter froze her in place.

Her mind shouted that it couldn't be: her heart drummed that it was.

The man laughed again—a deep, full sound that flowed over her body and made her spine tingle, drawing her eight years into the past. Light brown eyes darkened, then closed in remembered pain and betrayal.

Slowly her eyes opened. She took one, then another deep, calming breath. What was the matter with her? To her knowledge Logan Prescott hadn't been back to Stanton since he left for Oklahoma. Of course, he could have returned a dozen times without her knowing it. Yet she didn't think he had. There was no reason for him to return to the small East Texas town. He had left an aging four-room house, few friends, and a lot of unhappiness behind. He had also left his bride.

Unwanted memories coursed through her. Logan, battered in body and spirit, asking for her to acknowledge him as her husband. To protect him, she had given him anguish and betrayal instead. With a steely determination developed from years of practice, she drew her mind from the past. Her slim, trembling fingers rubbed her suddenly throbbing temple. Maybe her weeks of fourteen-hour workdays were finally getting to her.

When an architect looked at blueprints and they made no sense, as had happened to Rachel that morning,

it was bad enough, but then to start hearing things...
Logan wasn't back. *But what if he was?* Overhead a
white ceiling fan twirled lazily to cool her flushed
cheeks. Flushed cheeks that had nothing to do with the
ninety-two-degree temperature beyond the high arched
windows of the boutique.

She had to be wrong. He hadn't come back. Well,
there was one way to find out.

Even as Rachel moved behind the swim-suited mannequin to locate the owner of the laugh, she questioned
the wisdom of her action. If there was any chance it
really was Logan, she should be running in the opposite
direction, not sneaking about to find him. She had
turned her back on him when he'd needed her most, and
Logan Prescott wasn't the kind of man who turned the
other cheek.

Through the fronds of a lush, green acrea palm on a
mirrored stand, she glimpsed the tall, muscular build of
a man. His broad back was to her. A chambray shirt
flowed over wide shoulders that tapered to a narrow waist.

His dark head and shoulders dipped; well-worn
denim shifted and hugged his strong thighs and long
legs to maddening perfection. A knot formed in her
stomach. She didn't need to see his face; the sudden
tightening of her body told her all she needed to know.

He was back. After eight years, Logan Prescott was
back.

Sultry laughter that could only belong to a woman
rose. Only then did Rachel notice the outline of another

person and the peach-colored silky material swirling almost caressingly around Logan's pants legs. Slender, amber-toned fingers cupped his wide shoulder, squeezed, then slid down his arm as if reluctant to break contact. With a final clinch of her hand, the woman turned and walked through the swinging white louvered doors behind her.

The sharp stab of jealousy that sliced through Rachel was as unexpected as it was unwanted. Her eyes shut as if that alone would block out the disturbing emotion. How could she have forgotten that eight years ago her lies had destroyed any chance for happiness they might have had?

She hadn't just rejected Logan, she had thrown his love back in his face. No matter how much she wished things might have ended differently between them, Logan was in her past. She mustn't forget again. Stepping back to leave, her booted heel banged against a glass counter, sending the display of jeweled-toned crystal perfume atomizers clanking and tinkling.

Her eyes snapped open. Her heart pounding, she waited for her past to collide with the present.

Logan spun in one smooth motion, his piercing black gaze finding and locking on Rachel in less than a heartbeat. Her befuddled brain refused to command her feet to move. She was trapped. The door between past and present, between dream and reality, swung open.

Across the space of twenty feet, coal-black eyes clashed with wide brown ones. Her throat was dry. Damp palms sought the steadying solidity of the countertop. It was impossible, but he was even more handsome and more devastating than ever.

Close-cut black hair defined his well-shaped head. Thick black brows slashed over magnetic eyes fringed by long lashes. His nose was elegantly patrician. A neatly trimmed mustache curved above the unyielding outline of his mouth. His skin was the warm, rich color of mahogany. She trembled. Logan still had the power to make her knees weak.

The unsettling reminder made her snatch her hand from the counter and draw herself to her five-foot-seven inch height. In order to survive, she had learned to forget the past, forget her dreams. Her chin lifted.

Just as quickly, Logan's eyes narrowed perceptively. He stepped forward to answer her unspoken challenge.

Rachel stared at the sudden ruthlessness etched in his face and shuddered involuntarily. Before her was a different man from the one who had left. No longer sure of her ability to face his wrath, she turned to flee.

She had taken four frantic steps when calloused fingers clamped around her forearm. It flashed through her mind that he moved with the lethal quickness of a panther. She was his prey.

Rachel spun toward her captor, her hand coming up in a defensive gesture to push Logan away. Instead, her fingers slid inside his partially opened shirt, grazing over warm, hair-roughened flesh. A hiss erupted from her trembling lips. Jerking her hand away, she tried to ignore that the sound had come from her.

"Leaving without saying hello, Rachel?"

Her head snapped upward at Logan's biting tone. Black eyes glittered down at her. Memories and sensations vied for her attention: the seeping warmth of his body reaching out to hers, the tingling feeling in the palm of her hand, the foreign sound of her name on his lips she'd once known and loved so well. It was too much too soon.

"Or didn't you think I'd recognize you?" he questioned, letting his gaze sweep over her in a cool, calculated appraisal.

His unsettling reminder that she was dressed in faded jeans, a blue cotton blouse and steel-toed work boots stung her pride and helped to restore her courage. "Hello, Logan, and goodbye," she told him, answering his first question and ignoring the second.

Ebony eyes studied her upturned face. "You're very good at saying goodbye and walking away, aren't you?"

"Turn me loose," she ordered as she simultaneously tried to ignore her pang of guilt, the heat and hardness of Logan's body pressed against hers, the tantalizing scent of his woodsy cologne. It was impossible.

Logan stepped closer and gently tucked both her arms behind her back and captured them in one hand; his free hand caught her chin between thumb and forefinger.

Motionless, Rachel stared at Logan's determined features and sensed it was useless to struggle. Her pulse racing, she waited for him to finish taunting her. Perhaps he deserved his pound of flesh.

His work-roughened thumb slid across her bottom lip

and she couldn't suppress their trembling again. His smile could have chilled an icicle. "I don't take orders anymore, Rachel. I give them. And what I want I take for as long as it pleases me." His head lowered, his warm breath fanned her face. "Guess what I want."

"You want to hurt me, but I won't let you," she blurted without thought.

His handsome face hardened. "You have to care to be hurt, and we both know you never gave a damn about me." Ignoring her gasp of incredulity, he released one of her hands and lifted his head. His voice impersonal he said, "Ida Mae would never forgive me if I allowed a customer to leave without seeing her. Especially one so prominent in the community."

Firmly holding Rachel's arm, he started toward the white louvered doors. "Ida Mae, you have a customer."

"Tell them I'll be there in a minute, honey," came the answer from back in the store.

Hearing another woman call out an endearment to Logan left Rachel off balance and shaken. She dared not examine the reason too closely. Logan was enough to deal with. Minutes ago he had intentionally made her aware of him just to see her reaction. He wanted more than his pound of flesh. He wanted her skinned and nailed to the nearest tree.

Surreptitiously, she glanced at Logan and looked straight into riveting black eyes. His steady gaze held a burning emotion that chilled her. Hate stared unflinchingly back at her.

He hated her, yet he still had the power to make her want him.

The louvered doors swung open and a slim, attractive black woman in her mid-fifties came toward them. The smile on her amber face froze as her wary gaze swung from Logan to Rachel standing stiffly by his side.

"Ida Mae Jones, meet Rachel..." Logan paused and looked questioningly at Rachel. "How do I introduce you? Since you didn't want me, I'm sure you didn't want to keep my name."

The older woman rushed forward. Taking Rachel's arm, the shopkeeper retraced her steps to the back of the store. "Welcome to *Whispers.* Sorry I wasn't here to greet you. Your mother wasn't sure if she could get you in this afternoon. I put the dress in the last fitting room just in case. You go on back. Just let me know if I can be of any help."

Rachel needed no further urging to escape. She called herself a coward for running and a fool for caring, but neither helped keep the stinging moisture from her eyes. Once out of sight, she leaned against the rose-colored silk padded wall near the first dressing room and hugged her churning stomach. She deserved his condemnation; she just hadn't realized how much it would hurt. Hushed voices drifted to her.

"Honey, I'm sorry, I should have warned you she might come in. But I was so happy to see you finally walk through that door I forgot," Ida Mae said.

"For what? I told you before Rachel Malone means

nothing to me and she proved long ago that I mean nothing to her."

Pushing away from the wall, Rachel raced to the fitting room. The faint jingle of the store's bell caused her to breathe a sigh of relief. Apparently Logan had tired of baiting her. But what was he doing back? How long did he plan to stay? Questions without answers swirled around in her head. With jerky motions, she laid her glasses on a small table, then began unbuttoning her blouse. She'd stay and try on the dress her mother had picked out, if only to prove to herself she wasn't a complete coward.

Pulling off her boots, then her jeans, she took the gown from the hanger and stepped into it. Reaching behind to fasten the three hooks in the neck of the gown, she glanced up. Her lips formed a silent "Oh" of wonder. The long red knit jersey garment hugged her body in revealing detail.

The high neck and cap sleeves gave no hint of the gown's backless style or the mid-thigh split on each side. It was the kind of dress that allowed nothing beneath except goosebumps and guts. Exactly the kind of dress she had envisioned Logan seeing her in if they met again.

Instead, he had seen her without a trace of makeup on, her shoulder-length, curly black hair windblown from a ride in the truck with the windows down because the air conditioning wasn't working. She was dressed like the Malone Construction Company General Manager she was. She hadn't brought Logan to his knees as she had once envisioned; he had nearly brought her to hers.

Shaking off the past, Rachel picked up the dangling price ticket. Four hundred and seventy-five dollars. Considering her mother's disregard for expense, the gown cost less than Rachel had expected, but it was still more than she could afford. She'd tell her mother the back was too revealing. Martha Malone might be desperate to marry Rachel off, but her mother understood propriety.

Too bad she didn't seem to understand recession and what it had meant to the once prosperous Malone Construction Company. Rachel's father understood and she often wondered if he held her responsible.

For a second, anguish darkened Rachel's eyes, but just as quickly it was replaced with resolve. Everything would be fine once Malone Construction was awarded the contract to build Stanton's new municipal complex. Then, from out of nowhere a twinge of worry pricked her.

Twice in the last year, she had thought the company's financial worries were over only to learn Bridgeway Construction Company, not Malone, had been awarded the contract they'd sought. She shook her head. This time would be different. Even if the Malones hadn't been community leaders for the past three generations, their bid was so low Stanton's city council *had* to give her father the contract.

No other construction company could outbid them and make a profit. Malone would barely break even, but more important than money was the council's display of confidence. The contract would provide the springboard for Malone to regain its solid financial footing.

Without the contract, she wasn't sure Malone Construction could survive.

Pushing her thoughts aside, Rachel grabbed the waist of the garment, bent forward and pulled. The narrow neck opening stuck beneath her nose. Berating herself, she reached inside the dress, unhooked the fasteners, and pulled again. Hooks snagged her hair. After a few tries and the loss of several strands of hair, she admitted she wasn't going to be able to free herself.

Her choices were limited. She could wait for Ida Mae to check on her or she could call for help. Knowing she had acted like a coward earlier in front of Logan enabled her make up her mind.

"Please, could you help me?" she called. When no one answered, she said more loudly, "I'm stuck. Can anyone hear—"

The creak of the swinging door behind her halted her plea. "Thank you. The hook is caught in my hair."

Without a word, the person began freeing her. In a matter of moments the dress slipped over her head.

A smile on her face, she turned to her rescuer. "I can't thank you—" Her jaw slackened.

Dark and forbidding Logan loomed in front of her. The red dress spilled from his clutched fist.

No memories, no dreams had prepared him for this. Rachel's face and body were perfection. A low-cut, lacy white bra bared the upper curve of her lush breasts and made his hands ache to take its place. The matching

French-cut bikini sensuously detailed her womanly softness. If his tortured memory was right, her silky-looking skin tasted as forbiddingly delicious and addictive as its rich chocolate color. Once he'd loved tasting her almost as much as he had enjoyed watching her eyes darken and her body spin out of control beneath his.

Standing in front of the mirrored wall, Rachel afforded him a gut-wrenching view of what he had lost. Sleek and elegant and curved in all the right places, she was a walking fantasy. *And she could never be his again.* It took all of Logan's considerable control to let none of his longing show in his face.

He had calculated the risk of heeding the panic in her voice and followed the sound. He hadn't calculated high enough. He had made another mistake where Rachel Malone was concerned. There could be no more. Once she had shredded his pride and trampled his love. Never again. She had taken enough.

"Get out of here!" Trembling arms crossed her breasts. "Now," she shouted when Logan didn't move.

"You called for help."

"I wanted Ms. Jones."

"She's helping a customer," he told her calmly.

Deciding that Logan wasn't going to leave, she picked up her blouse and quickly shoved her arms through the sleeves. Fumbling fingers began matching buttons to holes. "What kind of place is this that allows a man access to the dressing rooms?"

"One with the highest reputation since your mother shops here," Logan said easily. "Besides, we've both seen each other in a lot less, a whole lot less."

"That was a long time ago." Grabbing her jeans from a chair, she wrapped both arms around her stomach to hold them in front of her. Somehow to put them on with Logan watching would be more intimate than standing in front of him in her underwear.

"So it was." His face expressionless, Logan turned to leave. "I'll tell Ida Mae to ring this up for you."

"I'm not buying the gown."

Logan spun around, his gaze cutting. "You don't want to patronize her shop because she's a friend of mine?"

"Of course not."

"Then why? Your mother picked it out for you; surely you're still doing what 'Mama' tells you," he stated caustically.

"I am not buying the dress."

"Suit yourself." Turning, he left.

Rachel jerked on the jeans, rammed the blouse tail in and snapped her pants shut; then shoved her feet into her dusty boots and tied them. Putting on her shades, she left the dressing room corridor at a brisk pace, hoping she didn't have to see Logan or Ida Mae again. It was not to be.

"Didn't the gown suit you?" came Ida Mae's questioning voice.

Rachel jerked in mid-stride, then accepted the inevitable and faced the older woman. "I'm afraid not."

Ida Mae's eyes crinkled at the corner as she frowned. "But your mother was very specific. Mrs. Malone expected you to buy the dress."

"Same thing I told her, Ida Mae," Logan said, leaning casually against the counter, the red gown draped across his broad shoulder. "Yeah, Rachel, buy the dress. You wouldn't want to start thinking for yourself for a change, would you?"

Rachel sucked in her breath. The cynicism of Logan's remark stung. The pain went deep because she knew he meant to hurt her.

For a long moment she met his contemptuous stare, then she turned to the older woman. "Thank you, Ms. Jones, and good afternoon." Holding herself stiffly, she walked from the store.

Logan moved across the room. Tapered, lean brown fingers lifted the rose silk drapery aside. With unnerving stillness, he watched Rachel run across the street and quickly climb into a dirty red pickup truck. The name of "Malone Construction Company" emblazoned on the door caused his fist to clench. In a matter of seconds, the truck backed up and sped away.

"If you scare off our customers like that, we won't be able to keep making a profit," Ida Mae said.

Logan said nothing but simply watched the truck until it turned onto Main Street and disappeared.

"Change your mind about going through with your revenge?"

He pivoted abruptly to see Ida Mae watching him

closely. They had met over nine years ago when he was a frequent and inept shopper at the grocery store she managed. She was one of the few people he'd counted as a friend when he'd left Stanton in a blaze of dust and a gut full of pain. "What makes you ask?"

She nodded toward the window. "Her. When you telephoned me last night to tell me you were coming home and your plan to ruin Old Man Malone, I didn't tell you there had been a change of players because I didn't think it mattered. Now, I'm not so sure."

"What do you mean?"

"Malone had another heart attack about six months ago, and now Rachel runs Malone Construction Company."

His jaw hardened as he glanced out the window. "It doesn't make any difference."

Ida Mae shook her head of light auburn hair and moved toward Logan's rigid back. "If you could have seen your face a moment ago, I don't think you'd be so quick to say that."

His dark head whipped around. "Leave it alone."

"Don't you go ordering me around. You're not too big or too old for me to take a switch to," she shot back, her hands on her slim hips. "You know, until today, I would have agreed with anything you wanted to do to those Malones after the way they mistreated you; but that was before seeing Rachel Malone's face when she walked out of here. The shattered look was unmistakable."

"Ida Mae."

Undaunted by the obvious warning in his voice, she stepped closer. "And do you know why it was unmistakable, Logan Prescott? Well, I'll tell you. Because eight years ago I saw the same look on your face the morning you came to tell me what happened at the construction site and at the hospital. I wanted to shake Rachel until her teeth rattled for hurting you. Instead, I prayed you'd make it safely to Oklahoma. The tires on your raggedy truck were already slick and you left the remaining rubber on my driveway."

"I'm seeing this through." He moved away from the window, trying not to remember how alone he had felt the morning he'd left for Oklahoma or how good it felt to have Rachel in his arms again.

"Honey, you know how I've hoped and prayed you'd come back to Stanton one day. I refused to sell your house like you wanted. I badgered you to open this place. But now that you're finally back, you have me worried. You're going to pay a high price for your revenge if she still cares for you," Ida Mae predicted.

"What she cares about is money and position."

"Then why don't you tell her that you own the Victorian House and the construction company that turned it into a showcase." Ida Mae waved her hand expansively around the shop. "Tell her Logan Prescott is rich enough to match dollars with her old man any day of the week."

"Do you think I want a woman if all she cares about

is how much money I have?" he said tersely. "Besides, if what I've heard is true, Malone doesn't have very many dollars to match."

She frowned. "Logan—"

"It's over between Rachel and me," he interrupted sharply. "Whatever chance we had for happiness was lost long ago. I didn't come back for her. It's her father I'm after—the great J. T. Malone. Only he won't be so great once I'm finished with him. He may have everyone fooled into thinking Rachel runs the company, but I know how tyrannical Malone is. He wouldn't let her buy a load of Sheetrock without his approval. I want to see his face when he learns he has nothing and realizes the man he caused to be run out of town took it."

"After the shameful things he did to you, Malone deserves whatever he gets, but Jake Johnson and the others ganged up on you and beat you up," she told him.

"They'll get theirs in time, but Malone is first," Logan said with biting finality. "And despite what Charles thinks, I don't plan to lift a finger to help Malone stay solvent."

"Logan, honey, give it up." She gently touched his tense shoulder. "In the short time Rachel has been in charge, she has earned a reputation for being a fighter. Walk away while you still like yourself."

"My mind is made up. We both know there is nothing she can do."

"She can hate," Ida Mae shot back.

"I already know about hate. She was my best teacher."

Ida Mae's hand fell in defeat. "You'll lose, Logan."

Dark, haunted eyes stared back at her. "You're wrong. I have nothing left to lose."

Chapter 3

"You can make it. You can make it."

Hands clamped around the steering wheel, her entire body shaking, Rachel repeated the litany as she stopped at a red traffic light. She refused to look across the street to the refuge of the grocery store's busy parking lot. It would be foolish to stop with so many people around.

One problem with living in a small town all your life was that almost everyone knew you and spoke. If she tried to say a word, the tears burning the back of her throat and stinging her eyes would start falling. The person would immediately assume her father's health had declined and be on the phone to her mother within minutes. The news of Rachel Malone blubbering in

H.E.B.'s parking lot would start questions she wasn't sure she knew how to answer.

An impatient horn blasted behind her. Stepping on the gas, Rachel went through the green light. Swallowing convulsively, she fought tears and forbidden memories. Taking a left, she headed down a heavily wooded two-lane graveled road. Gradually the overgrowth of trees and vegetation climbing over the barbedwire fence paralleling the road gave way to a sparkling white wooden fence, mowed pastures, and pretentious homes on sizable lots.

Slowing down, Rachel turned into her parents' driveway. Seeing the rambling ranch house caused her hands to tighten once again. Logan couldn't have returned at a worse time. Both her parents were going to be upset if they learned he was in town. But unlike her, Logan wasn't a native and if he left quickly enough, they might never know he had returned.

Logan had come to Stanton with his parents when he was fourteen. By the time he was eighteen and a semester away from finishing high school, he had lost both parents. His mother had died of cancer less than a year after they'd arrived. He had once told Rachel that when they buried his mother, they might as well have buried his father because he never recovered emotionally from his wife's death. Although Logan didn't say it, Rachel got the distinct impression he sometimes resented his father for giving up on life when he still had a son to live for.

After his father's death, Logan stayed by himself on the outskirts of town. From what she managed to learn through the years, almost everyone expected him to run wild. Instead, the eighteen-year-old held down a full-time job and finished high school with honors. His accomplishment should have earned him the respect of the entire town, but by that time people were too wary of a fiercely independent loner who never seemed to fit in and seldom smiled. Rachel knew jealousy also brimmed beneath the town's dislike of Logan.

The house Logan lived in was small, but it sat upon two acres of land with its own stock tank full of trout. When his parents died, the debt-free property passed on to Logan. He had what most men worked half a lifetime to achieve. He had something else; youth and devastatingly good looks. If the men stayed away, the women came in droves—including Rachel. However, she tried to make herself believe her reason was more humanitarian.

The first time she saw Logan eating lunch away from the other men at one of her father's job sites, something inside her twisted when he looked at her, then away. It was as if he expected her to ignore him like everyone else there so he was beating her to it. That hint of vulnerability drew her to him. Somehow, she was going to make him feel as if he wasn't alone in the world.

In her naiveté, she told herself she only wanted to be his friend, but when he had turned those riveting black eyes on her a couple of weeks later, her knees had gone weak, her breath caught, something fluttered low in her stomach. What she wanted from Logan went deeper than friendship. She had intentionally set out to meet him.

A flat tire on her car near his house accomplished her goal. It was all she could do to keep her eyes off the sculptured fit of his jeans on his hips, his long, powerful legs, his strong, competent hands. Finished, he pushed to his feet. Since she had been practically standing on top of him, their faces were inches apart. Her gaze dropped to his mouth. Stepping back, he bid her a terse goodbye and left.

The following Saturday she gathered her courage and went to his house with lunch as a thank-you. Shirtless, he had opened the door. Ignoring his order to stay there until he put something on, she entered the house and promptly tripped over one of his shoes. He caught her by the arms and kept her upright. Her lips accidentally brushed his cheek. Logan had pushed her away with a muttered curse, then proceeded to tell her all the reasons she shouldn't be there.

A noble Logan didn't fit with the image of a stud. But by then she already knew the town's perception of him was wrong. Behind the gruff, stern-faced exterior was a decent, caring man. So she politely listened until he finished, then she did the only thing she could think of to let him know she understood the dangers and trusted him anyway. She hugged him. After an ageless moment, his arms slipped around her waist and drew her to him. Nothing had ever felt so perfect.

Shutting out the past, she stopped the truck in front of her parents' house and got out. Instead of going to the front door, she took the stone walkway leading to the back of the sprawling house and the enclosed garden room. As expected, her mother was sitting inside. Her papers were strewn across a small writing desk. She was an officeholder or committee member for half the charities in town, but she made sure her husband and daughter were always well cared for. The house was always immaculate, the meals were always prepared. If something conflicted with a family commitment for her mother, the family came first.

To the casual observer, Martha Malone, at five feet and one hundred pounds, appeared frail and timid. Shamefully, Rachel admitted she had agreed with them until her world had shattered and her mother had displayed a backbone of steel and an unshakable determination to give her daughter the strength and courage to put her life back together again.

Opening the door, Rachel stepped into the room. "Hello, Mother. I see you're at it again."

Martha Malone looked up, a smile taking the frown of concentration from her otherwise smooth, cinnamon-hued brow. She removed her half-frame glasses and opened her arms. "Hello, honey. I didn't hear you come in."

Rachel ignored the jab of memory on hearing the word "honey" and bent to hug her mother. She felt warm and secure. For a long moment, Rachel just held on. Just now, she needed to know someone loved her despite the mistakes she had made.

Finally, Martha lifted her head, the frown once again creasing her forehead. "Where is the dress? Did you forget and leave it in the truck?"

"At the dress shop. I didn't buy it. The back was too revealing."

"I knew I should have gone with you." Martha shook her head of stylishly cut gray hair. "You haven't been out enough socially to know what the latest fashions are. The gown I picked won't show nearly as much as some of the women did at the Cotillion Idlewild Ball or at the Martin Luther King, Jr. banquet. I was actually embarrassed for some of those ladies."

Taking a seat on the floral-patterned sofa across the room, Rachel sent the petite woman a smile. "Then aren't you glad some other woman isn't going to say the same thing about me?" she teased. "And red, of all colors! You must be tired of me hanging around so much."

"You know that's not true," Martha quickly defended. "You're a beautiful woman, yet, you're the only one in my close circle of friends with a marriageable daughter still single. Worse, you refuse to go anyplace where you might meet an eligible man. And if you do, you're wearing denim. Well, no more. I refuse to let you hide away because of an unfortunate incident."

Rachel's smile faltered. "I'm not hiding, Mother."

"What else do you call it when you refuse to meet

any of our social engagements? I can't remember the last time you went out on a date."

"Mother, we've been all through this. I'm just not the social type. After I leave work, I'm ready to go home."

"I know. I'm so proud of you taking over the company for your father, but you're too young to stay at home," Martha reasoned.

"That's the only way I can catch up on my paperwork."

"Not this weekend you won't. You're coming to Mayor Davis's Fourth of July party, and that's final."

Rachel groaned and leaned back against the cushion. "I couldn't be happier that Stanton has its first black mayor, but I've done my bit. I campaigned and voted for him. Isn't that enough?"

"No, it is not. On our own state's celebration of be-latedly learning of the Emancipation Proclamation eighteen months after the fact on June 19, 1865, you barely stayed through the singing of the Negro National Anthem. A person of position owes it to the community to put something back," Martha told her.

"I'm sorry I had to leave the Juneteenth celebration, but it was a weekday and therefore a workday, since the date hasn't been declared a national holiday," Rachel said.

"Well, you can make up for it at the mayor's party. I saw him today and he mentioned his son, Lamar, is coming from Austin for the affair. Mayor Davis told me the only reason he thought Lamar was coming was to see you."

Rachel rolled her eyes. Lamar was a nice man, but

friendship was all she had to offer him. "Sounds as if we've gone from civic duty to matchmaking."

Martha was undisturbed. "You haven't given me much choice in the matter. I want to see you happy and a woman can't be totally happy until she's married and has a family," she said dogmatically. "You and your father are the joy of my life."

"What are you doing here this time of day?"

Rachel tensed in spite of herself at the brusque voice and turned to see her father. Her heart winced as it always did lately on seeing him. His face was gaunt from the thirty pounds he had lost since his last heart attack. His shoulders, once proud and straight, were thin and stooped. Worry instead of laughter shone in his brown eyes.

"Hello, Daddy," Rachel said, trying not to remember the old days when her doting father had always greeted her with a smile and a hug. "Everything's fine. I just stopped by on my way to the office."

J. T. Malone's narrow shoulders slumped even lower as he seemed to lean heavily onto the carved walking cane clutched in his right fist.

"The doctor told you not to worry about the company, J.T. Our baby is taking care of things just fine." Martha looked back at her daughter thoughtfully. "Although I never thought, after her upbringing, she'd end up looking like one of your construction crew."

A memory of Logan's blatant stare flashed through Rachel's mind. "It goes with the territory." Out of the corner of her eye, she watched her father slowly lower himself into a straight-backed chair.

"Martha, would you get me a glass of water, please?"

"Certainly." She was up before his sentence was completed.

Rachel knew it was just a ploy to get her mother out of the room. So did her mother. Yet she never seemed to mind letting her husband make all the family and business decisions. Only once had she adamantly refused to leave the room or let her husband's word be final. Martha Malone had stood toe-to-toe with her six-foot-two husband and told him how things were going to be and that was that. To Rachel's dying day she would always regret her mother's intervention had been for nothing.

As soon as Martha was out of sight J.T. said, "Nothing can go wrong this time."

"All three of the projects are on schedule, Daddy."

"Just see that it continues," he said tightly, his gaze to the left of his daughter's face. "If anything goes wrong with the college dorm, the city council won't give us another chance."

"I know, Daddy. I'm working hard."

Silence stretched across the room. She hadn't expected his vote of confidence, and she tried not to let it bother her when it didn't come. Once her father had told anyone who stood still long enough of his "Princess's" latest award or accomplishment. Eight years ago, that had changed. Now, she and her father did a delicate balancing act of being civil instead of being loving.

For a moment, Rachel toyed with the idea of asking him to look her in the face and, no matter how painful for either of them, to get everything out in the open. Until they did, they could never regain their former closeness. She had always been Daddy's girl. After school and on weekends, she'd been his living shadow. Maybe that was why her deception was so difficult for him to forgive or forget.

Fighting down the hurt, she rose. "Please tell Mother I'll call later."

She was halfway to the door when the sound of her name stopped her.

"Rachel."

She turned. Hope stirred at the unexpected concern she heard in his voice. "Yes, Daddy?"

His gaze skittered across her face before falling to the space between his feet, his fingers flexed on the walking stick. "Nothing. Just get the job done."

She walked from the house at a brisk pace. The desperation and uncertainty in her father's face and eyes were nothing new; the fear was. They both knew if Malone went under it would be because of the decision she had made long ago. How could something that had felt so right at the time be so wrong and have such far-reaching consequences? Memories of the past came rushing back....

Arms wrapped around her waist, Rachel had leaned against the wall outside the ICU of Stanton Memorial

Hospital and fought a losing battle with the tears streaming down her cheeks. This couldn't be happening. It wasn't supposed to turn out this way. Her love for Logan Prescott shouldn't have caused so much pain and heartache.

"Rae."

Her head jerked up and around at the raspy sound of someone calling her by the name only Logan used. Shock widened her eyes as they traveled slowly over his battered face, his torn dirty clothes. She was the cause of this. She shut her eyes and tucked her lower lip between her teeth to keep from crying out.

"I didn't start the fight with your father. I thought he was having trouble breathing and sweating because he was so angry. I didn't realize what was happening until he was about to pass out." Logan's arm circled his waist. "I tried to keep him from falling, but I couldn't."

Her eyes opened and stared at his poor, battered body. He could barely stand himself, yet he had tried to help her father. "This is not what I wanted. Everything is turned upside down. Daddy in ICU. You...." Her shaky voice trailed off. Restless hands continued their relentless sweep up and down her arms. She didn't think she'd ever be warm again. Tears crested in her eyes, then rolled down her cheek. "I didn't mean for this to happen."

Logan looked at her a long time, his hand pressed against the wall to keep him upright. More than anything she wanted to go to him, to hold him, to soothe the pain she knew he must be feeling in his body as well as in his soul. But that was the one thing she couldn't do.

"Welcome to the real world, Rae."

Somehow his words made her feel young and foolish. "Is that all you have to say?"

"What do you want me to say?"

Say you love me. Say no matter what you'll never stop loving me. Before the thoughts could become words the door behind her opened. Pastor Rodgers, and his wife, Emma, came out of ICU with Rachel's mother. One glimpse at Logan and Martha Malone burst into tears. Rushing to her mother, Rachel gathered the smaller woman protectively in her arms. Rachel's worried gaze locked with Logan's over her mother's head.

The minister cleared his throat. "Son, maybe it would be better if you left."

"I have a right to be here." Logan never took his eyes from Rachel's. "Tell him."

Martha Malone's grip on Rachel tightened as she lifted her pinched, tearstained face. "Leave my baby alone. You've caused enough trouble."

"Mrs. Malone, I'm sorry for what happened, but I have a right to be here. Rae is—"

"No!" The simultaneous shout came from Rachel and her mother. Her mother was trying to protect Rachel: Rachel was trying to protect Logan.

"What's going on here?"

Terror went through Rachel. She knew Logan wanted her to acknowledge him as her husband, but if she did, he'd be the one to suffer the consequences. Her father had made it very clear this morning when he left the house in a rage. Trying to protect Logan, her gaze skittered away.

"Is Prescott bothering you, Mrs. Malone?"

"Just make him go away," her mother whispered, her head barely reaching her daughter's shoulder.

The burly sheriff took a threatening step toward Logan. "You heard Mrs. Malone, move on."

Instead of moving, Logan kept looking at her as if trying to compel her to speak up and acknowledge him as her husband. She couldn't. Her chest felt tight. Her throat ached. She saw the love in his eyes and wept inside because she had to ignore it.

Sheriff Stone unsnapped his gun holster. "I'm not going to ask you again."

A horrified cry erupted from Rachel. Frantically she tried to disentangle herself from her mother, but her mother held on. Somehow she knew she was the only one who could get him to leave. "Mr. Prescott, we appreciate your concern, but you don't have to stay."

Logan didn't move. The sheriff's hand shifted toward the butt of his .357 Magnum.

With a supple twist of her body, Rachel broke free. Ignoring her mother's frantic cry to stop, Rachel continued until she stood between Logan and the sheriff. The relief in his battered face caused her heart to wince. Because she knew she had to ruthlessly destroy any love he had for her.

"Please leave." Fear and desperation gave Rachel's

words the hard edge she needed for Logan to believe her. "You're only making things worse."

Unable to bear the agony in his face, she turned her back on him, reclasped her mother's hand and thanked the sheriff. She never remembered what the sheriff said. All she heard was the slight shuffling of Logan's feet as he walked out of her life.

Slowly, memories faded and Rachel came back to the present and climbed into the truck. Her father had recovered, but he had never fully regained his health. Consequently, Malone Construction had suffered. The day in the hospital eight years ago all their lives had changed. She desperately wished she could say it had been for the better.

"Have you seen him yet?"

Shoulders hunched, head bent, Rachel continued pouring maple syrup over her pancakes. After a restless night of thinking about Logan Prescott, the last thing she wanted to do was start off the day talking about him. All she wanted was to enjoy the breakfast buffet at the Waffle House and forget yesterday happened.

A glance across the table at her best friend, Salina Hawkins, told Rachel she might not have any choice. Perhaps she had a right to know. More times than Rachel cared to remember, Salina had covered for Rachel while she was with Logan. "Yes, I saw him."

"Well?" came Salina's impatient response.

"How did you find out he's back?" Rachel asked, stalling for time.

"Daddy told me. He saw Logan at the gas station this morning," Salina explained. "Now, give."

Setting the syrup aside, Rachel studied Salina's anxious expression. From personal experience, Rachel knew that despite Salina's sweet, heart-shaped face and easygoing manner, she had the tenacity of a bulldog when she wanted something. That same tenacity had helped her become an award-winning investigative reporter for one of the top newspapers in the country. Still, it was worth a try. "Well, what?"

"Did...did you tell him?"

Rachel had known the question was coming, had thought she had prepared herself for it, but she was wrong. The pain she thought was safely under control now hit her in the stomach like a fist. She hunched farther over the wooden table in a reflexive motion to lessen the hurt. The shifting of her jean-clad bottom on the aged vinyl seat caused it to creak.

"He has a right to know," Salina said softly.

"I couldn't. He's changed." Rachel glanced up as she sought the right words. "He's hard, almost cruel. I can't help thinking maybe I helped him to become the way he is."

"You did what you thought was best for everyone at the time."

"Only it wasn't," Rachel whispered softly.

"You're not over him yet, are you." It was a statement not a question.

"Your waffles are getting cold and I'd like to talk about something else."

Hearing the forbidding tone in Rachel's voice, Salina sat back in the booth and picked up her fork. "Message received." Seconds later a mischievous smile deepened the twin dimples in her ebony-hued face. "You're still coming with me tonight?"

Rachel smiled her first smile of the day. One of the reasons she always liked Salina was her resilient nature. "I can't see why you want to spend your last night at Big Al's Place."

Mischief danced in Salina's eyes. "Girl, are you kidding? The infamous juke joint, known to one and all as the place of sin and degradation and rowdiness…it's practically a Texas monument."

"What will Nick say when he finds out?" Rachel asked.

"My straight-laced Baptist husband, whom I love dearly, will only smile and be happy I got it out of my system." Salina grinned. "It shouldn't be too crowded on a Sunday night and he knows I'll be safe with you."

Rachel pursed her lips. "Our safety is what worries me. I think this is the craziest plan you've ever had, and we both know you've had some humdingers."

Picking up her juice, Salina looked over the rim of the glass. "Some of my plans weren't so crazy. Planning that flat tire on your car sure got things rolling between you and Logan."

"Yes, and see how that turned out."

Instantly contrite, Salina reached across the table and

placed her hand atop Rachel's clenched one. "I'm sorry,
I shouldn't have said anything."

"It's all right." Rachel shook her head. "I just wish I had
the presence of mind yesterday to ask him what brought
him back to Stanton and how long he plans to stay."

Salina's eyes widened. "Oh, my goodness. You got
a chance to get your wish. Logan just walked in."

Rachel's entire body stiffened. She felt panicky,
breathless. The feeling increased as she watched
Salina's gaze dart from her to Logan. She had seen that
"take-charge-and-damn-the-consequences" look a hundred times. "Don't."

Salina lifted her arm and Rachel knew she had lost.
"Logan, over here," Salina called, beckoning him.

"I'll never forgive—"

"Morning, Salina, Rachel," Logan greeted, his gaze
going briefly to Rachel's bent head before bringing his
attention back to Salina. "For a minute I didn't recognize you until you flashed that killer smile."

Pleased, Salina smiled again. "I knew you right away.
Daddy told me he saw you this morning. What brings
you back to town?"

Out of the corner of his eye, Logan saw Rachel's pause
in reaching for her glass of water. "Unfinished business."

Salina threw a quick look at the silent Rachel. "Plan
on staying long?"

"As long as it takes," Logan answered cryptically.

"That sounds mysterious. What kind of business
are you in?"

Instead of answering Salina, Logan smiled. "Now, I remember something else about you. Your inquisitiveness."

Rachel sent her best friend a silent thanks for trying to get answers to Rachel's questions. Unfortunately, she didn't know any more now than she did yesterday.

Salina laughed. "I guess my time spent as a newspaper reporter is showing. Thanks for not calling it nosiness. My husband does."

"You marry anyone I know?"

"Yes, Nicholas Hawkins," Salina said proudly. "He's an electrical engineer. He recently received a promotion and was transferred from Seattle to Charlotte. After selling the house, I came back to spend a few days with my parents before joining him."

Logan shook his dark head. "You always said you were going to marry him. Although I was worried when you got so mad at him for taking another girl to a dance, you let the air out of his tires."

Salina looked abashed. "Don't remind me. I can't believe I was so childish. If Rachel hadn't convinced me to find Nick and tell him what I'd done and if you hadn't answered our frantic call to bring a portable air pump, I might not be Mrs. Hawkins today."

"At least you cared enough to fight for him."

At his words, an uneasy silence settled around them. Salina broke it. "Tonight Rachel is helping me have a grand send-off by going with me to Big Al's."

For the first time Logan centered his attention

on Rachel. He had been barely out of high school when he began earning his erroneous reputation as a tough guy at Big Al's. He didn't pick a fight, but he never walked away from one either. The stupidity of youth. Rowdy places like Big Al's didn't get better; they got worse. "I hope the men you're going with are prepared to fight for you."

"We're going by ourselves," Salina told him.

"I don't think that's wise."

"Nobody asked your opinion," Rachel snapped. He had some nerve, ignoring her, then trying to tell her what to do.

His hard black eyes looked over at Rachel, and for a split second she wished she had kept her mouth shut. "Did you finally stop pretending to eat?"

"I wasn't pretending." Picking up a piece of bacon, she took a sizable bite and chewed vigorously.

"I think you should reconsider and go someplace else," Logan advised Salina.

She grinned, deepening her dimples. "Come on, Logan. You of all people should understand. I heard you were practically a fixture in the place. We just want to see what we've missed."

"Rachel didn't miss it; she's been there."

Rachel choked on her bacon.

"Hey, I thought best friends had no secrets," Salina admonished, her large black eyes dancing. "So is it as lowdown and dirty as they say?"

Shooting Logan a lethal glare, Rachel went back to

her meal. "You can decide for yourself when you see it tonight."

"Stay away from Big Al's," Logan ordered. "This is one time your scheme might backfire. Some of them have far-reaching consequences."

The way he said it brought Rachel's head up. His gaze pinned her in place. "I once told you, I never do anything I don't want to. Flat tire or no, you could have walked the three miles back to town if I hadn't wanted to stop."

"I wish you hadn't," Rachel snapped.

"For once we agree on something," he tossed back. "Have a safe trip, Salina, and remember what I said about Big Al's. It's a mean place." Tipping his hat, he walked to the back of the coffee shop and took a seat.

Rachel watched a waitress rush over to Logan and give him a menu. For a second, Rachel had an irrational urge to go over and pull the grinning woman's blond hair out by its black roots. "What time shall I pick you up?"

Salina looked uncertain. "Maybe we shouldn't. Logan started me think—"

"What time?"

Salina sighed and bowed to the inevitable. "Nine, I guess."

Rachel took another bite of bacon. "Good. Logan can't tell me what to do."

With her chin propped in the open palm of one hand, Rachel waved the smoked-filled air in Big Al's from her face with the other. It was a losing battle. The elongated "shotgun" club's flat ceiling barely reached ten feet. Across the round, scarred table, Salina's gaze darted warily around the dimly lit room.

Rachel's feet shifted restlessly. She winced as dirt, and she didn't want to know what else, grated against the wooden floor. Sighing none too softly, she glanced at the dissipating foam in their mugs of untouched beer. They had felt compelled to order something from the glaring, gum-chewing, hip-swaggering waitress in black leather.

At the other end of the room, a raunchy song about a man's wild sexual night blared from a jukebox and competed with the noise of a disputed pool game, a pinball machine, and rowdy voices.

"Have you seen enough?" Rachel asked.

"Rather depressing, isn't it?" Salina muttered. "I thought this was going to be fun."

"The unknown is often not as hot as one expects."

Salina's mischievous nature surfaced. "I wouldn't say that. The first time making love was better."

A memory of entwined bodies atop a king-size bed in a honeymoon suite flashed into Rachel's mind before she shut it off. Her lips tightened. "You ready to go?"

"I put my foot in my mouth again, didn't I?"

"Not your fault. You and Nick deserve to be happy. If I can't handle Logan's memory, that's my problem, not yours." Standing, Rachel began to weave through the crowd. Salina, silent for once, was on her heels.

Rachel halted abruptly as a clean-shaven man pushed

away from the bar and stepped in front of her. "Would you like to dance?"

Before she could tell him no, he was roughly shoved aside by another man.

"A real man doesn't have to ask a woman, he tells her," the second man said. "Let's go, baby." Two other men standing at the bar urged him on.

Rachel looked at the beefy hand just inches from her, then to the burly dark-skinned man blocking her path, and stiffened. He looked mean and hard. The scar running from his left eye to the corner of his mouth intensified the impression.

Fighting back her unease, she said, "Sorry, I was just leaving."

The first man laughed. The sound died abruptly as the hand that had been inches from Rachel backhanded him in the face. With a howl of pain, he sagged to the floor.

Frightened by the second man's casual brutality, Rachel stepped backward and bumped into her friend.

"Maybe we should have listened to Logan," Salina whispered, clutching Rachel's arm.

"Where were we?" the man asked, extending his hand.

"I told you, I'm going home," Rachel said firmly, and started to walk around the burly stranger only to find her path blocked.

"You think you're better than me or something?" he growled, his voice now as mean and as hard as his face.

"R-Rachel," Salina said shakily. "What are we going to do?"

A good question. Rachel wished she had a good answer. Frantically, she looked around for anyone she knew or any of her crew. She saw neither. The people she socialized with wouldn't set foot in Big Al's parking lot. And thanks to her threat of firing any person who came to work unable to do their job because of drinking, none of her crew was there, either. *She was on her own.*

Chapter 4

The man stepped closer. "You're no better than me. Wearing those fancy clothes don't mean nothing."

Fighting down the fear creeping through her, Rachel straightened her spine and met the challenging gaze of the stranger. With black cowboy boots, a simple white cotton blouse, and black jeans, she wasn't dressed any differently from the other women in the room, except that her clothes weren't as tight and didn't expose as much skin. Turn a man down and right away he'd accuse you of thinking you were too good for him. A man's ego was colossal, she thought.

"Please move ou—"

A low, throaty rumble of familiar male laughter

stopped her in mid-sentence and had her twirling toward the sound. *Logan.* He sat at a small table against the wall across from her. The gum-chewing waitress leaned over him. This time she was all smiles. It was obvious she was willing to take more than cocktail orders. So *she* was the reason he didn't want them here. Unconsciously, Rachel took a step toward them.

"Rachel, where…oh, my goodness," cried Salina. "It's Logan. We're saved."

"Lee Roy, it looks like she's more interested in the man over there than she is in you," called one of the men from the bar.

"You got competition, man," said the other heckler.

"Ain't nobody cuttin' in on my time," yelled Lee Roy, as his gaze followed the direction Rachel had started in.

Rachel froze. An old memory pricked her. Logan, battered and in pain, fighting to stand. All because she had been too selfish to tell the truth, and then too big of a coward to stand up for herself, for him. Lee Roy had proved he didn't fight fair. This time Logan wasn't going to pay the price for her mistake.

"No one is cutting in on your time," Rachel said, turning toward Lee Roy and trying to draw his attention back to her. "The waitress didn't return the change from the ten I gave her for our two beers."

"Rach—" Salina broke off at Rachel's stern look. Obviously puzzled, the other woman looked longingly at Logan, then at Rachel.

Once Lee Roy's hard glare switched to Rachel, she said, "You've had your fun, but now I want you to get out of my way or I'm calling the police."

"A real smart mouth," Lee Roy snarled. "I know how to fix you." His hand shot out. Salina screamed. Rachel leaned to one side and brought up her knee. He deflected the blow, caught her arms, then dragged her up against him. His foul breath pelted her face. He grinned, showing stained yellow teeth.

"I'm going to enjoy teaching you a lesson." His head bent. Rachel kicked him as hard as she could with the pointed toe of her boot. He let out a bellow of rage and clutched his leg. Rachel grabbed Salina and started for the door. Three running steps later they were caught by the two agitators from the bar. Their struggles were met with laughter.

Lee Roy slowly straightened. The scar on his rage-filled face pulsated wildly. Cruel fingers closed around Rachel's forearm and jerked her up against a rock-hard chest. "You're gonna pay for that."

"Let her go."

The deep, chilling voice rang clearly in the sudden quietness of the club. In spite of herself Rachel went weak-kneed in relief. *Logan.*

Lee Roy didn't release her, but only searched the dim room until he located Logan slowly emerging through the parting crowd.

Five feet away, Logan repeated the challenge. "I'm not going to tell you again."

The man shook his head as if to clear the alcoholic haze, then looked at Logan a long time. Finally, as if discovering what he sought, he raised his shaggy head and let out a roar of contemptuous laughter. "Logan Prescott, I already ran you out of town once before like a whipped dog. Guess I'll have to do it again."

A muscle twitched in Logan's dark jaw. Rachel sensed his anger, but she also sensed it was strangely controlled.

Lee Roy laughed again. "Here, Sonny, hold her for me. This won't take long." He slung Rachel into the arms of the tall light-skinned black man beside him, and came back with a balled fist aimed at Logan's face.

Rachel screamed Logan's name in warning.

It wasn't necessary. Logan ducked the punch. His foot shot out. Lee Roy grabbed his groin. His eyes bulged. Like a ballerina, Logan twirled on the balls of his feet, and when he came full circle, his foot rammed the braggart in the chest and sent him stumbling backward. He fell over a table, then slid to the floor, gasping for breath and clutching his groin.

Logan calmly walked to the man holding Rachel. Sonny drew back his fist. With a quick slice of the heel of Logan's hand to the side of the man's neck, he dropped like a lead weight. He didn't move.

Slowly, Logan, his face harsh and ruthless, looked at the third man holding Salina. He was already backing up, his hands raised. "Hey, man. They're all yours."

Apparently everyone thought it was a good idea to

distance themselves from the two men on the floor, because people who had crowded closer to see the fight began cautiously moving away, their eyes watchful. Rachel knew how they felt; if Logan hadn't just rescued her, she might flee from the savage intensity in his face herself. Instead, she reached for a trembling Salina.

She did it again, Logan thought.

Fingers of steel closed around Rachel's arm. Once more she had made him forget she was no longer his responsibility and had him coming to her rescue. Maybe if it had been any other man bothering her, Logan might have stayed out of it. But a loud-mouthed coward like Lee Roy took perverse pleasure in inflicting pain on both men and women. Logan knew from bitter personal experience.

And if Logan hadn't been there to stop him…

A mixture of fear and rage swept through Logan. He wanted to feel neither emotion for the trembling woman he held by the arm. He yanked open the club's door with one hand and dragged Rachel through with the other. Since she kept her death grip on Salina, her best friend hurried to keep up.

Logan didn't speak until they stood by Rachel's truck. "Get in and take Salina home. I'll follow you."

The whiplash of his voice almost caused Rachel to recoil. "L-Logan, I'm sorry you got involved, but thank you—"

"I didn't do it for you," he interrupted coldly. "I had a score to settle with Lee Roy. You just gave me the excuse I needed."

Afraid he would see how much his curt dismissal of her thanks affected her, Rachel climbed into the truck. Sitting very still, she tried to accept what she had no way of changing. Logan wanted nothing from her, not even her thanks. The thought that he hated her so much filled her with anguish.

As soon as Salina got in and closed her door, Rachel started the engine. The truck spun out of the graveled parking lot onto the deserted two-lane highway.

Fury shimmered through Logan as he followed Rachel home. He should have known asking…all right, ordering her to stay away from Big Al's was like waving a red flag in front of an enraged bull. Figuring she'd do anything to defy him, he hadn't been able to sit quietly at Ida Mae's house. He had told her he had something to do and left. When he saw Rachel's truck in Big Al's parking lot he had wanted to shake her. She couldn't have forgotten their first visit there.

A month after they had started secretly dating, he'd had some crazy idea to test her by showing her the gritty side of his world. He'd wanted to see if she'd run. Once inside Big Al's she had clutched his arm so tightly that he had had fingernail marks the next day. Yet all Rachel had said was, "I don't care where we are so long as we're together."

The turbulence Logan felt intensified as he remembered the pride and love he had felt at that moment. Eight weeks later she had clung to her mother and wanted no part of him. She'd believed lies instead of truths, chosen her parents instead of her husband.

Tonight, instead of remembering her betrayal, he had looked into her face and wanted nothing more than to take the fear from her eyes.

He had accomplished that, but he had also made sure she didn't think he had taken Lee Roy out just to protect her. It was bad enough rushing off to Big Al's. Then, when he saw her in trouble, he thought of getting back at her by having her beg for his help.

He had laughed out loud on purpose, fully expecting her to turn to him. Instead, she had taken on Lee Roy by herself. Admittedly, she had handled herself well. Ida Mae was right about Rachel being a fighter. But she couldn't fight dollars and cents.

He stopped his car as Rachel turned into a driveway of a small frame house. By the time she pulled to a halt, the single car garage door was halfway up.

Logan frowned. Why was she stopping here? She had already dropped off Salina. The obvious reason of seeing a man sent another shaft of anger burning through him. His gaze narrowed in an attempt to read the name on the free-standing mailbox near the curb: Rachel Malone. He glanced again at the house. She couldn't be living there.

He reread her name in flowing script on the mailbox with the family of wooden ducks marching across the top. His frown deepened. Although he had never been inside her parents' house, he had seen it enough to know their living room was probably bigger than this entire house. It didn't make sense.

Rachel had grown up being the pampered, indulged daughter of one of the richest families in the county. Eight years ago she had never completely made a bed, washed a load of clothes, or fixed more than a simple meal of toast and eggs.

His gaze switched to watch the automatic garage door inch down. Moments later he tracked Rachel's progress through the house by the lights winking on and off. They finally stayed on in a room on the far side of the house, the bedroom. The feeling of being shut out hit him without warning. She had made a home for herself, but she wanted no part of him in it.

How many times had he gone to bed thinking Rachel hadn't trusted him enough to build a home, a life with him? How many times as a young kid had he watched other families from the outside looking in? He had thought he had finally made it inside to share the warmth, the happiness, the love until Rachel had reminded him of the lesson his parents taught him.

He was a mistake, unplanned, an inconvenience to be pawned off on relatives or friends at every opportunity. His parents liked nothing better than going out and having a good time partying. The only reason they left Chicago and came to Stanton was to claim the property his father's uncle had left. They stayed after his mother became ill because M. D. Anderson Cancer Center in Houston was the best in the nation. After she'd died, his father had crawled into a bottle. Logan never stopped hoping his father would reach out to him.

He hadn't.

As Logan pushed the bitter memories away, his gaze went back to the bedroom. An unsettling thought crossed his mind. Rachel's name might be on the mailbox, but that didn't mean she slept alone. Why would she give up a life of ease to clean house and cook her own meals? It wasn't in her nature to be this independent. Seeing him secretly was the first time she had ever gone against her parents. They'd planned her life and chosen her friends and she'd obeyed like a dutiful daughter.

The light winked out. Logan's hands clamped around the steering wheel as his imagination conjured up another man pulling Rachel into his arms. Roughly shoving the car into gear, he spun away from the house and the image.

Rachel Malone was his past.

A little after ten the next morning, Rachel's truck jolted to a halt on the deep-rutted road gouged out by heavy equipment and rain. Noises assaulted her from all sides. Grabbing her yellow hardhat, she climbed out. Her steps were slow. Sleep had eluded her most of the night.

No matter how she tossed, turned or punched her pillow, Logan's face, full of hatred, was there to taunt her. Well, today she was going to put Logan out of her mind and get on with her life. She had told Salina as much when she had called early this morning to say goodbye.

Logan Prescott was her past.

Off in the distance, she heard several of her crewmen call enticingly to a passing group of college coeds dressed in halter tops and shorts. From experience, Rachel knew the light-hearted flirting would stop once the men saw her. They had always shown her the greatest respect and she felt totally at ease working around her crew. With one exception.

"Morning, Miss Malone. What can I do for you?"

Startled, Rachel swung around to see the foreman, Jake Johnson, standing in front of her. As usual, he was grinning from ear to ear. For some reason all those bared teeth made her think of a piranha just before he bit into his prey. A couple of times she had caught him looking at her in a speculative manner, but he never once did anything she could call him on. Just the opposite was true. He was overly courteous and went out of his way to please her and yet, she couldn't shake the feeling that behind that smile was a man she shouldn't trust.

"Good morning, Jake. I came to look things over," she finally said.

"Your daddy send you?"

"My father doesn't *send* me anywhere. I'm a partner and general manager," she told him. "I come and go as I please."

The grin slipped from his bearded face. "I didn't mean anything by that, Miss Malone. It's just that I talked with your daddy this morning and he was worried about the dorm coming in on time. Of course, I told him not to worry and what a fine job you were doing."

Jake's wounded expression made Rachel feel utterly foolish for overreacting and being annoyed with her father. She knew his faith in her ability to run the company was shaky, but did he have to let Jake know as well? Especially when by calling, her father had shown he trusted Jake completely. Their fifteen year history of working together and being fishing buddies was difficult to compete with and she didn't plan to try. The dorm coming in on time would speak for itself.

"I'm sorry, Jake, for being short with you. Thank you for the vote of confidence."

"You're welcome and don't give it a second thought about being a little testy. Running an operation this size is a big job," Jake told her. "How about a cup of coffee?"

She shook her head. "I'll take a rain check. What I'd like to do is look over the plans and inspect the operation."

The smile tilting the bearded corner of Jake's mouth faltered, but all he said was, "Whatever you want, Miss Malone. I'm at your service."

Wondering if she had imagined the suggestive tone in the foreman's last words, Rachel sent him a faint smile and started toward the work trailer. Her father trusted this man unequivocally, why couldn't she? There was only one incident in the six months of them working together that she had questioned her father's unshakable faith.

A month ago she caught one of the electrical subcontractors about to install low-grade, substandard wiring.

He had said Jake okayed the wiring change from the one in the specifications plans for the dormitory. However, when she questioned Jake he had denied everything and appeared genuinely hurt that she hadn't taken up for him immediately.

When he turned and asked the man to repeat himself, the electrician confessed he had lied. She might have believed the smaller man was intimidated by Jake if he had raised his voice or did anything threatening. Yet he hadn't. She fired the electrician and apologized to Jake. However, at odd times, she often thought if the electrician had looked at Jake's grin and saw a piranha. Pushing the incident to the back of her mind, Rachel walked up the three steps of the work trailer.

Later that morning she and Jake were about to climb into the freight elevator to check out the wiring on the top floor of the five-story building when one of the men shouted to her.

"Miss Malone. Miss Malone. A man wants to see you."

"Me?"

Jimmy nodded his sandy head. "Yes, ma'am. He asked for the person in charge."

"Did he tell you his name?" Rachel inquired.

"He didn't say, and I forgot to ask." Jimmy looked crestfallen, then he grinned at himself as only an eighteen-year-old can. "I guess I was so busy looking at his car, I forgot. Man, it's something."

"He did the same thing yesterday when a rep from a concrete company came by." Jake bared his teeth in a wide grin. "You better be thankful you work for a fine person like Miss Malone. Another boss might not care if you were the sole support of your mother and little brothers and fire you."

Jimmy's green eyes widened in alarm. Rachel looked at Jake and couldn't tell if he had meant to frighten Jimmy or make him more conscientious. Either way, as foreman, he shouldn't have stooped to threats involving Jimmy's family.

"As long as Malone Construction has a payroll, Jimmy's name will be on it." She turned her back on the foreman and smiled encouragingly at Jimmy. "Why don't you show me where the man is waiting."

Jimmy took off and Rachel followed him across the cluttered site, stepping over cable, beams and scrap lumber. She was still trying to figure out the man's identity when she came around the work trailer.

The instant her gaze touched his deceptively lean profile, she knew. Unconsciously, her hand touched the tendrils of hair fluttering against her cheek. Realizing what she had done, she dropped her hand. He hadn't come to see her. His refusal to accept her thanks showed he wanted nothing to do with her.

"Here she is, mister," Jimmy yelled, then headed back the way he had come.

Logan looked around, and at that moment she could have strangled Jimmy. Now she had to walk the thirty-odd feet separating them with Logan tracking her every movement.

Lifting her chin, she started toward him with stiff dignity. As expected, he openly studied her. As for Rachel, she found it impossible not to notice the way the midday sun glinted in his hair, the way his beige knit shirt clung to his wide, muscular chest. Nor did she fail to notice the shifting of his biceps as he shoved his hands deep into the pockets of his wheat-colored slacks, the silent power in his hard thighs and long legs. He was a beautiful specimen of manhood, and he despised her.

A few feet away from Logan, she stopped. Her eyes indifferent, she shoved her hands into her back pockets to hide their slight trembling. Today, she wasn't going to lose her cool with him. She'd show him she was as indifferent to him as he was to her.

Logan stared at the twin peaks straining against the green fabric of Rachel's blouse, the tiny waist, the gentle flare of her hips, her long, slender legs. His body stirred. A part of him realized she'd always have the power to make his heart beat faster, to make him want to take her to bed even as another part of him struggled to remember his reason for being there. He couldn't forget the lesson she taught him long ago.

"Good morning, Logan. You wanted to see the person in charge?"

"Where is your father?"

Uneasiness swept through Rachel. She dragged her hands from their hiding place. The last thing she wanted was for her father and Logan to meet. "He's at home. You can talk to me. I'm running things now."

"I thought you wanted to be a fashion designer."

"Architects' creations last longer."

His hand shot out and grabbed one of hers. Before she could snatch it back, his thumb grazed the palm of her hand. "An ex-debutante with calluses. What is the world coming to?"

"Is there some point to this?" she asked, pulling her hand free and resisting the urge to hide it behind her back.

"Just an observation." He glanced around the site. "Steel and concrete is a long way from silk and satin."

"We all have to wake up from our dreams. As I recall, you wanted to own the largest construction company in the Southwest."

Something hard flickered in his black eyes, but no harsh word came back to lash out at her. The silence was just as condemning. She felt ashamed for being so vindictive. "I'm sorry. What can I do for you?"

"I heard Malone Construction Company is for sale."

Her body stiffened in defiance. "You heard wrong. Malone Construction has been in business for four generations. It will be around for another four."

Logan cast a raking glance at the shell of the five-story building. "If what I've heard is true, you may be wrong. It seems your father has taken out a sizable loan, and he's behind in the payments."

Logan watched shock widen her eyes and part her lips. *She hadn't known.* Her father was apparently acting like the true southern gentleman who believed in protecting his women from all unpleasantries.

"Where did you hear such a lie?" Rachel asked finally.

For some reason he refused to examine too closely, he didn't want to be the one to tell her. He shrugged. "Rumors aren't considered lies."

Her stance relaxed. "Nice try. If you don't have any more mischief to stir up, I have work to do."

"Get off this site."

Both Rachel and Logan spun around to see Jake, his beefy fists balled, his chest heaving, his face twisted in fury.

Logan pushed Rachel aside and stepped forward. "It took three of you last time. Lee Roy and Sonny found out last night it's not so easy in a fair fight. Now it's your turn."

Surprise tensed Jake's body, then his anger appeared to redouble. "I don't need no help to beat the tar out of you," Jake bragged.

Without thinking, Rachel jumped between the two men, her back to Logan. She knew trying to reason with Logan would be like trying to get the concrete wall in front of her to walk. "Back off, Jake."

"He shouldn't be here, Miss Malone. Not after what he done to your daddy," Jake raged.

"I decide that, not you. Now, get back to work, and don't interfere in my conversation again."

"Miss Mal—"

"I know how devoted you are to my father, but I don't give orders twice."

Throwing one last, murderous look at Logan who had stepped to one side of Rachel, Jake whirled and stalked away. Rachel let out a tension-filled breath. She had never seen Jake so enraged. He really loved her father. But with Jake gone, she still had the hardest thing to do, face Logan. He wasn't going to be grateful. She pivoted slowly. As expected, Logan was livid.

"Don't interfere again," he warned harshly, his fists clenched.

"I won't have my men fighting," she explained. "A battered man can't work."

"Your father had the same policy," Logan said, a cool edge of irony in his voice.

Rachel lifted her hand to push through her hair, felt the hardhat, and rammed her hand in her pocket instead. "If you and Jake want to tear each other apart away from here, that's between you and him. When you want to do it on my job site, then it's my business. This project is going to come in on time, and to do it, I need every man."

"Excuse me, Miss Malone," Jimmy said. "Ted has a question about the blueprints."

Grateful, Rachel barely glanced at Jimmy, who was already leaving. "Goodbye, Logan. I'm sure you can find your way out, and next time wear a hardhat." Nodding curtly, she headed for the cluster of men fifty feet away.

She tried to listen, but she kept glancing at Logan, who remained immobile. After what seemed an eternity, he started toward the parking area. He had gone a short distance when he stopped and hunkered down.

What in the world was he doing? He was getting off the site and now. She started toward him. A flicker of movement above his head caught her attention. Horror wiped the annoyance from her face.

The cable around a steel beam being hoisted by a crane was fraying like rotten twine. She sensed from the way the hoist jerked crazily that the crane operator was trying to swing the beam to a safe area. He wasn't going to make it.

And Logan was beneath it.

Rachel was running over the uneven terrain before she realized it. Logan would never hear her warning over the roar of the machinery. He had only one chance.

Afraid to look up, to see the beam fall, she fought the heavy weight of her workboots. Her heart screamed in silent protest as she heard the loud snap of the cable.

Logan was going to die.

Chapter 5

"W-what?" Hunched down retying his shoe, Logan caught a flash of yellow out of the corner of his eye, then he was tackled and knocked off his feet.

In desperation Rachel grabbed Logan around the waist, hoping she had enough strength and momentum to carry them beneath the safety of the building's shell. A cry of pain erupted from her lips as she landed on her right side with her arms locked around Logan. A minisecond later the sound mingled with Logan's muttered curse and the thud of the steel beam hitting the ground.

Babbles of excited voices broke over her. Pinned beneath Logan, she shuddered. Her eyes clamped shut.

Quivering hands felt the warmth beneath the coiled solidness of his muscled arms, his broad back. He was safe.

Logan's gaze flicked to the swirl of dust surrounding the beam less than ten feet away, then centered on the trembling, silent woman beneath him. His eyes were flint hard.

"Miss Malone, are you all right?"

"What happened?"

"She saved him! He'd have been flatter than a pancake."

"Why ain't they moving?"

Her sooty lashes lifted. The first thing Rachel saw was the rigid line of Logan's jaw. "L-Logan, I can't breathe."

Unrelenting fingers closed around her forearm, tightening momentarily before Logan stood, bringing Rachel with him.

"Let me through," demanded Jake. The cluster of men parted. Jake's eyes widened, he started toward Rachel.

Logan's fingers flexed. Rachel lifted her free hand to halt the foreman. "I—I'm all right, Jake," she barely managed to get the words out. Logan wasn't going to let go of her arm and she didn't want Jake making an issue of it.

Jake halted abruptly. He looked at Logan's tense body, then at Rachel's shivering one. The foreman's upper lip curled. He spat a stream of brown chewing tobacco juice in the dirt.

"Miss Malone! Miss Malone!" yelled a short, wiry black man as he shoved his way through the crowd that

had merged once the foreman passed. Shaking from
head to toe, the second man stopped in front of Rachel
and Logan, his frantic gaze going from one to the other.
"Miss Malone, I...if you...I'm sorry...I..." His barely
audible voice trailed off. Unsteady fingers wiped the
sweat from his dark face.

"It's not your fault, Ed," Rachel said, knowing her
voice sounded as wobbly as her legs and unable to do
anything about it. "I saw you trying to get the cable
unstuck. I want you and Jake to go over the pulley before
putting a new drag line on. Make sure nothing like this
happens again."

Ed's brown eyes widened. His head whipped in
Jake's direction.

"Would have done the world a favor if you hadn't saved
him after what he did to your daddy," Jake snarled con-
temptuously. "Look at him. So scared he can't even talk."

Out of the corner of her eyes, Rachel saw the arch of
Logan's jaw as he brought the full force of his gaze on
Jake. Logan's fingers tightened. Rachel fought to keep
the grimace of pain from her face and to stay on her feet.
"That will be enough, Jake."

"I don't think he's scared," Jimmy murmured. "He
looks mad enough to chew nails."

Rachel could well imagine Logan's rage. That was
the reason she had yet to look him in his face. "Jake,
keep things moving. I'm going to take Mr. Prescott to
the doctor to make sure he's all right. In the meantime,
I don't want word of this to leave the site. Everyone back

to work." One by one, the men began to leave, a few of them glancing over their shoulders.

Knowing Logan wasn't going to turn her arm loose, she started for the parking lot. She had no difficulty locating the car Jimmy had mentioned. Surrounded by dusty, dented trucks and cars, the shiny black Corvette stood out. All she saw last night of his car was low-slung headlights.

Obviously, Logan had done well for himself. She wondered if he had remained in the construction business. Fingers flexed on her arm. Time was running out. She wanted to be well away from everyone when the rigid control Logan held on his temper broke.

Shoving three fingers of her left hand into his front pants pocket, she retrieved his car keys. Opening the passenger door, she said, "Please, Logan. Get in." She sighed in relief when he complied. Tossing her hardhat into the back seat, she got inside and started the engine. The sports car easily answered her demand for speed. They were two miles from the construction site when the explosion she expected came.

"Stop the car!"

"Logan—"

"Rae, stop the damn car!"

The Corvette fishtailed to a stop. Dirt and gravel flew in all directions. She had heard that tone of voice only once before.

Logan looked at Rachel's dirt-smudged face, her blouse torn on the shoulder, and shuddered. With jerky movements, he opened his door, got out, then walked around to the driver's side. Calloused hands lifted a wide-eyed Rachel out of the car.

Black eyes met wide brown ones. "If you ever do such a stupid, asinine thing again, you won't be able to sit down for a week."

"Logan, I—"

"Damn it, Rae. Is that clear?" he shouted, shaking her suspended body in mid-air.

"Yes," she agreed meekly. Logan was past his endurance. He probably didn't even realize he was calling her by his pet name for her. Twice today she had stepped in to save him, and to a maverick like Logan, once was enough.

He set her none too gently on her feet. "Do you know you almost got killed? Why didn't you just yell?" he asked, his voice rising with each word.

Rachel swallowed as she recalled her fear when she had first seen Logan in danger. "You couldn't have heard me over the noise of all the machinery," she told him, and watched his face harden again. She rushed on, "Besides, I had my hardhat on."

Black eyes blazed. It was the wrong time to joke. She whirled to get back into the car. She never made it.

"Oh, my God, Rae. Your back is bleeding."

Rachel froze. Hunching one shoulder, then the other, she twisted her head around in an unsuccessful attempt to see what he was talking about.

"Stop that," Logan ordered, his voice oddly shaky. Gentle fingers probed the bloody area. "Why didn't you say something?"

Rachel winced as he touched a tender area. "I didn't know it until now."

Logan snatched his hand away and stared at the shredded, bloody blouse smeared with concrete shavings and dirt, and wished for anything except to know that she had been hurt trying to save his life. "I'm sorry."

Facing him she saw the agonized expression on Logan's dark face. "It's not your fault."

Logan knew it was. If he hadn't been trying to take his revenge on her and her father, he never would have gone to the site, and she wouldn't be hurt.

Without thinking, she laid her palm against the hard curve of his jaw. "It can't be more than a scratch."

Yes, it was, he wanted to say, but the tender expression on her face forestalled his words. She was trying to console him when he should be the one comforting her. His need for revenge had caused her to be injured and had almost gotten her killed. Roughened fingers gently closed around her hand. "Come on. Let's get your shoulder taken care of."

Picking her up in his arms, he carefully placed her in the passenger seat. Quickly circling the car, he hopped in and took off. One hand gripped the steering wheel, the other alternated between Rachel's hand and the balled gear shift.

"I can see why you drive a convertible." At his frown, she smiled. "You never take time to open the doors."

He vividly recalled dragging her out of the car by her

arms. His hand clenched. Disgust rolled over him. "I'm sorry for handling you so rough."

The smile almost slipped from her face. "I'd say I was lucky. The last time you thought I had put myself in danger, you shook me so hard my teeth rattled."

Logan cut a sharp glance at Rachel as he paused at a stop sign by the main highway. "You deserved it."

"I did not." Rachel lifted a delicate brow as he jerked the gear shift and accelerated onto the highway. In the past, even at his angriest, he had always changed gears smoothly. "I only wanted to show you my new prom gown. So instead of going with some of the gang to Salina's house for a pool party as I told my parents, I came to see you."

"And almost got yourself molested," he ground out, passing the other cars on the road as if they were parked.

"How was I to know I was being followed by a carload of boys from a rival high school?" Rachel defended. "They didn't start flashing their headlights, honking the horn, and yelling obscenities about my school football team until I was out of town."

"I had told you at least a dozen times it was too dangerous to come out to the house after eight at night," he reminded her roughly. He shot her a fierce look as he stopped at a light. "What if I had gone to play cards or gone for a beer? They could have blocked you in."

Rachel was undisturbed by his anger. As long as Logan was talking you could reason with him. It was when he stopped talking that you had to worry. "I told you. I was so scared that all I could think of was getting to you. I knew I'd be safe. And I was." The promise of another smile touched her lips. "You came charging out of your house with a baseball bat. I hardly noticed the car turning around. I was so busy getting out of my car and running to you. You didn't say a word for five minutes. When you did, my ears stung."

"But you never did anything so stupid...until today," Logan said, as he pulled to a stop in a squeal of brakes.

Rachel glanced around and every nerve in her body tensed. Wildly she looked away from the red glow of Stanton Memorial Hospital's emergency room entrance sign back to Logan. "Why are we here?"

For a moment Logan stared at her as if she might have hurt her head as well as her shoulder. "To get your shoulder fixed up."

"I don't want to go inside," she told him stiffly, pulling her hand from beneath his.

"What?"

"I—I don't like hospitals," she said. "I thought you were going to fix it."

"Me!" Logan yelled. "Lord, woman! How—" he roared, then caught himself. She hadn't seen the wound. "Your shoulder has to be cleaned and bandaged. Some Methiolate and a Band-Aid won't cut it." His voice lowered to a persuasive drawl. "Besides, you may need a tetanus booster."

"My tetanus is up to date," she told him. Once again her gaze went to the emergency room, then slithered

away. She pressed against the seat despite the pain beginning to throb in her shoulder and down her right arm.
Silently, she shook her head. Too many nightmares waited
for her inside. The last time she had been brought to an
emergency room, the doctor hadn't been able to fix her
up, no matter how hard she begged. "Just take me home."

"Are you crazy? You're bleeding all over the car and
you want to go home."

"Send me a bill," she snapped. She wasn't going in
there. Just sitting in the parking lot she remembered the
anguish, the blood, the overwhelming sense of loss that
time wasn't able to dim. She had lost too much that day.
She bit down on her lower lip to keep the tears stinging
her eyes at bay. And it had all been her fault.

Logan held his temper only by seeing the torment
and desperation in Rachel's face and remembering the
deep lacerations on her shoulder. It would hurt like hell
to have the cuts cleaned, and she had received them
trying to save his life.

"If I take you home, is there someone there who will
come back with you?"

"I live alone."

"Let me put it another way," he said slowly, surprised
at the effort it took to ask the next question. "Is there
someone else you'd rather have with you? Because if
there is, I'll stay with you until they can get here."

Once again, she shook her head. "No one."

"Then that settles it. It's going to be you and me."

Opening his door, he came around and opened hers,

then hunkered down by her. His dark brown fingers interlaced with hers. "Rae, honey, you need to see the doctor. If I could take care of you, don't you think I would?"

The throbbing sincerity in his voice caused her heart to wince. Yet, how much more would she hurt him if she told him why she was afraid. "I don't like hospitals," she repeated.

"I don't either."

Their gaze met and held. Each knew the other was thinking of the last time they'd been in a hospital together. "Why didn't you come with me?" he asked, the question out before he realized it. He promised himself never to ask.

"I..." her lips trembled.

"Never mind. It doesn't matter."

Rachel saw him retreat behind an impersonal mask and swallowed the growing lump in her throat. She had hurt him so much, taken so much from him. If he knew what her selfishness had caused, he'd never forgive her. She knew things could never be as they'd once been between them, but she didn't want to remember him looking at her with hate.

"If-if I went into the hospital, I might be recognized," she told him. "I don't want my parents or the bond company learning about the accident. I don't have time for OSHA to come snooping around and halting work. It would be better if I went to my doctor."

Logan reached over and handed her the cellular phone. "Make the call."

Trembling fingers closed around the receiver. In less than a minute, she hung up. "He's here making rounds."

"Like I said, it's you and me. Don't look so scared. It's only around ten. There shouldn't be that many people. Hide your face against my shoulder and we'll play it by ear." Logan slid one hand beneath her knee, the other around her uninjured arm and picked her up. "Don't worry. I'll stay with you as long as you want."

Left without a choice, she nestled her head against the muscular solidity of his chest and fought her old nemeses, fear and heartache. This time Logan would be with her. This time she wouldn't be alone in the sterile room fighting a losing battle of keeping their baby.

The automatic double doors of the emergency room whooshed open. Logan and Rachel were enveloped by the air-conditioned, disinfectant-scented air of Stanton Memorial Hospital. Several people were milling in the hall. Although Rachel didn't recognize any of them, she pressed closer to Logan's comforting warmth. With each of his steps, her need for him became greater than her fear of being recognized.

A young nurse in green surgical garb spotted them. Grabbing a wheelchair, she rushed over. Logan shook his head and kept walking. He didn't stop until he was in front of the glass enclosure of the receptionist.

"She's been badly hurt. We need to see a doctor."

The gray-haired woman glanced up from the form she was writing on. Her indifferent gaze went first to the hard-faced man, then to the dirt-smeared, trembling woman in his arms. "How was she injured?"

"She fell. Now, can we please see a doctor?" Logan asked.

A clipboard with a black ballpoint pen attached by a string was pushed through the half-circle glass opening. "Fill out these forms and take a seat."

Logan's black eyes blazed. "Woman, you can stick those forms—"

"Rachel, is that you?"

Logan whirled with Rachel in his arms. An elderly, kind-faced man walked toward them. The name written in script letters on his pristine white lab coat was Dr. L. Perry. Tension eased out of Logan.

Eight years ago the doctor had been one of only two people who'd believed Logan innocent of maliciously attacking J. T. Malone and causing his subsequent heart attack. Dr. Perry's staunch belief had kept Logan from being arrested by the sheriff. He was a fair man.

"I'm afraid so, Dr. Perry," Rachel's voice wobbled. "I hurt my shoulder, and Logan insists a doctor look at it."

Thick, white eyebrows rose up to meet the thinning swatch of white hair. "Logan? Logan Prescott? Well, I'll be a son-of-a-gun. Never thought I'd—" Dr. Perry stopped upon noticing the avid interest of the receptionist. "Betty, is exam room C available?"

The woman behind the glass partition stood, her elongated face pinched in disapproval. "Dr. Perry, she hasn't signed in yet. I don't even know who she is. The hospital can't be stuck with her bill if she can't pay."

Logan set Rachel on her feet. One hand curved around her waist, the other dragged out his wallet. Somehow, he managed to pull six one-hundred-dollar bills out and toss them on top of the clipboard. "Is that enough?"

The receptionist's eyes bugged out as much as from the money as from the angry face of Logan, who picked Rachel up again.

"We'll talk about the bill later, Betty. For your records her name is—"

"Rachel Simmons," Logan interrupted smoothly.

Dr. Perry's gray eyes narrowed. He looked at Rachel's tense body and trembling lips, then stepped forward and gently examined her. "Admitting diagnosis is multiple abrasions and contusions to right arm, shoulder, and back. I'll take care of any other information after I've finished."

Taking Logan by the arm, Dr. Perry led them down the hallway to a door marked "C." Pushing the door open and seeing it empty, he ushered them inside. Over his shoulder he said, "We'll be in exam room C." The door swung shut on the receptionist's angry face.

"Thank you, Dr. Perry, for not correcting me out there when I used Rachel's middle name as her surname," Logan told him.

Rachel nodded. "I was in a construction accident and

I don't want to deal with my parents or anyone else if word gets out."

"I thought it might be something like that," Dr. Perry said. "You're lucky that you have your mother's maiden name as one of your middle names."

The door opened and the young woman, minus the wheelchair, stood hesitantly in the doorway. "If you need some assistance, Dr. Perry, I'll be happy to work with you."

The elderly man smiled. "Thanks, Molly. I got a feeling Betty might be a bit slow in getting me some help. Please get Miss Simmons into a gown while I wash up."

"If you'll please put her on the table. The waiting room is down the hall," Molly instructed.

Rachel's arms tightened around his neck. She was trying not to think of the past only the present, but she couldn't do that without Logan being with her. "I—I want him to stay."

"I told you I'd stay with you, and I meant it," Logan said. Over her head, he spoke to Dr. Perry's back. "If you have any objection you better speak now, because I'm not leaving her."

Dr. Perry never ceased rubbing his hands together under the blast of tepid water. "If I wanted to object to your being here, you would have heard it by now. Rachel wants you here and it's good enough for me."

Logan set Rachel on the table. Almost immediately Molly was there. "Miss Simmons, I need to get your blouse off," Molly said, a blue patient's gown draped over her arm.

Rachel glanced frantically around for the doctor. Too many memories were crowding in on her. "Dr. Perry, can't we do this in your office?"

"We could, but we're here now." Dr. Perry snatched a paper towel from the rack and dried his hands. His back to Rachel, he said, "Give Mr. Prescott the gown, Molly, and come over here and help me set up. The last time I was in an exam room, I couldn't find a thing. I swear, they move things every day. Where are the gloves?" Dr. Perry opened a cabinet only to shut it and open another one.

Logan took the gown and watched Rachel's quivering lips. "It's going to be okay, Rae," he assured her, his fingers undoing the buttons of her blouse, his eyes never leaving hers. "The doc knows his stuff. He'll have you fixed up in no time and you'll be back to work. I bet you run a tight operation. How many men work for you now?"

Rachel didn't answer, but just kept looking around the room as if she wanted to jump off the table and run. Logan knew the real depth of her fear when she made no attempt to stop him from removing her blouse or her bra. Her gaze locked with his as if she were trying to draw strength from him. "Let's put this gown on, and then I want you to lie on your stomach."

Cold fingers grabbed a fistful of shirt. "You won't leave, will you?"

"I'll be here for as long as you want me." Gently, he

uncurled her fingers, eased her down on the table, then drew the sheet Molly had placed there earlier up to her waist. With the toe of his boot, Logan snagged a stool and pulled it over. He sat down at the head of the table facing Rachel, both of her hands in his.

Dr. Perry pushed a stainless steel stand closer to the exam table. "Logan, keep my favorite patient occupied while I take a look at her. Once we're finished, I'll want a full report of how this happened."

Logan grimaced. "She was being Superwoman." Out of the corner of his eye, he saw the nurse tear open several packages of gauze.

"Turn onto your left side," Dr. Perry said.

Sweat popped out on Logan's head. His mouth dried as Rachel shifted.

"Logan, could you talk to me?" Rachel asked, her eyes shut.

He talked of anything that came into his mind—places he'd been, things he'd seen—and prayed it was enough.

Rachel kept her eyes closed and let Logan's presence flow over her, his soothing words banished the night she called for him and he didn't answer. After what seemed an eternity of cleaning the wounds, the nurse positioned Rachel on her stomach. Her grip on Logan's hands tightened. If only he could have been with her then…. Her lashes fluttered upward, and she stared into his drawn features. "I never forgot you."

Logan blinked, then sucked in his breath as the full import of her words hit him. Slowly, he blew the air out of his lungs and nodded. "Maybe this time neither of us will have to try."

"All finished," Dr. Perry said, snapping off his plastic gloves. "Logan, why don't you go see if there's anything else Betty needs while I have a talk with Rachel."

"Will you be all right?" Logan asked.

Rachel sat up and slowly nodded. "I'll be fine."

As soon as Logan left, Dr. Perry turned to Molly. "I can take it from here." When he was alone with Rachel, he folded his arms and said, "He's the one, isn't he?"

Rachel bowed her head and whispered, "Yes."

"I should have figured it out sooner. I'll never forget the day the ambulance brought Logan and your father into the emergency room." Dr. Perry stuffed his hands into the pockets of his lab coat. "I gather you haven't told him about losing the baby?"

Rachel's head snapped upward. "No. I haven't. I couldn't."

He sighed heavily. "Rachel, I make it a strict rule never to get into the personal lives of my patients. But I brought you into this world, so I think that gives me a little more privilege."

"Dr. Per—"

"Tell him," he interrupted. "Get it all out into the open. You've both been through a lot and you need to put it all behind you," he advised, removing his hands from his pockets. "From the way he was hovering over you, I think it's safe to say he still cares for you."

Rachel shook her head wildly. If she closed her

eyes she could still feel the warm, tingling sensations of Logan's fingers combing through her hair as she lay on the table. "I can't live on 'think.' I've lost too much already."

"No more than he has, and he still doesn't know about the greatest loss of all."

A broken sob caught in her throat. "Don't you think I know that? I want to tell him, but I don't know how. His coming back to town was so unexpected. I'm not even sure how long he plans to stay in Stanton or why he's here."

Logan's palm was pressed against the door when he heard Rachel's words and the sadness she made no attempt to hide. Pushing the door open farther, he asked, "All set to go?"

Rachel reached for her blouse and bra. "If you'll wait a minute, I need to get dressed."

"Don't you dare put that blouse back on and mess up my clean bandage," Dr. Perry admonished, and handed her another hospital gown. "Just bring it back, or Betty will really have my hide."

"That won't be necessary," Logan said and handed her a teal-colored silk blouse.

Rachel shrank from the blouse in Logan's hands. "The hospital gown is fine."

Logan's hand fisted in the blouse. She was doing it again, just like before. Reaching out to him, then turning from him. He had had enough. "All right, Rachel, what is it? One minute you're trying to climb in my skin to get closer, the next minute you're acting as if I'm horsesh—"

"Logan!" she gasped. Her gaze went to Dr. Perry, who had an "I told you so" expression on his face.

"I'm waiting," Logan snarled.

From the sound of his voice, Rachel knew he wasn't going to wait long. There was an old saying, "Tell the truth and shame the devil." She didn't know about shaming the devil, but she certainly wasn't going to shame herself. "Whoever the blouse belongs to might not want me wearing it."

"Since it's a birthday gift to the wife of my best friend and it's been in the trunk of my car since I picked it out Saturday at *Whispers,* I don't think she's going to mind," Logan said evenly. "I'm not in the habit of giving used gifts."

Rachel winced. Jealousy had made her act like a selfish child, and everyone in the room knew it. "Guess I acted without thinking again. Forgive me. I appreciate your thoughtfulness and your staying with me. If the offer of the blouse is still open, I'd be happy to wear it." Rachel held out her hand.

Logan gave her the blouse. He gave her some privacy to dress. When he faced her again, she was slowly trying to button the blouse. Pushing her hands aside, he quickly finished.

"You're going to be pretty sore for the next twenty-four hours. The right side of your body is badly bruised. In a couple of hours it'll probably be an effort to move, and by tonight you won't want to move. I shouldn't have to say this, but take it easy. Pamper yourself for a change and let someone else run the company," Dr. Perry instructed. "And whatever you do, don't get the bandage wet. I want to see you in a week to remove the sutures."

"She'll be there," Logan said.

Dr. Perry walked over to the counter and wrote out two prescriptions and handed then to Rachel. "Something for the pain, and an antibiotic. The pain pills may make you a little woozy, but since you'll be at home for the next couple of days that shouldn't be a problem. Take the antibiotic until they're all gone. I don't want that shoulder infected. Logan, I'm counting on you to see that she follows orders."

"I plan on keeping an eye on her."

Rachel tucked her head for a moment at the intimacy in Logan's voice. "I don't want to keep you in town. You've done enough."

Guilt swept through Logan. "I had planned on being in town for a couple of weeks anyway."

"Oh." Rachel lowered her head to hide the unexpected pleasure his words caused and wished she had the courage to ask what had brought him back after all these years.

Her bowed head bothered Logan. She was retreating again. "Even if I hadn't planned on being in town, nothing could keep me away after you risked your life to save mine."

"What?" Dr. Perry cried. "I want to know everything and don't leave out a thing."

Logan told him every frightening detail. His voice became more strained with each sentence. By the time he finished, he looked at Rachel as if he didn't know whether to turn her over his knee or to pick her up and keep her safe in his arms forever.

"I'm not surprised," Dr. Perry told him. "Too often Rachel puts what's best for her behind what's best for others."

"Well, it's going to stop," Logan said with biting finality.

Rachel looked into Logan's face lined with concern and again felt the need to console rather than challenge his authority over her. "I'm fine, Logan."

"And I'm going to make sure you stay that way."

The intensity of Logan's statement coupled with the intensity of his gaze shook Rachel to the core. He was acting like a man who cared about her. A grateful man might pay her medical expenses and even stay with her in the emergency room, but he wouldn't take it upon himself to make sure she stayed safe in the future. Or was she reading too much into his words?

If she was wrong, she was going to pay a very high price. Logan had simply walked away eight years ago. If she dared allow Logan back into her life and he learned how she had unintentionally almost ruined his life, then lost his child, if he walked, he wouldn't go quietly. His words would likely flay her very soul. She wasn't sure she was strong enough to risk the danger.

"I kind of thought you'd keep an eye on her. Even as a teenager you didn't take responsibilities lightly. I always admired the way you managed to attend school, hold a job and visit your mother, then your father every day while they were hospitalized." Dr. Perry extended his hand. "I'm glad you haven't changed."

Logan's large hand closed gently around the doctor's frail one. He usually didn't care what people thought about him, but the doctor's unexpected high regard of Logan pleased him. "I'm glad you haven't changed, either. Are you ready, Rachel?"

"Yes," she said then gasped softly as he picked her up. "I can walk."

Logan's expressionless face stared down into Rachel's uncertain, upturned one. "You could have walked in here, but you didn't. Or do you suddenly have a problem with me holding you?"

Yes, she wanted to say. Earlier he had helped her get through an extremely difficult time, but if she continued to let him hold her it implied for the time being both of them were putting aside the past and testing the other for a possible new beginning. She both wanted and dreaded it happening.

There were so many things she wanted to say to Logan, to explain to him and she could not do it with him looking at her with loathing in his eyes. If there was a chance for them to put the past behind them and call a truce for a little while, she was going to take it.

Her uninjured arm slid around his neck. He gathered

her closer to his chest. "I'm glad you were here, Dr. Perry. Thank you."

"You're welcome, Rachel, but I'd be a lot happier if I had one of your chocolate cakes when you feel better."

"It's a deal."

"You sure you want to do that to the doctor after he helped you?" Logan said half-teasingly.

"I'm a pretty good cook," she told him, then angled her face toward his. "After this shoulder heals, why don't you come over for dinner and see for yourself?"

Logan debated only for a moment the wisdom of accepting her invitation. By that time the winner of the bid to build the city hall complex would be announced and he was almost certain it wasn't going to be Malone. Rachel wouldn't want him in the same state with her, let alone fix him dinner. But the thought of finding another hidden facet in this new independent Rachel was an irresistible lure. "I'd like that."

Telling the doctor goodbye again, Logan strode down the hallway with Rachel in his arms. The automatic door opened and they walked into the bright sunlight and saw the angry face of J. T. Malone.

Chapter 6

"D-daddy." Rachel scrambled out of Logan's arms and stood. Vaguely, she heard him curse, but her gaze stayed on the angry face of her father. "What are you doing here?"

"Where did you expect me to be?" he snapped. "Jake came to the house and told me about the stupid stunt you pulled. God, Rachel! You could have been killed!"

"I'm fine. Jake had no right to worry you," Rachel insisted.

"Of course he did. What possessed you to risk your life for a worthless—"

"Please, Daddy. Not now." Her voice wobbled.

J. T. Malone's brows furrowed. For the first time in years, his eyes searched her face. "Are you all right?"

"Aren't you asking a little late?" Logan said.

J. T.'s attention switched to Logan. "If she's hurt, it's because of you. Haven't you done enough?"

"Daddy, please," Rachel repeated, trying to calm her father down before he revealed too much. "I'm fine. There's nothing to worry about."

"No thanks to Prescott," Jake said, as he came up behind Mr. Malone. "If he hadn't been there, Ms. Malone wouldn't have put herself in danger. You should have seen him, Mr. Malone. He was so scared he couldn't talk. She had to lead him to his car."

Rachel rounded on the foreman. "I gave you orders to stay and check out the crane. Why did you disobey them?"

"I... I..." He fumbled for words.

"He did right," Mr. Malone defended. "Someone had to let me know what a dangerous thing you had done."

"I see Jake continues to run your errands and does your bidding like a trained lapdog," Logan said.

Jake bristled, took a step toward Logan, then faltered. He glanced at Rachel. "One day soon we're gonna settle this."

Logan simply smiled.

"Get back to the site, Jake, and don't ever ignore another order I give you," Rachel said in the heavy silence.

Jake's gaze went to Mr. Malone and Rachel's followed. "I've already reminded you once, Jake, my father put me in charge. There won't be a next time."

"Mr. Malone?" Jake queried.

J. T.'s hand trembled on the cane. He looked from

his daughter to the foreman. "Rachel, Jake has been with me—"

"If you can't back me up, I'm handing in my resignation." Rachel watched her father's eyes widen and his left hand join his right on the walking stick. She saw fear and indecision in his brown eyes. But this was one time she wasn't going to back away from a confrontation with him for worry the stress and strain might be too much for his weak heart. Dr. Perry had repeatedly told her and her mother that they coddled her father too much. `

"Daddy, I won't have Jake or any other man working for us who thinks he can run to you if I tell him something he doesn't like."

"Pumpkin, don't."

The fight almost went out of Rachel. Almost. An hour ago she would have wept for joy on hearing her father call her by her nickname. He hadn't called her that since the night she'd lied and told him she was spending the night with Salina and instead had eloped with Logan. She knew it was her father's stubborn way, of telling her they could start over…if she backed down. Eight years ago she had backed down, and she'd lived to regret it every waking moment.

She shook her head. "It's him or me."

J.T. bowed his head and when he lifted it he stared straight at Logan. "One day you're going to wish you were dead, and I'm going to dance a jig."

"Daddy," Rachel cried out in horror.

J.T. ignored her, his attention totally on Logan. "Get

back to work, Jake. I'll take a cab home." J.T. didn't say another word until the sound of an engine disrupted the stillness. For the second time in years, he sought his daughter's gaze. "Have it your way this time, Rachel, but the business had better not suffer."

"It won't," she said with absolute conviction.

"Then you'd better get back to work," her father told her.

"Dr. Perry told Ra—"

"That he wanted a chocolate cake for his fee," Rachel said, cutting Logan off.

J.T. snorted. "Couldn't have been that much wrong with him, then. Scared, just as Jake said. You were a pitiful excuse for a man then, and age didn't make you any better." With that, he started walking toward the emergency room door.

Rachel's heart winced as she watched each laborious step her father took. In his high school years he had been on the all-state baseball and football teams. He had lettered in track. There was nothing he used to like more than physical labor. Before his first heart attack, if they needed an extra man at the construction site, her father often stepped in to do the job—not because he couldn't afford to hire someone, but because he enjoyed working with his hands. Now, he barely had enough strength to walk a hundred feet without getting winded.

She easily caught up with him. "Daddy, I can call a cab and wait with you if you'd like."

"I can take care of myself." He kept walking. "You

just make sure there is a business left for me to run when I return." The automatic door opened and he walked inside.

Rachel hung her head, tears glistening in her eyes. Her throat stung. Lord. When were the pain and anger going to end? She hadn't stood up for Logan so much as she had stood up for herself against an insubordinate employer.

"Why didn't you tell him you had been hurt?"

Drawing on her last strength, she faced Logan. "He has enough on his mind. Besides, he's right about me getting back to work. And if Mother knew she'd raise such a fuss, I'd have to take off."

"Maybe I should call her, then."

"No," Rachel cried, reaching out to him in supplication. "It would solve nothing and just create more problems."

"Damn it, Rachel," Logan said tightly. "You heard the doctor. You need to rest. When the local anesthetic wears off, your shoulder and back are going to hurt like hell."

"I've been in pain before and survived," she said softly. "What I really need is for you to take me home so I can change and get back to work."

"Is it that important for you to please him?"

"Logan, you know the bottom line for construction projects is for them to come in on time and on budget. At the moment, Malone has three buildings going up," Rachel said, willing him to understand. "Everyone looks to me and I have to be there. The men are good workers, but we both know that most crews work better when the owner is around. You couldn't afford that little black number parked over there if you hadn't learned to work despite some aches and pains. Sometimes you have to put what you'd like behind what has to be done."

For a long time he studied the determination in her face. "You've learned more than just how to cook I see."

"I tried."

Logan took her arm. "Come on, but first we're getting your prescriptions filled."

"Thank you, Logan," Rachel said, and allowed Logan to lead her to his car. Her legs wobbled, and her head hurt. She felt like a brick building had fallen over her. All she wanted to do was crawl into bed and sleep. As Logan shut her car door the clock on the town square struck eleven. In spite of herself, she allowed herself the luxury of leaning her head back against the warm leather seat. How was she going to stay on her feet for another six hours?

How is she going to stay on her feet for another two hours?

Arms folded, legs crossed at the ankle, Logan watched Rachel enter the work trailer with two of her crewmen on her heels. She hadn't stopped since they'd returned. It was a good thing he had insisted on stopping to get something to eat. She had refused until he'd pointed out she might get sick if she took her medicine on an empty stomach. But it bothered him that she had taken only the antibiotic and not the pain pill.

She had flatly refused, then repeated Dr. Perry's warning that the pain medication might make her drowsy. She went on to remind him unnecessarily that not having a clear head around a construction site was too dangerous and could easily involve her in another accident. That she was right didn't stop him from getting angry all over again when he'd catch sight of her rubbing her arm and shoulder.

Logan had to admit she was a hard worker. She didn't give up. He gritted his teeth. But it was all for her father. She'd work in pain to please him, but she hadn't cared enough for him to say three words: *he's my husband.*

As he recalled the reason for her being in pain, his anger fled. It also brought him back to his as yet unsolvable problem. After saving his life, how could he destroy the company she was working so hard to save? If Rachel had sole control, he might be tempted to forget his idea of revenge. But he had heard J.T. tell Rachel at the hospital to make sure there was a business left for him to run when he returned. And J.T. was as self-righteous and self-centered as Logan remembered. His heart attacks hadn't made him any easier to like. Even struggling to stand, J.T. had made his hatred known.

The trailer door opened. Rachel came into view. Instead of continuing down the steps, she paused. Even from where he stood, Logan could see the lines of pain bracketing her tightly compressed lips. Her head and shoulders slumped. Logan straightened from leaning against his car and started toward her. This playing Superwoman had gone on long enough. She was going to take her pain pill and go to bed if he had to drag her.

His gaze locked on her, he saw her lift her head and say something over her shoulder. At the same time, she began her descent...and stumbled. Logan broke into a run. The man behind her caught her right arm and tried to bring her upward. With a broken cry, she went down on one knee.

"You're hurting her," Logan yelled, and took the four steps in two.

The baldheaded man holding her arm released her and stepped back. "Miss Malone, I'm sorry. Are you all right?"

"No, she isn't," Logan growled. Gently, he helped her to stand, then leaned her against his side. His arm slid possessively around her waist.

Rachel spoke despite the searing pain in her arm and shoulder. "I...I will be in a moment. It's not your fault, Sonny."

"No, it's mine for getting under a steel beam," Logan said through clenched teeth. "All you did was save my life and get your shoulder torn to shreds for your trouble."

"She's hurt?"

"Why didn't she say something?"

Rachel sent Logan an accusing stare. He ignored her and the small cluster of men beginning to form around the steps. More were approaching. They might not be able to hear over the machinery, but they couldn't help but notice the silent man who followed her every movement with the watchfulness of a hawk.

At least Jake wasn't here. She had sent him to check another building site. She tried unobtrusively to free her arm from Logan and failed.

"No way," Logan said flatly.

Realizing he wasn't going to release her, she contented herself with another killer glare, then turned to the anxious faces of the men. "Since Mr. Prescott has chosen to blurt out my medical condition, there is no need to go into further detail. However, as I said before, I don't want a word of this getting out. That means not to your best drinking buddy, your barber, your wife, or your girlfriend. I won't have my parents worried or the bond company getting nervous. If word leaks out, I'll find out who, and believe me, I'm not going to be happy. Is that clear?"

The men nodded.

"You can count on us, boss."

"Sure thing, Miss Malone."

"You forgot mothers, but I won't tell mine, either," Jimmy said with a wide grin on his freckled face.

The men laughed. It broke the tension.

"Let's go, Ms. Malone."

She looked into Logan's set features and groaned inwardly. He wasn't going to budge on this. Besides, her legs were trembling so badly she could hardly stand. "Sonny, you're in charge. I'll be in the office in the morning, if you need me. Make sure the wiring is done right. The inspector is scheduled to be here in a few days."

"Don't you worry about a thing, Miss Malone," Sonny said, his brown face a study in determination.

"From what I've seen this afternoon, she couldn't have a better crew," Logan said.

All eyes converged on Logan.

"She needs her pain medication now and she probably shouldn't drive," Logan told them. "Would one of you see that her truck gets back to her place?"

"I will, Mr. Prescott," Jimmy said in a rush of words. "I live two blocks over from Miss Malone, and I usually grab a ride back home anyway."

Logan nodded and held out his hand palm up to Rachel for her keys. After a moment's hesitation, she automatically lifted her right arm to retrieve the keys from her pocket. Air hissed through her teeth.

With a muttered curse, Logan shifted to her other side and slid three long fingers into her pocket and obtained the keys in an exact imitation of her retrieving his keys earlier. He took off the ignition key and handed it to Jimmy. "Leave the truck in the driveway and the key under the floor mat. Now, if the rest of you will excuse us, we'll be going."

Too tired to protest his taking charge, Rachel allowed Logan to lead her to his car. As soon as she was inside, he handed her some bottled water.

"Open."

Rachel looked at the two pills between Logan's blunt-tipped fingers and moistened her lips. "Shouldn't it be one?"

"Four hours ago, yes. Now open."

She sighed in resignation. "I can do it myself."

"Mighty funny, you haven't. Now open."

"Logan, the men—"

"Are watching. I know. They've been watching me since we returned. I recognized a lot of them from eight years ago and I'm sure they aren't too pleased with you leaving with me," Logan told her. "I thought a couple of them were going to speak up, but I guess they remembered you don't like your orders questioned. But from the concerned way most of them were looking at you, I wouldn't be surprised if your crew came charging to your rescue if I forced these pills on you. So open."

"You don't appear bothered by the prospect if they did."

He shrugged. "Not many things bother me. Now open."

"Logan Prescott, I'm going to pay you back for this once I feel better."

He touched her mouth with the tablets. The pad of his fingertip pressed against her lips. Sensation totally alien to pain coursed through her. She had the craziest notion to extend her tongue and explore the taste and texture of the man watching her so intently.

Afraid he'd see the yearning in her face, she opened her mouth and took the medicine. On retreating, his fingers grazed her inner lips. She shivered. Averting her eyes, she lifted the bottled water and drank.

"Are you satisfied now?" she asked. He waited so long to answer, she turned to him.

Black eyes smoldered. "Depends on your point of reference." He switched on the ignition and backed out.

Her fingers gripping the bottle, Rachel sought a safe

topic of conversation. "You handled the crew like you did it every day. What type of business are you in?"

Logan's hand on the steering wheel tightened for a fraction of a second. The answer he had planned to give her was no longer possible. Her accident had taken care of that. If he told her he was half owner of the company that was going to bankrupt her, she'd get out of the car and out of his life for good.

He'd never again see the need in her eyes he'd glimpsed earlier. He wasn't ready for that yet. As illogical as it sounded, he needed to be able to see her and know she was all right. He wasn't ready to let her out of his sight. Fishing around in his mind for an answer, he decided to stick with a variation of the truth.

"I'm still in construction."

Suddenly wary, Rachel sat up. "What do you do?"

"General manager," Logan said truthfully as he pulled onto the main highway. He and Charles had decided at the beginning that Logan would oversee the actual building and Charles would handle the office.

"Who do you work for?"

Logan's fingers tightened on the steering wheel. This was getting tricky and dangerous. "C. Dawson," he said and watched for a reaction from Rachel.

She frowned. "Never heard of him."

"He just started in Texas. I wanted to know if Malone was going to be a tough competitor." Logan knew he was only postponing the inevitable, but at least it would give him enough time to make sure she was well cared for.

"Tell your boss there's enough business for us all," Rachel said, once again relaxing in her seat. "I just wish Bridgeway knew that."

Logan tensed again. "They're giving you trouble?"

Afraid she might have revealed too much about the company's failing finances, Rachel closed her eyes and said, "Nothing I can't handle."

"Glad to hear it. Now sit back and relax until I get you home."

Rachel nodded. Home...she wondered if he knew how much the word made her ache. If only...but there was too much anger, there were too many secrets still unspoken for them to be able to start over. A lot of things about Logan might have changed, but his willingness to forgive wasn't one of them. His initial anger at her when they'd first met had shown that very clearly. The only reason he tolerated her now was because she had saved his life. He was repaying a debt—nothing more.

Logan kept a close eye on his silent patient as he drove the nine miles to his house. By the time he turned off the winding blacktop road into a one-lane driveway bordered by a tightly strung barbed-wire fence, the lines of pain bracketing her mouth had disappeared. Half a mile farther, a small frame house came into view. "We're here."

Rachel sat up and opened her eyes. Although it had been eight years since she had seen Logan's house, she recognized it instantly. Yet, the house she remembered was weathered, the grounds were barren of even weeds, the asphalt roof looked like a patchwork quilt because of the different colors of roofing Logan had used from leftover jobs.

This house had a new coat of white paint, and the gray asphalt roof matched the gray shutters bordering the two windows on either side of the front door. Instead of a few skinny shrubs struggling to survive in the hard-packed dirt, lush, neatly trimmed boxwoods ran the length of the house.

In spite of promising himself he didn't care, Logan watched the play of emotions on her face, waiting for her reaction and her approval.

"You've been back before the day I saw you."

"No."

Rachel looked from him to the house. "Then who took care of all this?"

"Ida Mae." He didn't add that she had blatantly ignored his desire to sell the house and had instead rented it out. Using the rent money, she had paid the taxes and kept the house up. However, after the last late-paying renters and their four rambunctious kids had moved out at the end of May, she'd decided, after repairing all the damages, she needed a break from being a landlady.

Strangely, at the mention of the woman in the store, Rachel didn't experience any jealousy or remorse. Silently, she added another crime to her long list. Because of her, Logan had stayed away from the only place he had truly called home. Before his family came to Stanton, his family had apartment hopped. They never stayed anywhere more than a couple of years. "I'm sorry."

"We've both said those words too much today. Why don't we make a pact from this minute not to have a reason to say them again," Logan said.

"I'd like that." She smiled.

"Good." He got out of the car and opened her door. "Now, let's get you inside."

Rachel stared straight ahead. "I'll wait here for you to come back."

"You're going inside with me."

She shook her head. "I'll stay and then you can take me home."

Logan realized Rachel thought he had meant her home when he'd said he was taking her home. He had meant his. He glanced at her hands and saw she had a death grip on the bottled water. She was nervous. He wasn't so sure about what he planned himself. All he knew was that he could call the shots at his house. If he took her home and her parents came over, he'd be out the door in nothing flat.

She was hurt because of him and he had an obligation to take care of her. Besides, if he didn't help her, he wasn't sure who would. Dr. Perry had made it plain that, at least for today, she wasn't going to be able to do much with her right arm.

"It might be awhile. I'm expecting an important phone call and I need to be here." She glanced at the cellular phone. "Out of range," he explained, easily and gently grasping her elbow.

Knowing she shouldn't, but unable to stop herself, Rachel allowed Logan to help her out of the car. Once she had dreamed of a lifetime with him in this house, now she was left with counting minutes and thinking of what might have been.

When they entered the house, he still held her arm. Memories swept through both of them. Both remembered the last time they had come through the door. It was the night before they'd eloped to Houston. They had been nervous and giddy with excitement and so sure they would share a lifetime of happiness together. Less than two days later they had bitterly parted. The look they shared asked questions neither had the nerve to voice.

Pulling free, Rachel walked farther into the sparsely furnished living room. The overstuffed couch she and Logan had snuggled on had been reupholstered in a multicolor plaid of predominantly mauve and blue. Throw pillows of the same print were on two blue cushioned chairs. The walls were a pristine white. Gleaming pale blue linoleum stretched through to the open door leading to the kitchen.

"I wonder if Ida Mae would take on my house?"

"Your mother would shudder at the thought of anyone doing anything to your place if they didn't have a mile of initials behind their name," Logan said.

Rachel looked for a trace of malice behind his statement and when she didn't see any, she relaxed. "Mother has mellowed. Besides, it's my house and what I say goes."

Once Logan might have believed otherwise, but not after seeing Rachel stand up to her father and work through pain. She had grown up to be a woman of substance and he hadn't been there to see it or shape her growth. Inexplicably, he felt cheated. "Come on, it's bath time for you."

"What?"

Logan smiled at the shocked expression on her face. "If you think you're getting into my bed as dirty as a four-year-old who's been playing in a sandbox, think again."

She backed up a step. "I—I'll wait until I get home to lie down. I'll just sit."

"Ida Mae would have a fit if you sat on the couch or chair in your dirty work clothes. She had them reupholstered and stored for me. I had barely walked through the front door before a truck pulled up with them," Logan told her. "Besides, I know you'll feel better after you're cleaned up."

"That's exactly why I need to wait until I get home." Her mouth dried. "I'll need clean clothes if I take a bath."

Logan grinned coaxingly. "You can wear one of my shirts again."

Rachel's cheeks heated. "That was different. I had no choice. I accidentally fell in the tank while we were fishing."

"Since I can't leave to take you home, you don't

have much choice this time, either," he told her. "I know by now, you feel gritty and sticky and would like nothing better than to be clean again. Isn't that right?"

"Yes, but—"

"No buts," Logan interrupted. Taking her by the hand, he started from the room.

She was mildly surprised to find herself following him with only token resistance. Somehow, as the aches in her body subsided, so did her ability to stand up against Logan's persuasiveness. Going down the short hallway she caught a quick glimpse of a double bed through an open door. Her pulse raced at the thought of sleeping there. Then they were in the tiny bathroom.

"Y-You can leave now," her voice quivered.

Logan smiled a smile that could have melted steel. "You might need some help."

She shrank back until she bumped against the clawfoot tub. "Help for what?"

"Washing any of those places you can't reach."

The thought of him seeing her naked, of his hands brushing against her body, caused her to shake. She plopped on the edge of the tub.

Oh, Lord, she dreaded the image as much as she shamelessly anticipated it happening.

Chapter 7

"See, you're so tired you can hardly stand, let alone manage your bath by yourself," Logan pointed out.

Rachel got to her feet. "That's because you made me take two pills." His dark brow quirked. "You are not helping me take a bath."

Logan folded his arms across his wide chest. "Then who is? You're faced with the same problem you had at the hospital, finding someone who can be trusted to keep quiet. If you get those stitches wet and they become infected because of your refusal to let me help you, what's going to happen then?"

"I'm not going to get them wet," she insisted. "I can take a bath by myself."

"One-handed?" he scoffed.

"Yes."

Logan looked at her a long time. "Have it your way for now, Rachel." Opening the door, he closed it behind him.

Rachel sank down on the commode. How had she let herself get backed into this? Taking a bath in Logan's house was impossible. She should have never taken two pills. The throbbing pain was gone, but now she felt light-headed and drowsy and it was an effort to think clearly.

"Rachel, are you all right?"

Her head lifted at the worry in his voice. "I'm fine."

"All I want to do is make sure you're taken care of," he said through the door. "You trust me enough to believe me, don't you?"

"Yes," she answered, without hesitation. She'd trust Logan with her life, her heart, her soul.

"Then why don't you let me help you?"

Because I don't want you to find out I still care about you, Rachel thought. Out loud she said, "This is awkward for me."

"I know and I'll do anything I can to make this easier for you."

"Does that anything include taking me home?"

There was a long pause before he answered. "You're hurt because of me and I'd like you to stay. But I'll take you home if I'm making things worse. Or is it you don't think I'm capable of taking care of you?"

The stiffness in his voice came through clearly. She could go home, but once again she would hurt the only man she'd ever loved. She had taken enough from him. It was time she gave. Unsteady fingers began unbuttoning her blouse. "I hope you remember this when I become short-tempered."

"You're entitled," came the soft reply.

Taking her blouse off, she started to reach behind her to unclasp her bra. "O-o-h-h."

The door swung open. "What happened?"

Rachel looked at Logan's worried face and couldn't decide if she wanted to ask him to hold her or to reach for her blouse. She did neither. "I forgot again."

Logan took in the situation and correctly guessed the problem. Grabbing a bath towel, he gently inserted it under her arms, then unhooked her bra. His fists clenched on seeing the multiple bruises on the right side of her body, the various scrapes, the large white bandage. He was the cause of this.

"Logan."

The uncertainty in her voice set Logan in motion. Picking up the ends of the towel, he anchored them under Rachel's left arm. "Stand up and let's get you ready for your bath."

Swallowing, Rachel did as directed. "I'm…I'm not so sure about this anymore."

"I'd change places with you if I could."

"Oh, Logan, I know that," Rachel said, trying to find the right words. "It's just that it's not easy standing here knowing you're going to…well, you know."

"Get you out of your pants?"

"Logan," Rachel groaned.

"Sorry. Let's get this over with before I say something else wrong. All right?" His hands went to her waist and paused.

Rachel studied the long, slender fingers, the smattering of curly hair on the back of his hands, hands that were strong and competent. Hands that used to drive her crazy with desire.

"Hey, did you go to sleep?"

She jumped guiltily. She was never taking two of those pills at the same time again. "N-No. I'm ready." Air wobbled out of her lungs as Logan's fingers grazed her lower abdomen as he slipped one, then another metal button free. Breath hissed through her teeth when, whether by design or accident, the back of his finger grazed against her belly. The muscles of her stomach clenched.

His thumbs hooked inside the loose jeans to slide them down. Bending from the waist, he continued over the satiny texture of her panties. Rachel looked down at the top of Logan's dark head, so close to the primal heat of her body. Her legs felt rubbery. He might have his eyes closed, but all of his senses, like hers, were probably working overtime.

The jeans slid over her thighs, past the bend of her knees, then bunched around her feet.

"We forgot to take off your boots."

"Logan, this is becoming intolerable."

"Not from where I'm sitting."

Rachel felt heat flare up from the soles of her feet to the top of her head.

"I wish I could see that blush."

"H-How did you know?"

"Instinct. I know this isn't easy for you," he said, as he untied one shoe, then the other. "You better sit down so I can take off your shoes." He glanced up her long legs, then to the blue bath towel draped over her breasts and stayed there for several heartbeats. Finally, his gaze swept downward. "If it's any consolation I'm paying for that slip."

"I am, too," came the soft reply.

Intent evident in his flaring nostrils and smoldering eyes, Logan started to stand.

"No." Rachel reached out her right hand to stop him and winced.

Immediately, Logan crouched back down, then took the trembling hand in his, his eyes shadowed. "I don't seem able to keep from hurting you."

"Not your fault I keep forgetting."

"And I remember too much," Logan said, releasing her hand.

Pressing her left arm to her side, Rachel sat on the commode and let Logan remove her shoes. She wondered if she dared ask him about his memories. Were his as painful and as lonely as hers, or were they full of anger toward her for not standing up for him?

Rising, he placed her shoes and jeans on top of a small hamper and ran the water for her bath. When the tub was a quarter full, he shut off the water and studied her face. "Your eyelids are beginning to droop. We'd better finish this in a hurry."

Logan was right. She was becoming more fuzzy-headed with each passing minute, but she couldn't make herself release the towel or move toward the bathtub.

"The tub is kind of high, so I'd better help you get in, then I can wash your back and let you do the rest."

Rachel glanced down at her bare feet. "Could you turn your back for a minute?" Logan didn't hesitate to do as requested. Not wasting time with doubts, Rachel slowly pulled off her underwear, stuck them under her jeans, then laid her towel on the rim of the tub. Using her left hand, she slowly got inside and replaced the towel beneath her arms. "All right."

He spun around and nodded his approval. "Leave the towel in the tub and I'll take care of it later."

More of the tension in her body subsided. "Thanks, Logan."

Wetting a washcloth, he began to bathe her back. At the first touch, she jerked and stiffened, but as he continued the long, controlled stroke on her left side, she sighed and gradually relaxed. Logan couldn't relax.

He was too intent on making sure cloth, not his skin, touched Rachel, too intent on trying not to let his gaze drop below the small waist to the graceful flare of hips, too intent on not imagining the path of the water running over Rachel's left shoulder, over her breasts and beyond. Most of all, he tried not to remember a time when soft flesh accepted hard and nothing else mattered.

Gritting his teeth against the need throbbing through his body with a wild cadence, he continued. By the time he was finished, it was an effort to stand.

Keeping his eyes averted, he handed her a fresh washcloth. "I'll go see about something to eat. Use the bathrobe on the hook. Yell if you need help getting out of the tub."

Closing the door, Logan let out a shaky breath. This was going to be harder than he had anticipated, but he was going to do it.

Several seconds passed before Rachel began to bathe. Her body felt hot, flushed. It had been too easy to imagine Logan's strong hands, not an unwanted washcloth, stroking her, needing her, too easy to remember a time when nothing had been between them, too easy to forget she was on borrowed time.

In the kitchen Logan looked at the assortment of canned goods and knew he was in trouble. There was nothing he could remotely think of to fix them to eat. He was a pretty decent cook, but he didn't have anything to work with. Pushing aside a can of canned meat, he lifted a box of instant grits only to put it down again.

The refrigerator wasn't much better. All it contained was a half-pint of potato salad left over from his last takeout meal, a quart of milk, and some bottled water. In the three days he had been in town he had eaten out or gone by Ida Mae's. He had meant to stock up, but he'd never seemed to have the time.

The ringing of the phone was an unwelcome interruption. He snatched the receiver. "Prescott."

"You sound grouchy," said a female voice. "Remember, I'm the partner who raised our profits by ten percent with those string bikinis."

Logan smiled into the receiver as he leaned against the counter and crossed one long leg over the other. "And you aren't going to let me forget I thought the good people in Stanton were too proper, are you?"

"Nope. You'd be surprised at what I've learned since we opened up," Ida Mae said. "You still coming to dinner tonight?"

He glanced toward the bathroom. "Something has come up and I'll have to cancel."

"Oh." The voice on the other end of the line perked up. "You left last night halfway through dinner without giving me much of an explanation. Now you're standing me up again. Is there something or *someone* you're not telling me about?"

"Most women wouldn't ask such a personal question," Logan said evasively.

"Probably not, but I'm not most women. I'm the one who has an uncut strawberry cake, a barely touched pot roast, and as we speak, a brisket in the smoker that looks like it's going to join the pot roast in the refrigerator," she said. "Now tell me everything and don't leave out a juicy detail."

Logan straightened and opened another cabinet. "Do you know anyone that delivers food?"

"All the pizza places," came the sweet reply.

"Ida Mae."

"Oh, all right. I take it this mystery woman can't or won't cook."

Logan closed the cabinet. "I didn't say there was a woman involved."

"Logan, you must think I'm as dumb as dirt," Ida Mae said.

"I—"

"Call the Trail Blazer," she interrupted. "I'm sure for a generous tip someone will be willing to bring an order out."

"Thanks, and there's one other thing I need to ask."

"I can't wait."

"I need a size eight dress that is easy to get into and out of and what goes underneath."

Without a pause, Ida Mae came back with, "The mind boggles at that little tidbit, but *Whispers* sells only outer-wear. If your next question is, can I get the things you need and send them out with the clothes, the answer is yes. A cab can delivery everything, but it's going to cost you."

Logan rolled his eyes heavenward. Ida Mae wasn't talking about money. And once she got something in her stubborn head, it was easier trying to stop a stampede. He wished she wasn't so perceptive. But he had to admit, her instincts were right on target about their joint business venture.

When she'd first approached him about her idea for the Victorian House, she'd already had half the prospective tenants lined up. No matter how he'd tried, he couldn't talk her into just opening a dress shop and letting it end there. No, she'd envisioned small, personal shops that offered a unique, multicultural shopping experience for the discriminating buyers who didn't mind paying more if the quality was high enough. Before he knew it, he had bought the condemned mansion and asked Charles to oversee the renovations. On occasions Ida Mae could talk water out of a stone, but not this time.

"A gentleman never tells."

"I could come out there—"

"If you do, I might decide I need to take more interest in things at the shop."

"I never thought you'd stoop to playing dirty," Ida Mae told him. "I guess I'd better get those things together. And Logan, be sure and tell Rachel hello for me."

"How—"

The line went dead. He frowned at the phone and realized it probably wasn't too hard for her to figure out who was with him. Rachel was the only woman who ever put him in a spin, and she was also the only woman he had ever brought to his house. He had never taken any woman to his house in Arkansas, either. He just considered his place off limits.

Pushing his thoughts aside, he dialed Information and obtained the telephone number of the restaurant he fervently hoped delivered. A few minutes later his wish had been granted. Hanging up the phone, he started for the bathroom. He stopped in the hallway on seeing the door open and his bedroom door closed. He knocked.

Getting no response, he opened the door and stopped dead still. Rachel, her arms folded, was leaning against the wall, looking out the window. She looked small and vulnerable in his too large bathrobe. Her hair was tousled, her pose pensive. Despite himself, his body stirred. He wanted her.

This was how it should have been—him, with this woman in this place. But theirs was a time that had passed and could never be again. He just wished he didn't keep forgetting it.

"You're supposed to be resting," he chided gently.

She turned, and instead of a smile, she looked so sad, he felt his stomach clench. All her thoughts lay mirrored in her eyes. She was thinking of the past. He wondered if she ever thought of the night they'd spent together in Houston when memories were made, promises sealed, and a new beginning sought. And it hadn't lasted a day.

"I let you down, didn't I?" she asked quietly, her voice shaky.

This was the opportunity he had wanted. He could wound her as deeply as she had wounded him. Yet the words of recrimination wouldn't come. It was more than her saving his life, she looked as if she was barely hanging on. He knew how it felt to be down. Her father had laid a heavy burden on her small shoulders and

Logan wasn't going to add to the weight. "We were both young," he finally answered.

It was more than she deserved, more than she expected. "I did try to find you once."

Shock swept across his face. "When?"

"After...after you left." She turned away from the blazing intensity in his eyes and looked out the window. "I just wanted you to know."

Logan stared at Rachel and didn't want to believe her, yet, somehow he knew she was telling the truth. "You must not have looked very hard. Your lawyer certainly knew where to find me and serve the divorce papers."

Slowly she faced him, accusations in her eyes. "At least I looked for you. You never called or wrote."

"Because on two occasions you made it very clear that you didn't want me anywhere near you. Why would I set myself up to be rejected again?" he asked bitterly.

"If you had loved me enough you would have tried to contact me," she flung without thought.

"If you had loved me enough you wouldn't have sent me away," he tossed back at her.

Logan and Rachel stared at each other across the space of seven feet. However, eight years of recrimination and heartache separated them. "May-maybe it's best if we don't discuss the past."

He was about to tell her he couldn't agree more when he noticed her arms were folded around something. He peered closer and saw in the overlapping material of the robe's sleeve a gold-toned photograph frame.

The only photograph in the room was one of him and his parents when he was about six years old. Ida-Mae had kept the picture and returned it to him the day he'd come back to Stanton. It was one of the few family outings he remembered and the only time a picture was taken. At six he had been young enough to hope and foolish enough to believe dreams came true. At thirty he knew better.

"My child will never have to worry if he's wanted," Logan said tightly.

Rachel's stricken gaze swung to him and Logan realized he had spoken aloud. The two people he loved the most had loved him the least. A shutter came down over his face. "I'll call you when dinner is ready." The door closed on his retreating back.

Rachel closed her eyes, but nothing could stem the flow of tears. How was she ever going to tell him about the baby she had lost? Their baby. It wouldn't make any difference that she was coming to him when she had the car accident. The only thing which mattered was that she had lied to Logan about her age when they'd first met and to protect him, she had let him think she didn't love him and sent him away.

A tiny lie she had told herself. She was two-and-a-half-months from her seventeenth birthday when she and Salina had staged the flat tire. She lived in terror of him finding out she was sixteen and walking out of her life. At the time, she had thought her overprotective parents were enough of a problem to overcome without adding her age.

That lie came back to haunt her the morning her parents discovered she had eloped with Logan instead of spending the night with Salina. All her father kept saying was that she was underage and he'd see Logan in jail for seducing her. He'd added she had to be eighteen to get married without his written consent and he wasn't letting her ruin her life with a man who only wanted her money.

Her father had left the house in a rage, swearing Logan would pay for what he had done. Less than two hours later her father was in ICU and Logan could barely stand he was so badly beaten. If her father had been angry enough to hit a man who obviously refused to defend himself, then he wasn't just making an idle threat about pressing charges against Logan. Guilt and her fear of Logan being arrested caused her to turn her back on him both times in the hospital.

After he had left Stanton, she'd tried to convince herself he hadn't cared enough to stay and fight for her. Her father pressuring her to file for divorce or he'd track Logan down and press charges, had only added to her turmoil. Since Logan was probably in Oklahoma, as they had planned, he wasn't going to be very difficult to find. So she had filed for divorce and tried to forget how much she loved him.

Six weeks after Logan had left, she'd discovered she was pregnant. All her doubts about Logan loving her had vanished. She wanted to be with him and she was willing to fight for a life with him.

She had packed a bag, left her parents a note, got in her car and headed for Oklahoma. Halfway there, she'd been broadsided by a woman who ran a red light.

Clutching the photograph, Rachel crawled onto the bed: That was the worst part of losing the baby; she had nothing to hang on to, no memory to cherish or relive. Only a black void. Through all the pain, the woman crying she was sorry, the ambulance ride, Rachel begged for Logan.

By the time her parents arrived, she had lost the baby and was heavily sedated. A nurse told her afterward, that she continued to mumble Logan's name. The one thing Rachel remembered was her father telling her Logan had moved and left no forwarding address. She had stopped asking for him out loud then, but never in her heart, in her soul.

"Logan. Logan. Logan." Tears slid down her cheeks as she curled into a tight knot of pain....

Almost one hour later, Logan opened the bedroom door to check on Rachel and saw her huddled on the bed with a tearstained face. He'd discovered a deeper level of pain and guilt than he'd thought possible. In his need to protect himself after his revealing comment about his parents, he had purposefully stayed away. He had promised to take care of her and instead he had thought of himself. She had saved his life and he had walked away from her when she was in need.

In three long strides he crossed to her. "Rae. Honey. It's all right. Everything is going to be all right."

Tear-spiked lashes fluttered, then lifted. Desperation and misery stared back at him. Cursing his callousness, Logan carefully lifted her, then sat on the bed with her in his lap. Without hesitation, she burrowed into his chest as if he was the source of all her strength. His arms closed around her in reassurance.

"Rae, don't cry." Gently he pried the photograph out of her left hand and placed it on the bed. She was crying for him and he had abandoned her. "Please don't cry. I'm not worth one of your tears."

"Oh, Logan, I hurt so bad."

God, he thought. How much was a man supposed to take? He was the cause of her suffering and he didn't know of anything that could alleviate it. "I'm sorry, but it's too soon for another pill."

Unrelenting fingers grabbed a fistful of shirt. Tear-stained eyes pleaded with him. "Why did it have to happen?"

"Honey, don't. Please." He alternately begged and crooned and rocked until he felt her fist loosen, her sobs turn into whimpers, then silence.

Logan continued to hold Rachel and rock. A drop of moisture splashed on his forearm and his entire body tensed. She had started crying again. It was only when he looked down at her and noticed his blurred vision that he realized his mistake.

The tears hadn't come from her. His mind shouted he was the biggest sucker *and* the biggest fool in the world. This woman had made his life hell. Ignoring the taunting voice, he continued to hold the woman sleeping so trustingly in his arms.

Chapter 8

She couldn't move.

Heat and hardness ran from her shoulder blades to her buttocks. Panic drove Rachel from the fringes of sleep to full awareness. Cocooned by the bedcovers, she stared at the dark, muscular arm draped over her waist. Logan. Instant awareness shot through her. The soreness of her body brought the accident back. Vaguely she remembered crying for him after she'd fallen asleep in his bed, but unlike the situation eight years ago, this time her pleas were answered.

She recalled waking in Logan's bed sometime last night and seeing him staring down at her with a strange expression on his face. He told her his call had come through and she'd probably rest better in her own bed. Despite a temperature in the nineties, he had bundled her up in a blanket and put the top up on his car.

Once she was home, she thought he would abandon her. Instead, he had stayed and fixed her a light meal of eggs and toast. She smiled at the memory of him grumbling about her kitchen being barer than his.

When he had turned to leave with her tray, she had taken his hand and asked him to stay until she fell asleep.

He said, "For a while." But it was morning and he was still with her.

Her lashes dipped as she relived the horror of seeing him beneath the steel beam. What if she hadn't been in time? Her throat stung. Tears pricked her eyes. Needing reassurance, she slowly relaxed against the solid warmth. He was safe. She hadn't lost him.

Then she felt something else, the growing need to be held and comforted. It had been so long. She wanted to press her hips against him, to pull his arm tighter around her, to place his calloused hand on her breast. Most of all she wanted a chance to start over and share the loss of their child, to let him know she had never stopped loving him.

To do that, she had to regain his trust enough for him to listen with an open mind. On their first meeting he had looked at her as if he hated her. At his house yesterday afternoon, their attempt to discuss the past had almost turned ugly. Yet his comforting presence last night as she slept and this morning indicated she hadn't completely turned him against her. But she had to get out of bed before she realized just how desperately she needed him.

"Logan, I can't move."

Instantly the arm withdrew. A suspicion that he hadn't been asleep pricked her. Perhaps he liked holding her as much as she liked to hold and be held by him. With a tentative smile on her lips, she glanced over her shoulder and froze.

The savage intensity of Logan's face was frightening. Whatever progress they'd made was gone. "What's wrong?"

"Nothing." He rolled from the bed and sat on the padded bench at the foot of the bed. "I'll see if I can find you something to eat for breakfast. There's no more eggs or bread."

She flinched at the coldness of his voice. He could have been talking to an obnoxious stranger. "So the unspoken truce is over?"

Logan's broad shoulders jerked, but he finished tying up his shoes before he faced her. "I owe you a debt and I intend to pay it."

"That's very magnanimous of you." She sat up in bed, the sheet and bedspread pooled in her lap.

The muscle leaping in his temple was the only outward sign her words annoyed him. He turned away. "I'll be in the kitchen. Afterward, I can help you get dressed if you need it."

"Don't bother with breakfast."

He spun around. "You need to eat something."

"I agree, but you don't have to prepare it. In fact, I insist you don't." Shoving the covers away, she stood. She was at enough of a disadvantage in his bathrobe without being in bed, too. "I also won't need your help getting ready for work. I feel much better this morning."

"That's because you took two pain pills a couple of hours ago," Logan argued.

Rachel didn't bother denying the probable truth or berating Logan for giving her two pills. They had something far more important to discuss. Apparently it was time to let him nail her to that tree. "I saved your life yesterday and last night you took care of me. What do you say we call it even and let it go at that?"

His expression grew harsh. "I place a higher value on my life."

"I do, too, or I wouldn't have risked my life to save yours." He flinched. She let out a sigh. "Look, Logan, you're happy to be alive, but you wished you owed it to anyone else except me. As impossible as it may be for you to believe, I can understand how you feel. But I'm glad it was me. Eight years ago I wasn't there for you, yesterday I was."

"So that makes you guilt free in your book. You tried to trash my life, then saved it, and now you think I'm supposed to be grateful?"

"No. I only meant I—"

"I. I. Stop thinking about yourself first," he interrupted harshly, and took a step toward her. "Does the world have to revolve around you? I thought you had changed, but you're as self-centered as your father."

Rachel recoiled, but she met his angry gaze. "All right, Logan. We've two-stepped around it long enough. Maybe we should discuss the past. Tell me how I messed up your life, what a bitch I am."

"I said 'tried' to trash. You give yourself too much credit in one area and not enough in the other." His gaze tracked her from head to toe. "You figure out which."

She smiled coldly. "Believe me, I can. You know the way out." She started for the bathroom.

Strong fingers closed around her uninjured arm. "Don't you *ever* turn your back on me again."

A rage she hadn't known existed without violence shimmered in his hot gaze. "What did I do to you?"

"You want a list?" he shot back.

"I'd settle for an answer. You couldn't have been more attentive after the accident, but this morning you act like you woke up with a viper in your bed." His smile chilled her. Her head lifted. "You knew what I was when you climbed into my bed. Now, please let go of my arm. I can't work if they're both bruised."

Immediately his fingers unclamped. "I'm waiting for my answer." When he didn't say anything, she decided to up the ante. "After risking my life for you, don't you think I'm entitled to know why, all of a sudden, the sight of me turns your stomach?"

"Leave it alone, Rachel. You won't like where this is going." He spun away.

"I never thought you were a coward."

Her whispered words stopped him. He jerked back around so swiftly that Rachel let out a startled cry. His face looked as if he was holding on to his self-control by sheer force of will. Trembling fingers clutched the robe together at the throat.

"I'm sorry, Logan, that was a cheap shot. I didn't want you to leave and I said the only thing I knew that would make you stay." She sat on the bed and clamped her hands in her lap. "I—I thought this morning when I woke up that…never mind. I'll have your robe laundered and returned. I'm sure you'll understand if I don't show you out."

The brittle voice and bowed head reached Logan as nothing else could. He realized they probably always would. Why did she have to look so pitiful and alone? Then he realized perhaps she was.

Yesterday there'd been no one she could trust enough to stay with her in the hospital, no one to hold her when she was upset. There'd been no one else to give her her pain medication last night and this morning. She hadn't had it easy.

Now she was hurt because of him and she continued to look at him sometimes like he was a long, tall glass of water and she was dying of thirst. That was the main reason he had gotten her out of his house so fast last night. She could turn him inside out with a look and make him forget everything except his ungovernable urge to take care of her and make her happy, just as she was doing now.

"It was what you said." She looked up at him with so much longing in her sad brown eyes he had to clench his fists to keep from dragging her into his arms. "You said," he paused and drew in a ragged breath before continuing, "you said the same words, 'I can't move' the morning we woke up in Houston after we were married. Hearing you say the same thing brought back too many memories of what happened afterward."

Rachel's hand went to her hair, shorter by several inches. "My hair was trapped beneath your arm and I couldn't get free. You woke up smiling and…" Her voice trailed off as she vividly recalled what had happened next.

Logan had freed her hair and trapped her beneath his body. She had gloried in his possession of her and the power of his body. Afterward, she had lain in his arms and promised to love him forever. Yet, less than twenty-four hours later she had refused to acknowledge that love or Logan as her husband. From the way his eyes narrowed and his nostrils flared, he remembered as well.

"Now you know. I trusted you, and look what happened. I won't be kicked in the teeth again."

Rachel looked into the harsh face of the man who she couldn't stop loving and closed her eyes against the misery she felt. She was a woman without hope.

Her eyelids lifted. She looked at him with dark, haunted eyes. "Thank you for answering my question," she said, her voice a thin wisp of sound.

He had finally gotten back some of his own, and he felt like horse manure. "Why did you push it?"

One shoulder lifted beneath the robe. "Guess I thought if you said the things you obviously wanted to say, we could clear the air and perhaps be friends." Her voice thickened. "Friendship requires trust and I'll never regain yours. I just wish you had one good memory to go along with the bad ones."

Although she didn't ask, the yearning was visible in her face and tense body. She wasn't asking anything else from him. Because she didn't ask, he gave.

"They were all good until the morning at the hospital. That's what made your walking away from me so much worse. You never blinked at my aging house, riding in my raggedy truck, eating greasy hamburgers. You never minded that we couldn't go out much because you might be recognized. Whether watching me work on my truck, helping me do minor repairs around the house or sitting with me while I watched a sports show on TV that you had no interest in, you always insisted it didn't matter what we did, as long as we did it together. I would have bet everything I owned on your loyalty." He laughed harshly. "In fact I did."

She frowned. "What do you mean?"

"The day I was in the emergency room the sheriff told me to leave town by sunset. I ignored his order and would have continued to do so, but after you walked away from me the next morning at the hospital, I decided there wasn't any reason for me to hang around."

"Oh, God. I never knew. I thought you simply walked away and never came back because of what happened between us," she cried. "This is so much worse. No wonder you never called or wrote. I don't blame you for despising me."

The bed dipped as he sat beside her. "I tried, believe me I've tried, but I can't. In some ways, I think you went through as much as I did." He glanced around the bedroom. "How long have you lived here?"

Rachel frowned at the change of topic, but she answered the question. She'd answer anything to keep him beside her. "Three years. I bought the place just after I graduated from college."

"It looks like you just moved in."

Rachel didn't have to glance at the bedroom. The only pieces of furniture besides the full bed was a chest of drawers and the padded bench. The living room with a couch and two chairs wasn't much better. "Mother shudders when she visits. I always intended to decorate, but I guess I never got around to it."

"A month after we started seeing each other you were throwing hints about area rugs, slipcovers for the furniture, and paint," Logan reminded her. "You didn't mind not going out, but you badgered me for weeks for us to go to the nearest town where you wouldn't be recognized and shop for curtains for the front room. We went to three stores before you found the ones you liked. They were simple blue curtains, but you kept saying how beautiful they looked once we got them hung."

"It took so long because the blue curtains were the only ones you looked at and didn't shudder. And they did look beautiful." She shrugged again. "Anyway, that was different."

He didn't have to ask why that was different. She had been making a home for them. She hadn't bothered to make one for herself. Neither had he. His place in Arkansas was only slightly more furnished than hers. However, he wasn't sure they could make it this time any better than eight years ago. Nothing had changed between them physically. He wanted her in his bed, beneath him, her sleek legs wrapped around his. Apparently, she wanted him just as much.

Yet once she'd found out he planned to put her father out of business, she'd turn her back on him just as before. Logan glanced at the bowed head beside him and gritted his teeth. Why did she have the power to make him want her, and why couldn't he control the need?

Her father stood between them the same as he had eight years ago. And no matter how much he wanted her, before he left Stanton, he intended for old man Malone to pay for what he had done to Logan, and Rachel was going to be caught in the middle. Again.

This time he was going to make sure there would be no misunderstanding. "What about your father?"

Her head lifted. "My father?"

"I don't like him, and he feels the same way about me," Logan said bluntly. "If the company I work for comes up against his, we plan to win."

"I admit I wish you and Daddy got along, but that's something you'll have to work out between you," she told him. "As for the business, do your best, but Malone is going to be a tough contender."

Logan sank lower than fertilizer. "Knowing how I feel, have you changed your mind about wanting to be my friend? Because this time I don't plan to sneak around or act like I don't know you if we pass on the street."

"Neither do I and I haven't changed my mind."

"I can't promise anything, but I'm willing to try." He offered his hand.

Her lips trembled as she lifted hers. "To new beginnings."

His hand closed around hers for a long moment. "To new beginnings."

After a long moment Rachel pulled her hand free and stood up. "I better get dressed for work."

"I'll go see what I can scrounge up for your breakfast." Logan pushed to his feet.

"You don't have to do that, I can manage."

"Friends help friends and you need to eat something before taking your antibiotic." He nodded toward the bathroom. "You better get going."

"All right, but don't worry if there isn't very much to choose from. I haven't been to the grocery store lately."

"Tell me something I didn't know," Logan said as he walked from the room.

"Mind if I disturb you?"

Rachel glanced up from the stack of papers on her desk. Surprise widened her eyes. Pleasure tilted the corners of her mouth upward. "Logan, what are you doing here?"

"Making sure you follow at least a couple of Dr. Perry's orders," he said easily as he entered Rachel's office and closed the door behind him. "No one was in the front office."

"Teresa has gone to lunch," Rachel explained.

"And when had you planned to go?"

Rachel glanced at the papers on her desk and wrinkled her nose. "I'm not sure."

"That's what I thought." From behind his back Logan pulled out a large carryout bag from the Trail Blazer restaurant.

"You didn't have to buy my lunch. I would have gotten around to eating eventually," she told him.

Logan grunted. "Eventually is what worried me. It's been almost six hours since you had a frost-bitten waffle and day-old coffee."

"Sorry I couldn't offer you anything better. I keep forgetting to go to the grocery store," she explained lamely.

"It's you we're talking about. You're the one who's hurt and needs to take her medicine," Logan said accusingly. "I keep telling you you aren't Superwoman."

"How did you know I haven't eaten?"

"I've noticed you have a tendency to put your work ahead of your health." He took out a compartmentalized Styrofoam container and frowned at her cluttered desk. "Would you rather move something over or eat on the loveseat?"

"The loveseat." Accepting the food, Rachel rounded the desk and sat down. The glass-top table in front of the small couch was almost as cluttered as her desk. She shoved everything to one side and set her lunch down. "Did you bring something for yourself?"

Logan took a seat beside her, then pulled another container and two large fountain drinks from the sack. "As a matter of fact, I did. You still like chicken-fried steak with brown gravy?"

"Yes," Rachel admitted and opened the container. "Ummm. Thank you, Logan. I didn't know how hungry I was."

He smiled as he watched her take a generous bite of the batter-fried steak. "You also still have a hearty appetite."

"Guilty. You kept fresh fruit and my favorite snacks around your house for me." Rachel shook her head. "You always took care of me."

The smile slowly slipped from his face. "I tried."

"You did more than try," Rachel said, willing him to believe her. "If I drove my car to meet you someplace you always followed me back home or to Salina's house. You never let things go too far between us. If I had a problem, big or small, you always took time to listen and then you'd challenge me with questions so I'd reach my own decision. You made me feel as if I could accomplish anything. That's why I wanted you at my graduation."

Logan swallowed a mouthful of cole slaw and shook his head. "I didn't believe you were serious about not going to your graduation if I didn't come. Salina's worried phone call convinced me in a hurry."

"After she called home and told me you were coming, I had the fastest recovery from a virus in history. You should have seen me getting dressed and getting my things together." Rachel smiled and bit into her yeast roll.

"I didn't know you could be so stubborn."

"I learned that from you." At his surprised expression, she continued, "In spite of losing your parents, the town's unfair opinion of you, you never lost sight of what you wanted out of life. You never gave up, you never blamed anyone else, you just looked for ways to make your life better. You did it then and you're still doing it."

Shame swept through Logan. He didn't deserve her admiration or the caring look on her face. He had blamed others, namely her and her father and that was the only reason he had returned to Stanton.

"Is everything all right? You look funny," Rachel said.

"Yeah, I guess I'm not as hungry as I thought." He closed the container and pulled out a small medicine bottle from his shirt pocket. "Doc says since you're determined to work you can take these without worrying about being drowsy."

Her fingers curled around the bottle. "Thanks again."

Although she didn't say the words Logan saw it in her tender expression that she thought once again he was taking care of her. What else was he supposed to do?

She wasn't going to take the other pain medication no matter how much she needed it. He had done the only sensible thing. It wasn't a big deal.

He pushed to his feet and stuffed his container and drink back into the carryout bag. "I better let you get back to work. Take care of yourself and don't forget to take your antibiotic."

Rachel smiled and Logan practically ran from the room. One of the things that made Rachel unique from all the other women was the way she used to look at him with total trust and complete devotion. Just then, for a moment he had caught a glimpse of that look again. It had shaken him to the core to learn how good it made him feel and worse, how much he wanted to see it again and again. He was repaying an obligation, nothing more. He mustn't forget his goal. Malone was going to pay.

She may never move again, Rachel thought as she settled slowly against the cushioned sofa in her living room. Her right side was one big ache. Except for the brief lunch with Logan, the day at work had been nonstop. She smiled on visualizing Logan's shocked expression when she told him who she had learned her stubbornness from. She'd have to be more careful in the future. The last thing she needed was for Logan to learn how she really felt about him.

The doorbell rang. Rachel's lids swept shut and she rolled her left shoulder deeper into the cushion. The sound came again and again. One eyelid lifted. She stared at the offensive door. Whoever it was must have seen Jimmy bring her home in her truck. They knew she was there and they weren't leaving. With a slight moan she pushed from the chair. She kept forgetting not to use her right hand for weight bearing. Slow, measured steps carried her across the room. She opened the door. Logan stood on her doorstep with two bags of groceries in his arms.

"Hello, Rae," Logan greeted. The smile slipped from his face. "The other pills didn't work as well or did you overdo?"

"I refuse to answer that," she said. She had taken her first pain pill of the day fifteen minutes ago. In her rush to get to one of the sites and check out a problem with the surveyor, she had left them in her office. Then from there she had gone to the dorm site.

Logan scowled. "Go lie down before you fall and I'll take care of things."

Rachel automatically stepped back as Logan started toward her. It was then she saw the three women carrying plastic, multi-compartmental totes filled with cleaning supplies. She dragged her gaze away from the smiling women and followed Logan into the kitchen.

"What are they doing here?"

"They're going to clean up your house." Logan set the overflowing paper sacks on the cabinet by the refrigerator.

Embarrassment and outrage flushed her cheeks. "I can clean my own house and buy my own groceries."

Logan looked up from filling the egg tray. "I'll be finished with this in a minute if you need some help with your bath."

Rachel gasped softly. Logan smiled. It was a clear warning. "I'll get you back for this."

"I'm looking forward to it."

Gritting her teeth she turned to leave. Logan's soothing voice stopped her. "I don't think there are many things you can't do, Rae. But sometimes even Superwoman needs the help of a friend."

Rachel didn't have to look around to know her entire house needed a thorough cleaning. She wasn't a neat person, but dust thick enough to write your name in and cobwebs on the ceiling were a little too much. "I don't want them in my bedroom or messing with any of my papers."

"I already told them. Take your time with your bath and take one of those lethal pain pills." Logan went back to unloading the groceries. "I'm still trying to decide what to cook."

"At least I know it won't be possum."

Logan glanced up. "I knew it was a mistake to take you night hunting with me."

"I wanted to go. But holding the flashlight while you aimed the gun was something different. His beady little eyes were so sad."

"You started crying."

"I expected you to yell. Instead you held me."

"You wouldn't stop crying and apologizing."

"Until you kissed me," she said softly. The kiss had led to another and another until they were on the ground and Logan was above her. She would have willingly given herself to him, but Logan had rolled away. They were going to wait until they were married. Neither would have any regrets because there would be a lifetime of loving. There had only been a glorious night and morning.

With a clenched jaw Logan went back to putting up the groceries. "No possum. Once I learn a lesson I don't forget it."

Rachel went into her bedroom and closed the door. In her attempt to lighten the mood she had unintentionally brought up a time when they thought nothing would ever separate them. Instead she reminded him of how badly she had betrayed him. She had betrayed him and he still cared for her. Dr. Perry was right. Logan never shrank from his responsibilities. She just wished he was helping her because he wanted to and not because he felt he owed her. If only there was enough time for him to learn to trust her. Again she wondered how long Logan was going to stay and how was she going to endure the heartache when he left.

"Concentrate."

Rachel heard the terse word. Her tired brain understood the self-given command, but her mind refused to cooperate. She kept remembering coal-black eyes, strong arms, a deep voice that kept her fears at bay. But most of all she remembered calloused fingers grazing over heated flesh.

The leather stool on which she was perched shifted. She glanced at the blueprints spread over the drafting table and realized her progress in the past two hours had been minimal. She had to have the draft finished by Monday for another construction job Malone was to bid on.

Twisting her jeans-clad bottom deeper into the padded stool, Rachel brushed her hair from her forehead and tried again to concentrate. Hard-won discipline and determination kept her seated, but her imagination created images of Logan. His dark head tossed back, laughter spilling from his throat as she tried to bait her hook with a live worm. His black eyes dark with passion. His handsome face distorted by rage.

Her left hand remained motionless around the cold metal of the T-square, her right hand held the engineering pencil immobile. Neither the bright sun shining through the window behind her nor the noise of the two dump trucks rumbling past distracted her.

The same imagination that helped her create from nothing but fragmented images in her mind now held her firmly in its grip. Logan had said he wanted to be friends. It wasn't his fault that after seeing him for three of the past four days, she wanted so much more. Or his fault that she was so restless because she hadn't seen or heard from him all day.

The abrupt ringing of the phone thrust her firmly back into the present. She reached for the wall phone over the drafting table with her right hand and felt only a slight twinge in her shoulder. "Yes."

"Ms. Malone, Mr. Anderson is on line one," came the lyrical voice of the secretary/receptionist.

Rachel's hand on the receiver tightened. Jim Anderson was on Stanton's city council, and they were scheduled to meet in a private session today to discuss plans for the municipal complex. She pushed the blinking red button with the eraser of the drafting pencil.

"Good morning, Mr. Anderson. I hope this is good news."

A long sigh drifted through the line. "I wish it was, Rachel. You know your father and I go back aways."

"We didn't win the bid, did we?" She gripped the phone.

"Nothing's definite, but when we broke up for lunch, most of the members were leaning toward another company," he confessed. "Their reputation for bringing in a project on time and on budget were strong factors in their favor. On the other hand, your daddy had some problems. People on the council might forget if Fred Mason didn't keep reminding them. He's still worked up over the unexpected costs of his apartment complex."

Rachel sighed. "I've tried to explain to Mason a dozen times what happened. We ran into the penalty phase of our contract and the cost overrides far exceeded our expectations. All the subcontractors were bonded and reputable, and monies were allocated to adjust for the override. The sad fact is, we both lost money."

"I know, your daddy told me as much. Unfortunately, Mason can be very opinionated. The sad fact being, he is one of the most influential members of the council," Mr. Anderson informed her.

"I know. I appreciate you keeping me posted."

"No problem. I walked the floor with your daddy at the hospital the night you were born," Mr. Anderson said. "You've done him and your mother proud."

"Apparently, it wasn't good enough."

"Now don't go blaming yourself. Your being in charge had nothing to do with the vote."

"Thank you."

"No thanks needed. Just telling the truth. You're doing a fine job. Folks have taken notice of how hard you work and how your men respect you. If the dormitory at the college comes in without problems, I may have a project for you."

She couldn't control her excitement. "That's fantastic. What is it?"

He laughed. "A medical building, and that's all I'm going to tell you."

"That's enough."

"Goodbye, Rachel, and good luck. The Fourth of July is tomorrow, and the mayor wanted the council to make a decision by then," Mr. Anderson told her. "But don't worry. A lot of people in town are on your side and watching to see how things work out."

"I know, Mr. Anderson, and thanks again for keeping me posted. Goodbye."

Hanging up the phone, Rachel straightened and absently began rubbing her shoulder. She stopped the nervous gesture on realizing what she was doing. Her shoulder was doing fine, unfortunately Malone Construction wasn't. If Fred Mason had his way, nothing would save her family's company, which had been around for generations.

Only a miracle would shift the odds in Malone's favor. To think she had bragged to Logan about being a tough contender. No wonder he had such a strange look on his face. It was amazing he had kept from laughing out loud.

But they hadn't lost yet. She'd pray for the best and worry about the worst if it happened. What she had to do now was make sure the dorm came in on schedule.

Getting up, she opened her desk drawer, took out a small billfold, and shoved it into her back pocket. When she returned from the building site, she was going to forget about pride and contact Bridgeway about the possibility of doing subcontracting work for them. She didn't have any doubt that they were the company in the lead. She only hoped they could come to some agreement, because if they didn't, she wasn't sure of where to turn next.

Fifteen minutes later, Rachel's truck bounced to a halt in the makeshift parking lot of the dorm construction site. Automatically putting on her hardhat, she got out. Halfway there, she spotted Jimmy dragging a piece of cable from the trash dump. She cut across the construction site to intercept him.

"Hi, Jimmy. What are you doing?"

Startled, Jimmy dropped the cable and turned around. He relaxed on seeing Rachel. "Trying to put this ornery wire in George's truck. I found it in the trash and I thought I might be able to sell it for chokers." When she continued to stare at the cable, he looked uneasy. "You did say I could cull the trash. Another crane operator might be able to use it for a smaller loop to make a choker and lift something."

Rachel's eyebrows bunched. "It looks new to me."

"This piece does. I cut the ruined part off and left it in the trash." Jimmy ran his hand through his sandy-blond hair. "I don't mind telling you, it took me all of my break to do it, too. It's hard to believe it snap—" Jimmy stopped abruptly on seeing Rachel's eyes widen, then lock on the cable at his feet.

"I'm sorry, Miss Malone, you know I wouldn't do or say nothing to upset you," he cried. "I'll just put it back."

"No, wait," Rachel commanded as Jimmy stooped to pick up the cable. Crouching, Rachel took the wire in her shaking gloved hands. She couldn't believe what her eyes were telling her. Her hands fisted. Someone was going to pay for this. She pushed to her feet.

"I'll take this. Tell payroll to give you twenty-five dollars," she said tightly, then started toward the crane.

The loud noise of the engine increased as she neared. Her fingers opened and closed as she waited for the two men on the ground to direct the operator. They worked as a team when the operator's visibility was hindered.

Francis Ray 173

They also worked together to thread the cable through the three pulleys for the crane. All three were responsible for this. As soon as the steel beam was in place, she motioned for Ed to cut the engine.

"Ed, Leon and Gunther—come here."

All three men were slow on approaching, their eyes on the length of cable in her hands. Her anger grew. They already knew. She waited until they were in front of her.

Steel-toed work boots shuffled. Three pairs of eyes looked anyplace but at Rachel.

"One of you better talk and talk fast," she said hotly. "I want to know whose initial idea it was to use this light cable to lift a half-ton of steel, then I want you to draw your pay and get off this site. I don't want that kind of careless, irresponsible man working for me and endangering the lives of others. Since the other two must have known and didn't tell me, I want you both right behind him. I won't have men working for me I can't trust."

All three heads snapped up. Words tumbled out of their mouths. All of them were talking at once. Yet Rachel understood because each man was pointing at her and calling her name.

Chapter 9

Rachel held up her hand and the babble of voices stopped as abruptly as it had begun. "Don't make things worse by lying."

"It's the truth, Miss Malone." Ed, the crane operator, glanced around at the two worried men, then continued. "I questioned Jake when he told us to rethread the roller with the lightweight cable. He said you changed the order to save money and if I wanted my job, I better keep quiet."

"Ed's telling the truth," Gunther said.

"I—I was afraid something like the accident would happen, and it did," Ed confessed. "We already went and got a heavier cable and changed it while you were gone with Prescott to the hospital." He studied his feet again. "Jake said you didn't want anyone to know."

Rage followed swiftly by disappointment swept through Rachel. She had always had her reservations about Jake being trustworthy, but never had she questioned the loyalty and respect of the men in front of her. That was the reason the thought of them being dishonest had both angered and hurt her. "You believed such a lie?"

The three men studied the toes of their mud-crusted work boots instead of the angry woman in front of them.

"Jake may smile when you're around, but once you're out of sight we have to walk a tight line. He don't like to be questioned," the crane operator mumbled.

"So instead of coming to me to check things out, you let Jake bully you into knuckling under and endangering the crew?"

The small man seemed to shrink even more before her wrath. He tucked his head. "I got a family to feed. You know Ishira is due any day now."

"Since I'm the godmother of your youngest child, I'm well aware of your family. So don't pull that sob story on me," she snapped. "You saw an easy way out and you took it rather than doing what's right."

"Jake can be mean when he's riled," said the third man, who had remained silent. He stroked a small scar on his upper lip.

"So can I." Rachel gripped the cable in her hand. "The only reason I'm not going to fire all three of you is I believe you won't make the same mistake again.

Don't make me sorry." Three Adam's apples and three heads bobbed up and down. "Leon, find Jake and tell him I want to see him in the trailer. If you say one word to him or any of the other crew about this, you can keep going. Ed, Gunther, that goes for you, too."

Rachel waited until the men gave their consent then she went to the work trailer to wait for Jake. She glanced at the inferior cable one last time, then tossed it across the room. If she had it in her hand when Jake arrived, she might be tempted to hit him with it.

The door opened and Jake walked in. "You wanted to see me, Miss Malone?"

Confident. That one word described the muscle-bound, black man standing a few feet from her. He stood there grinning as if butter wouldn't melt in his mouth. But it was all an act to keep her off guard while he lined his pockets at the expense of Malone Construction. She should have trusted her instincts.

Rachel walked behind the desk. She wasn't sure if she stayed close to Jake, she could control herself. Of all the times for him to turn rogue, now was the worst.

"How long did you think you'd get away with it?"

His eyebrows bunched. "What are you talking about? Get away with what?"

Rachel had to admire his cool. "Switching supplies and pocketing the money."

Surprise, then dejection swept across his bearded face. "I can't believe you're doing this to me again. This company means as much to me as it does to you and your father. I thought you learned that the last time you questioned me."

"Lies and indignation won't save you." She came from around the desk and snatched up the cable and shook it in his face. "There's no way in hell this was on the supply list I faxed to our supplier."

"That's what came. You ordered..." His voice trailed off, his eyes widened. "Now I see, you plan to blame me for your mistake. It won't work. You order the supplies."

Rachel tossed the cable aside and shook her head. "You still don't get it, do you, Jake?" She went to the file cabinet in the corner of the room behind her desk and took out a folder marked "Stanton Junior College/Dormitory."

"Every order I send is done in triplicate. One copy for the supplier, one for my records, and one for the bookkeeper. Then I make an extra copy to keep on the job site if there's a question if something was ordered. If you find that weight cable on here I'll apologize."

For the first time, his bravado faded. "Maybe the supplier made a mistake. Those young fool kids working for the summer on the dock are always playing around instead of working."

"If they did, you should have taken one look at the cable and sent it back."

"Things have been kind of tight. I thought you wanted to shave a litt—"

"Stop lying." She rammed the folder back into the file cabinet and slammed the drawer shut. "You're fired."

A moment of uncertainty flickered across his face. "Your daddy won't let you fire me."

"That's where you're wrong. The other day at the hospital Daddy proved he'll back me in any decision I make, including firing you. And if you're thinking of going to him behind my back, don't. Because if you do, I'll press charges against you for stealing," she warned him.

"You either exchanged the cable yourself and pocketed the money for one of lighter weight or someone at the supply warehouse is working with you. You look like a greedy man, Jake. I think you'd want it all. Hope you got enough because you're not getting any severance pay. Now get out."

"You think you can tell me what to do like I'm a nobody. I worked for this company for fifteen years. This company and your daddy owe me," he suddenly snarled, his face becoming terrifying. He took a threatening step toward her.

"We owe you exactly nothing." Rachel held her ground. She was too angry to be afraid. "Leave, or I call the police and press charges."

Menacing black eyes drilled into her. "It would take them ten minutes to get out here."

"If you hurt me, the police wouldn't be able to put what's left of you in a paper bag after fifty-three men get through with you." Calmly, she picked up the phone.

"You're going to pay for this." He stormed out the door and slammed it so hard the trailer vibrated.

Seconds later, the door opened and four men rushed

in. Jimmy was in the lead. She smiled as he stuck the tire tool behind his back. Ed, Leon and Gunther were barehanded. After working in construction over half their lives, all they needed were their fists.

"Did you need something?" she asked.

"No," Jimmy answered. "I have to go pick up a load of nails. Do you want me to bring you back something for lunch, or is Mr. Prescott sending something today, as usual?"

Rachel lifted a delicate brow. The older men found the calendar of heavy machinery intensely interesting. Jimmy, with his open boyishness, just smiled. She ignored his leading question and asked one of her own. "Jimmy, do you mind telling me why you're here?"

"I sorta watched when you left me to talk with Ed and the guys. Then I saw Leon go tell Jake something. He didn't look too happy and when I saw them," he looked at the three men, "hanging around the trailer after Jake came in here, I decided they might need a little help."

She looked at the four men. The corner of her mouth lifted in a small smile. "Thank you. Jimmy, get all the men over here. I need to tell them we lost a foreman."

"Yes, ma'am. They'll be glad to hear it," he predicted and left.

"We won't let you down again, Miss Malone," Ed said and the other two men voiced their agreement.

"I hope not, because we're going to have to work harder than we ever have. Starting now."

Rachel left the trailer and waited on the steps for the

men to gather. Once they were all present, she simply told them Jake had been let go, but not the reason. As Jimmy had predicted, most of the men looked relieved. Seeing their faces made her realize that Jake probably got the men to work by threatening them, not from respect.

She reasoned his intimidation must have been going on while her father was in charge also. Briefly she wondered if he knew, then she decided her father hadn't. Her father might have trouble forgiving, but otherwise, he was a fair man.

The appointment of Sonny Taylor, a twenty-year employee of Malone's, as temporary foreman received loud yells of approval. She knew she had made the right decision when Sonny turned to the men and said they were all adults with a job to do and he'd treat them that way. The volume of the yells increased.

She spoke after Sonny, reminding the crew that she thought they were the best crew of men anywhere, that she was always willing to listen, and ended with her thanks for their support. This time, the men's roar of approval was almost deafening. Watching them file back to work, she hoped they still felt that way after the city council made its decision.

The rest of the day, she walked the site and inspected each floor of the five-story building, and talked to the crew, trying to determine if any others were told to overlook faulty equipment. She came up with nothing.

As much as possible, she checked the copper wiring and the lumber to make sure it was straight and knot free. Two of the things she wanted to check and couldn't were the electrical wiring and some of the plumbing because it was already drywalled. In the basement, she studied the electrical board, the numerous wires hanging down to "make ready" for the inspector.

For the moment, she had done all she could. Going to the trailer, she dialed the number of their main supplier. Luckily, she and the manager had gone to high school together, and more important, he could be counted on to be discreet.

Ten minutes later she hung up the phone with Tom Wilson's assurance that he would check the records. However, he pointed out that Jake probably returned the ordered cable, picked out a lower-priced one, then asked for a cash refund. He was so well known and Malone bought in such large quantities, Tom doubted if anyone questioned that he didn't have a receipt.

For Jake's thievery to be profitable, all the "return switches" had to be for cash. Finding those return receipts, which had his signature, would be almost impossible to locate without the dates. As for someone working with Jake, Tom didn't think so. Only experienced and trusted employees worked at the cash register in returns for that very reason. It was too easy to write "no receipt" and hand out cash.

Getting up from her chair, Rachel walked to the small window and looked at the dorm. Uneasiness pricked her. The worst was knowing Jake could have "switched" something that might cause major problems for the occupants later on. Steel, nails, wiring…there were so many ways to cut corners and save money…if you didn't care about building an inferior structure and endangering lives.

Presently, Malone had three projects going on and Jake could have made "switches" at any or all of the sites. Luckily, the other two buildings were just getting started. Before the day was over, she was going to visit the other two sites and make sure everything was up to code specification.

She leaned her head against the warm window-pane. Before she'd let anyone be injured, she'd go public and tear the entire dormitory down. Saving Malone's reputation didn't stand up against someone's life.

Her knees shook as she thought of how Jake's thievery had almost cost Logan his life. Jake should be made to pay for what he had done, but if she filed charges now, Malone would be scratched as a candidate to build the city's municipal complex.

Her hand absently rubbing her shoulder, she looked back at the dormitory and knew the worst part was ahead of her…telling her father she had fired Jake.

He had left her in charge, and she had failed. Maybe if she had been more experienced, she might have discovered sooner that Jake was dishonest and that he was bullying the men. Straightening, she left the trailer; there was no sense in speculating in what might have been. The damage was done.

She had to accept responsibility and move on. She knew too well what happened when a person didn't. The one thing she refused to do was worry her father unnecessarily by telling him about Jake's pilfering. His insubordination was as good a reason as any to tell her father she'd fired him.

You're in trouble, Logan.

Logan accepted the truth of his thought with a clenched jaw. The very fact that he had been sitting in his car for the last thirty minutes outside Rachel's house when he should have been at home told its own story. True, he owed Rachel a debt, but he had also stayed away as long as he could. Even hundreds of miles away in Arkansas, he hadn't been able to stop thinking about her.

He had thought distance would put things in perspective and strengthen his resolve. All it had done was make him worry whether Rachel was taking her medicine and eating properly. A smile lifted his mustache as he remembered how angry she had been when he'd showed up with groceries and the cleaning ladies. She had probably called him a few choice words in her mind. This Rachel was as fiercely independent as the old Rachel had been dependent. While he admired the change, it made things worse for him.

He'd expected to find a self-centered woman who thought only about her own comforts. Instead, he discovered a woman who continually put herself last. Her parents, Malone Construction, and even Logan came before her own needs. Despite himself, he admired her selflessness, her courage.

He had been in enough uphill battles to appreciate the sheer willpower it took to see your life crumbling around you and continue to fight. Rachel had more inner strength and courage than most men. Which left him with one big problem: how could he destroy the company without destroying the woman who fought so desperately to save it, a woman who had fought just as desperately to save his life?

With each hour ticking closer to the announcement of the winning bid for the city hall complex, his anger at her lessened and his uneasiness grew. Perhaps he had asked too much of an eighteen-year-old. Perhaps he had judged too harshly. He honestly didn't know anymore. The only thing he did know was that he had stayed away as long as he could.

Late this afternoon, Logan had called Charles to tell him he was heading back to Stanton. Good friend that Charles was, he hadn't asked why he had left in the first place, how things were going in Stanton, or why Logan was rushing back. He was glad because he didn't know the answers to these questions. Getting out of the car, he went to the front door and rang the bell. It took four rings to get a response.

The door opened and Rachel's brown eyes widened in surprise. She quickly stepped behind the partially closed door. "L-Logan, what are you doing here?"

Disappointment went through him. He hadn't expected her to throw herself into his arms, but neither had he expected the weariness in her voice and in her face. She looked as if someone had taken all the joy from her. Anger coursed through him at whoever had upset her. Before he left, he intended to find out the reason.

His gaze raked the towel turbaned around her head, her sweats, faded and damp in spots, another towel draped around her neck. "Did I catch you at a bad time?"

"As a matter of fact, you did." She closed the door another two inches. "Maybe you could come back tomorrow."

"Expecting company?"

"Looking like this?" she cried, then snapped her mouth shut.

Logan relaxed and put his palm against the door. "Good, then you won't mind letting me in."

"Logan, I'm tired," she said, absently rubbing her injured shoulder.

"Is your shoulder hurting?" Logan questioned.

She snatched her hand away. "No."

"I have a feeling you wouldn't tell me if it was. I think I'll see for myself," he said, pushing the door open farther. Ignoring Rachel's glare, he strode inside and closed the door behind him. "Turn around so I can look."

She crossed her arms belligerently over her braless breasts. "No, and that's final. And don't bother threatening to call and worry my mother, because if you do, I'm going to do something very unpleasant to you."

"Why are you being so stubborn? If it's troubling you, it could be infected or something," he reasoned.

"Dr. Perry's nurse changed the dressing this morning and she said it was healing fine. And to your next question, my neighbor washed my hair. She just left. I thought you were her at the door." Keeping her back to Logan, she opened the door. "Good night."

"You told her about the accident?"

"I told her, I was too tired to do a good job by myself. Besides, it was payback for all the times I've helped her give her dog a bath. Good night, Logan."

Instead of leaving, Logan studied the slight droop of her shoulders, the dark smudges beneath her eyes. She was tired. Fighting to keep Malone afloat was taking its toll on her. If he did nothing to help, it was all going to be for nothing. Not for the first time he tried to separate what he had to do from what it would cost the woman in front of him. As always, he failed.

"Logan, please."

He didn't question why he didn't want to leave her, he just accepted that he couldn't. "Got anything to eat?"

"What?"

"I've been out of town for the past couple of days. I just got back and I'm hungry," he explained. "I'm tired of eating out and I thought you might take pity on me and show me your cooking skills. That is, if you don't mind?"

Rachel didn't know if she should laugh or cry. Her life was falling around her head and Logan was asking her to feed him. When she thought of her father's fury this afternoon after she'd told him she had fired Jake for insubordination, she decided she wanted to cry. Apparently, he thought Jake was more important to the company than she was.

"You'll ruin everything," J. T. Malone said, his face as strained as his voice. "It's only a matter of time now."

At the time, Rachel had fought against the pain her father's words had caused just as she now fought not to read too much into Logan's request. He wanted food, not her. Looking her worst with a towel on her head and old clothes, she couldn't blame him. Just once, she wished he could see her at her best.

"A scrambled egg will be just fine," Logan suggested.

Now, Rachel really felt like crying. It didn't matter what she wore or how she looked, she couldn't make Logan care for her the way she cared for him. She shouldn't be greedy. Friendship was better than hostility.

"Thanks to you, I can do better than a scrambled egg." She closed the door. "Have a seat and I'll be back in a minute after I change and finish drying my hair."

"I'll help?" Pulling the towel from her head, he began drying her hair. "Stop squirming."

"I will when you stop," she protested, trying and failing to grab the towel. "More than my hair is wet."

"So I noticed, but I don't think you wanted me to dry you off the way I did the last time I got you out of the shower."

She stilled then slowly lifted her head to look at him.

He wore an expression she thought never to see again: longing and banked desire.

"Do you remember?" he asked, his voice husky.

"Yes," she whispered. How could she have forgotten? She had hidden herself in the bathroom for thirty minutes on their honeymoon night. She wasn't afraid of him; her fear had been over disappointing him sexually. The very thought of failing him in bed terrified her.

The choice was taken from her when Logan opened the shower door and pulled her wet body to his hard, naked one. One hand shut off the shower, the other curled around her waist. She'd been too shocked to do anything but stare into his turbulent black eyes.

"Do you love me?" he had asked. Immediately, she had answered, "Yes." He'd smiled and turned her insides to jelly. "Then keep that thought, because I love you, too." He'd proceeded to show her and dried her body at the same time.

Firmly, Rachel pushed the intimate memories to the back of her mind. "That was a long time ago."

"Memories linger."

She nodded. Memories lingered, and she still dreamed. She looked into the face once lost to her, cataloging each feature; noting the changes in his face, from that of a young man set on conquering the world to that of a man who had apparently done just that. While she liked the changes, she regretted she had not been there to see them happen.

Using all her inner strength, she tugged the towel out

of Logan's hand and stepped away from temptation. "I—I can do this later," she said unsteadily, and went to the kitchen. Given a choice between having him see her looking her worst or embarrassing herself again by showing him how much she cared for him, she'd take the former any day. He might want her, too, but he had already showed her it wasn't enough to make him forget she had once turned her back on him.

Sensing him following her, she opened the refrigerator door. "I have pork chops—"

"Anything is fine," Logan said, cutting her off. "Have you eaten and taken your medicine?"

"Yes to both questions." She set the oblong plastic container with pork chops on the counter, then glanced over her shoulder at Logan. How about creamed corn and green beans?"

"Sounds great. What can I do to help?"

Rachel shook her head. "Mr. Microwave is going to do all the work. Just take a seat."

"You're the one who needs to sit down after working all day," Logan told her. "I can microwave with the best of them."

"Logan, I—"

"No arguing, or I might decide to help dry your hair again," he said firmly.

Grabbing the towel around her neck with both hands, Rachel sat in one of the straight-backed chairs at the small kitchen table. "I can certainly see why you're general manager. You like to give orders."

Logan's hand paused only briefly in opening the microwave door. After putting the food inside and setting the timer, he turned. "You're pretty good at giving orders yourself. By the way, how are things going?"

Momentarily, Rachel's gaze refused to meet his. "Everything's on schedule. How was your trip?"

"Fine," Logan answered slowly. He didn't like the sudden panicky look in Rachel's eyes. Had something happened at Malone? Was that the reason she'd looked so down when she'd opened the door?

"Since you're back, does it mean you're going to be around for a few more days?" she asked.

"Yes."

"I'm glad," she said, then yawned. "Sorry."

"I'm the one who should be apologizing," Logan said. "I'm keeping you from bed after I told Dr. Perry I'd look after you."

"It's only a little after nine. I just haven't been sleeping very well," she said, absently rubbing her shoulder again.

The microwave timer went off. Logan ignored it. "You're rubbing your shoulder again."

Snatching her hand away, Rachel straightened in her chair. "It's just a habit. It's fine."

"This time, I'm going to see for myself."

Rachel jumped up from her chair and started backing up. "No, Logan. It's fine."

"Then you shouldn't mind if I look at it."

The kitchen wall by the door stopped her progress. She folded her hands across her chest. "No."

"Yes." In one smoothly controlled motion, Logan turned Rachel around and pulled up her sweatshirt. Air hissed through his teeth when he saw the dark bruise from her right shoulder to her mid-back, the multiple crisscrossed tiny scars on her once flawless skin, the white bandage. It looked worse than the first time. "God, Rae."

"It's not as bad as it looks. I told you Dr. Perry's nurse said today I was doing fine."

Logan was too disturbed by what he saw to answer. He remembered the afternoon in *Whispers* when he had seen the sleek, smooth curve of her back in the mirror. Nothing had marred her creamy brown skin. Now, because she had risked her life to save his, it would never be that way again. "The red dress you were trying on. You can't wear it now," he said, his voice thick.

Rachel tried to pull the sweatshirt down and failed. She didn't want him to feel guilty. "My back will heal. The dress doesn't matter."

Logan slowly shook his head, his unsteady fingers tracing the outline of the bruise as he thought back eight years to his own bruised, battered body. It had burned like hell at first, then the pain had lessened, but it had been weeks before he could move without discomfort.

The physical pain was small in comparison to the emotional pain he'd felt knowing Rachel hadn't loved him enough to stand up for him and admit he was her husband. Seeing her bruised back, the gut-wrenching pain he now felt was worse than any he had ever experienced.

"I'm sorry. So sorry." Warm lips brushed across her

upper shoulder. Rachel jerked, and immediately, Logan lifted his head. "I didn't mean to hurt you again."

"You…you didn't," she answered breathlessly. "It's been a long time since someone wanted to kiss me and make it better."

His eyes narrowed, darkened, smoldered. "Lucky me."

He started at the top of her shoulder, worked his way down to her waist, moved across to her spine, then kissed his way up to her neck. His fingers glided over her skin, arousing, soothing, begging forgiveness and seeking solace. Rachel twisted restlessly under the double assault of his hands and lips.

Slowly, he turned her to him, his hands braced on her waist. She looked at the tension bracketing his mouth and wanted nothing more than to soothe it away. She didn't want him to feel guilty about her. She'd give anything to be able to touch him freely as he had just touched her, to be able to trace the spot in his chin, which on those infrequent times when he smiled, dimpled. But he was offering her comfort and she wanted more, so much more.

She closed her eyes to hide her longing and to resist temptation, but just as quickly opened them when her name, like a golden shadow flowed over her, deep and mystical.

"Rae."

Logan's ebony eyes had that same questioning look she remembered, but it was no longer shadowed with anger. This time she didn't hesitate to follow her mind.

Shaky fingers ran over the strong line of his jaw as she had done so many times in the past. And, as in the past, his hand cupped hers, his head turned to press his lips against her palm. She shivered and tried to keep her voice normal.

"I'm more comfortable in denim than evening gowns."

"But no woman can look as good as you in one. The night we were married and went out on the town. You wore a silver gown and I could barely keep my eyes or hands off you."

"I felt the same way about you. You looked like a handsome rogue in your black tux." Rachel pursed her lips. "Apparently I wasn't the only woman who thought so."

Logan's lips brushed against the top of her head. "You were the only woman I saw that night. You looked so elegant. You probably looked sensational in the red gown. I wish I could have seen you wearing it."

Rachel buried her face in his chest. "Don't remind me of that."

"I was a donkey's behind."

She lifted her head. "Yes, you were." For a split second he looked startled, then he smiled and pulled her back against his chest. "To be honest with you, I wished you could have seen me in the gown, not with it over my head."

"Then it's a good thing I had Ida Mae put it back for you."

Abruptly, she lifted her head again. "You did what?"

Logan shrugged. "Ida Mae was putting it back on the mannequin and suddenly I asked her to take it off. Your not buying the dress angered me. I had some crazy idea of making you wear the dress although I didn't know how I was going to accomplish it."

"I know why. You thought I was rejecting the dress like I rejected you at the hospital," Rachel said quietly and waited for the coldness to reenter Logan's eyes.

He stared down at her a long time. "Maybe you're right."

Rachel cried inside for the pain and heartache she must have caused him. Perhaps it was time for some of the healing to begin. "When I told you I started to go to you, you never asked what stopped me."

The harshness Rachel had expected earlier flared in Logan's eyes. "It didn't matter. You never came."

"Because I was in a car accident in Amarillo."

Shock swept through Logan. "God, no." He pulled her fiercely to him, his entire body trembling. "Were you hurt? Why didn't someone call me?"

Somehow she managed to say through the huge lump in her throat, "You're here now, Logan. That's what matters."

His arms tightened. "I'm so sorry I wasn't there with you."

Rachel just held on. "I—I wasn't well for-for a long time and when I was, the divorce papers had been finalized."

The thought of Rachel suffering took the remaining strength from Logan's legs. He sagged into the nearest chair with her in his arms. There were so many questions left unspoken, but from her trembling body he knew she wasn't ready to answer them. "If I had called or come back...."

"You can't change the past. Nobody knows that better than I do. All you can do is try not make the same mistakes again," Rachel said, hoping she wasn't making another mistake by not telling Logan about the loss of their child. For now, her accident was enough for him to deal with.

"You grew up without me."

"It wasn't easy," she whispered softly.

Gently, Logan eased her away from his chest. His gaze swept the perfection of Rachel's face he remembered at eighteen, that no longer promised, but was. Long, silky lashes fluttered over eyes the color of hundred-year-old brandy and just as potent. But unlike the last time eight years ago, they weren't dark and haunted. He drew in his breath as the memory of that time struck him, and instead of pain, he inhaled her unique woman's scent, alluring and innocent and haunting. Just like the woman.

His nostrils quivered in appreciation even as his lips parted slightly to ask, "I wonder if you taste the same? Hot, dark, forbidden."

Her sharp intake of breath splintered over and around him like a broken wave.

No power on earth could have kept him from lowering his lips to hers. His calloused hands cupped her face, his thumb stroked her cheek. His lips left hers and traced the curve of her neck, the lobe of her ear, and once done, his teeth nipped the sensitive flesh.

Her whimpering cry returned his mouth to hers in a deep, greedy kiss. His tongue stroked the inner softness of her mouth. Both moaned in remembered pleasure.

Abruptly, he lifted his head.

"You're not going to be noble again, are you?" Rachel cried.

"There's not a noble bone in my body. You're the only one who ever made that mistake." He gathered her up in his arms. They had a lot to work out, but tomorrow was soon enough. "The floor is no place for your shoulder."

Her finger traced the lines in his brow. "It doesn't ache anymore."

"Good." He never stopped until he reached her bathroom. He smiled at the frown on her face. "We're going to dry your hair first. Once we get into bed, I don't plan to let you out for a long time."

Trembling hands fumbled with the cabinet drawer and pulled out the hair dryer. Logan took it from her, plugged it into the socket, then proceeded to blow-dry her relaxed hair. Once he finished, he picked her up and placed her on the bed. His eyes on her, he started unbuttoning his shirt.

"Let me," she asked and came to her knees. Her hands shook. She couldn't get the button through the opening. "Maybe you'd better do it. I guess I need more practice."

He had the answer to his unspoken question about the other men in her life. Looking into the unsure face of the woman who just hours ago probably had fifty-odd men following her orders, he knew with a startling knowledge the other men in her life no longer mattered to him. Only she mattered.

"I'm not complaining," he said, and quickly unbuttoned his shirt.

Immediately Rachel's hands were there grazing over the hair-roughened chest, the coiled muscles. She leaned forward and flicked her tongue across his nipple.

He sucked in a rugged breath. Startled, Rachel asked, "Did I do it wrong?"

"No, you did it right." He kissed the frown from her face, then quickly pulled off the rest of his clothes.

Sitting back on her heels, she shamelessly looked at his gloriously nude body. "You're beautiful."

"You've been working in the sun too long. You also have on too many clothes," he said, then proceeded to remedy the problem. His breath caught on seeing her naked. "I've dreamed about this." Once again his mouth and hands teased and tasted, only this time both knew fulfillment waited.

"Logan, I ache."

"Where?" he asked, his lips on the full curve of her breasts. She moaned deep in her throat.

"Here?" His lips closed over her right nipple.

She whimpered.

"No. How about here?" His teeth captured her left nipple and his tongue laved it.

"L-Logan." She thrashed on the bed.

"I'll make it stop for both of us." In one controlled stroke, he slid into her waiting warmth. Her body arched beneath his, accepting him. Their gaze locked and held.

They were home.

Sometime later, Rachel lay on her left side facing Logan, feeling deliciously boneless and exuberant. They still had a chance. He couldn't have made love to her so beautifully if he didn't love her a little bit. Somehow she'd find a way to tell him about the loss of their child. He had to understand. She couldn't stand to lose him again. He stared down into her frowning face. "What are you thinking?"

"That I don't want this night to end."

"Morning is a long time away." He turned over and joined them in one smoothly controlled motion.

She forgot how to breathe. The exquisite fit of their bodies always amazed her. His breath fanned her face. She shivered and sucked in air for her starving lungs. Closing her eyes, she savored the rapturous feeling rushing through her body.

Logan rolled and Rachel found herself on top. He grinned at her startled expression. "I thought your shoulder might need a rest."

"Logan, I'm not sure about this."

"I am." With his hands splayed around her waist, he sat her up. Rachel folded her arms over her breasts and looked uncertain. Logan moved.

She sucked in her breath. Never had she felt such an exquisite feeling. He moved again. Uncertainty was forgotten. With her hands pressed against his chest, she threw her head back and matched his rhythm. Their combined shout of fulfillment came a long time later.

Chapter 10

"Don't answer it."

Rachel slowly surfaced from the fringes of sleep on hearing Logan's deep voice. From somewhere she heard a shrill sound, but her senses were more attuned to the warmth and muscled hardness of the man she was partially sprawled on top of. The upper part of her body was pressed against a wide chest, her leg sandwiched between hair-roughened ones. The steady sweep of a calloused hand up and down the slope of her back caused her to arch closer. She moaned. Her fluttering eyelids drifting downward.

The intrusive noise came again. Her eyelids snapped up. *The telephone.* Pushing out of Logan's arms, she sat up, bringing the sheet with her. Her gaze immediately sought the bedside clock: 11:37 p.m. Tension whipped through her. Without thought, she reached across Logan for the phone.

Sitting up, he blocked her way and captured her around the waist in an attempt to pull her back down into the bed. "Let it ring."

She shook her head. "I can't. Something might be wrong with Daddy."

Logan stiffened. The lazy warmth in his eyes cooled. Releasing her, he lay back down and stared at the ceiling. "Then by all means, answer it."

"Don't do this to me, Logan, please," she said, her hand touching the hard curve of his jaw. "Don't make me feel as if I'm betraying you because I care about my father."

The word "betraying" raced through Logan. He looked at the lines of strain on Rachel's beautiful face and knew he'd only add more if he continued his personal vendetta against her father. Unfortunately, they were two halves of an inseparable whole. He couldn't hurt J.T. without causing Rachel pain. He couldn't imagine hurting her ever again. He handed her the receiver.

She mouthed "Thank you," then said, "Hello." Her glance flickered to Logan as he sat up. His black eyes watched her closely. She didn't have to be a mindreader to know he was thinking once before they had made love and been torn apart afterward. The same thought was swirling in her brain.

Relief swept through her as she recognized the mas-

culine voice. It was short lived. "Is Ishira all right?"
Then, "Thank goodness. No, I'm fine. There's no need
for you to come over here." When no answer came, she
repeated her last sentence. The only response was the
steady drone of the dial tone. She hung up the phone and
turned to Logan. "I'm sorry, but you'll have to leave."

"Who's coming over, and why?"

"Just a few of my men," she answered, and glanced
at the clock. It was a seven-minute drive from Ed's
house. Logan had to be gone by then.

"Kind of late for a business call, isn't it?"

"Logan, please."

He studied the tension in her shoulders, the way she
kept looking at the clock. Something was wrong. He had
no right to probe, but he was going to make damn sure
if she needed him again he was going to be there. He
threw back the covers and got out of bed. "Mind if I take
a shower first?"

"Can't it wait until you get home?"

Undisturbed by his nakedness, he paused in
picking up his clothes. "Who don't you want me to
meet, Rachel?"

The gentle urging of his voice made her feel worse.
This was the man who had made love to her so beautifully and so thoroughly, the man she loved in return. If
she wasn't honest with him, she might lose him forever.

"I just don't want you involved. You might get hurt
again." She looked at him mutely, wanting him to
understand.

"Again?"

Her arms clamped tighter around her sheet-covered breasts. "If I hadn't begged you to keep our seeing each other a secret, my father wouldn't have beat you up the day of his heart attack. You were hardly able to stand." She bit her lip and looked away for a moment before she was able to continue. "You both suffered because I was too much of a coward to stand up for myself. I promised myself a long time ago that I would never again back away from a problem."

Logan saw the misery and determination in her eyes and something inside him lightened. She hadn't known her father ordered Jake and the other two men to beat up Logan. "And why should I get hurt this time?"

"I fired Jake today, and apparently he's taking it out on some of my crew."

"You what?"

"He was being insubordinate, so I called him into the work trailer and fired him," she said, repeating the reason she had given her father. "Tonight he slashed two of my men's tires."

"Are you next on the list?" Logan asked with deadly quiet.

"I don't think so, but Ed does so he's on his way over with some men."

"Get dressed. I'll wait in the living room for them."

"Logan, I don't want you involved. This is my problem," she cried.

"The second I made love to you it became my

problem." With his clothes clutched in his fist, he started from the room.

"I don't want you feeling guilty because we made love," Rachel said. "You don't owe me anything."

"I owe you my life, but that's not why I'm staying. Stop wasting time, Rae, and get dressed." The door closed behind him.

Rachel quickly got out of bed. There was no way she was going to let Ed talk to Logan without her being there.

Logan had never been so filled with rage or so frightened. Rachel apparently had no idea what a vindictive bastard Jake could be. He had been a bully for all the years Logan had known him. The big grin of his was all fake. When he didn't get what he wanted by using threats, he used his fists. But if he caused Rachel another second of worry, he was going to wish he had never been born. He wasn't the only one who knew how to fight dirty. In the years Logan had been away, he had survived in some of the worst dives in the world.

Pushing the living room curtain aside, Logan glanced out the window. On seeing no one, he looked back at the bedroom. Rachel was an independent, headstrong woman who liked to take care of her own problems. She had yet to understand that everyone wasn't going to fight fair. Hell, he sure hadn't. He had swapped kisses for unspoken truths, and by doing so, had backed himself into a corner.

If he told Rachel now he was part-owner of Bridgeway, she'd show him the door. He'd never get a chance to explain he had come looking for revenge and instead found a woman he still cared for. For her own protection, he had to remain in her life. She didn't have the nasty instincts needed to go up against a maggot like Jake and hope to win. That meant, at least for now, he had to go on living a lie. A lie that was becoming increasingly more difficult to bear.

Earlier he had looked at her sleeping so trustingly in his arms and realized he wanted to be completely honest with her. She had given so much, and he had given only deceit in return. The thought turned his stomach and left a bitter taste in his mouth, but not as much as the idea that if he didn't tell her soon, he might lose her forever. He didn't know what the future held for them, but he did know he wanted a chance to find out. He had decided to tell her everything when she woke up.

Now, he couldn't take a chance of Rachel shutting him out of her life. Jake was too dangerous for her to cope with by herself. As much as Logan hated deceiving her any longer, he had no choice. He just hoped she understood when the time came to explain who he really was.

The doorbell rang and he reached the door in two long strides and jerked it open. The three men on the porch shifted uneasily on seeing Logan. "Come on in."

The three looked around as if each expected the other to make the decision to enter first.

"If this concerns Ms. Malone, someone had better start talking, and fast," Logan told them.

"I appreciate your concern, Mr. Prescott, but these are *my* men." Rachel sent Logan a meaningful look, then stepped in front of him. She wanted no interference from him. "Hello, Ed, Leon, Gunther. Please come in."

"We didn't expect you to have company," Ed said, his gaze bouncing off Logan's grim face.

Rachel looked at the obviously embarrassed faces of her men. They were trying to make up for their mistake with Jake and protect her. "Mr. Prescott stopped by to see how I was feeling, and as you can see, I'm fine, so you can *all* go home."

"First, why don't you come inside and tell us why you're here." Logan grabbed the closest man's arm and pulled him inside. Rachel would just have to be upset with him. He wasn't leaving until he found out what was going on. As he expected, the other men followed.

"Logan, you really don't have to stay," Rachel told him as he closed the door.

"What kind of man would I be if I didn't make sure the woman who saved my life was safe and happy?" he asked smoothly.

Bowing to the inevitable, Rachel took a seat in one of the armchairs in front of the couch her crewmen were perched on. Introductions were brief. Logan came to stand beside her, his hand rested on the back of the chair near her head. "All right, tell me what happened."

Ed stopped twisting his baseball cap and finally met

her gaze. "Sometime after dark, Jake took something and cut up my and Leon's tires."

"Did you see him?" Logan asked.

"I didn't have to. The dirty, lowdown dog called." Ed's lips trembled. "Said he wanted to make sure I knew who was responsible. Said he always paid back his debts."

"I got the same call," Leon added, looking just as grim.

"I'm sorry," Rachel said, angry at herself for not foreseeing Jake's vindictiveness.

"Don't you go blaming yourself," Ed said. "Like you told us this afternoon, we should have stood up to Jake. But if he thinks I'm going to wait around for him to pay me a second visit, he's got another think coming."

Leon nodded. "Same here."

"I was out with a couple of the guys for a beer, but I bet the stinking bas...er...coward is just waiting for a chance to slash my tires," Gunther said.

"Why did he single you three out, and what has this to do with Ms. Malone?" Logan asked. Three pairs of eyes flicked to Rachel, then away. Logan's gaze followed, but his stayed on Rachel.

"I was talking to them before I called Jake into the trailer," Rachel explained. "He might think they had something to do with my firing him."

"Has anyone talked to the man with you when you fired Jake?" Logan asked.

"No one was with me."

Logan tensed, disbelief widening his eyes. He stepped in front of Rachel. "Why did you take such a chance? Jake is as mean as they come when he's crossed." Fear roughened his voice.

"Logan, it's part of my job," Rachel placated, craning her neck back to stare up into Logan's angry face. "What kind of general manager would I be if I were afraid of being alone with an employee I had to fire?"

Logan knew he was overreacting, Rachel had shown him she could take care of herself. But the thought of her being in danger made him sick to his stomach. "Don't you listen to the news? Disgruntled employees do stupid things. Why didn't you call in the security guard?"

"Reeves works only nights. Besides, like most bullies, Jake fights only when he's sure the odds are in his favor. If he had harmed me in any way, the crew would have made mincemeat out of him."

"We were waiting outside," Ed put in helpfully.

"Yeah," Gunther said.

"Me, too," added Leon.

"You see?" Rachel smiled triumphantly. "I was never in any real danger."

"And you won't be." Logan headed for the door.

Rachel came to her feet and was right behind him. "Where are you going?"

"To pay Jake a visit." Logan looked over Rachel's head to her crewmen standing just behind her. "Do you mind staying until I get back?"

"I wanna go with you," Ed said.

"Me, too," said Leon.

"No," cried Rachel. "No one is going anyplace

except to bed. Can't any of you understand, Jake's phone call was his way of luring you to him. He expects you to go after him and when you face him, he isn't going to fight fair."

Logan's smile was pure malevolence. "Neither will I."

"I don't want you to go," Rachel said.

The tips of his fingers gently brushed across her cheek. "I have to."

"No you don't. Not because of me. I told Jake if he tried to hurt me—" Rachel's words halted abruptly as she saw the change in Logan's face. He looked lethal and savage. In trying to stop him from leaving, she had revealed too much. "I don't want you hurt."

For a fraction of a second Logan's face softened. "I feel the same way about you." Opening the door, he turned to go.

"If you leave, I'll be right behind you," Rachel shouted to his retreating back.

Logan whirled and came back to face her. "You're staying here."

Her chin lifted and she met his blazing black gaze unflinchingly. "Only if you promise to stay away from Jake."

"I can't. He has to know what he does will be repaid in kind," Logan reasoned.

"I'll replace the tires." Rachel's hand curled around the coiled muscles in Logan's arm. "We don't know he has any intention of bothering me."

Logan looked over her head to the three men. "Do you think I should show her what's left of my car?"

"What?" Rachel looked from Logan to her men.

Gunther nodded his sandy head. "You were so calm, we thought you hadn't seen it yet."

"I saw it when I was watching out for you to arrive."

Rachel raced outside. She stopped several feet from Logan's Corvette. Even from that distance she could see the convertible black canvas top flapping in the gentle summer breeze. She forced herself to go closer. What she saw enraged her. The dim streetlight two houses away couldn't hide the destruction.

Jake hadn't just cut Logan's tires, he had mutilated his car. There were deep gouges running the entire length of the black sports car, the mirror was hanging limply from its mooring, the taillights were smashed. She felt Logan's arm slide around her waist.

"Jake's going to pay for this," she said with absolute conviction in her voice.

Logan turned her to him. "Leave Jake to me. The only reason I showed you this was to make you realize something has to be done tonight."

"We can call the police," Rachel suggested.

"It would be his word against theirs, and neither one of us saw anything." Logan nodded toward her employees. "They can call the police later. If I thought there was any other way to stop Jake, I'd take it. Violence is never the answer, but asking Jake nicely won't get us anywhere unless we show him every time he bothers us, we're going to come down on him twice as hard."

"Whatever you're planning, I'm going with you."

"Hold on a minute. You're staying here where I'll know you'll be safe."

She pushed out of his arms. "You're in this because of me. Either I go with you, or I'm following."

Logan knew that stubborn look. He had to talk fast. "Do you remember me asking you about the dress you can't wear because of your shoulder and you said it didn't matter?"

She frowned. "Yes. What has that to do with anything?"

"The car doesn't matter," he said simply.

"You can't compare a sixty-thousand-dollar car to a dress," she yelled.

"I can when I put it up against your safety. The car stays in the garage more often than it goes out on the streets," he said truthfully. The only reason he had driven it to Stanton was to show her what a success he had made of himself. Now, looking at her worried face, it seemed immature and petty. "It's about time I got something back from the high insurance I pay."

Rachel couldn't believe he was so calm. "You always loved anything you drove. Even your ten-year-old truck. I used to watch you for hours working on the Green Machine. One time a guy nicked it when he opened his car door and you had a hissy fit. You ranted for fifteen minutes."

"Let's just say I grew wiser as I grew older." Logan spoke to the silent men. "I had planned on walking to the nearest phone and calling a friend of mine to come get me, but since Rachel knows about my car, can one of you take me?"

"You can drive my truck," Rachel said.

"No. I don't want any connection to Malone." Logan's face hardened. "I intend for Jake to think twice before he pays anyone else a late-night visit."

Gunther stepped forward. "I'll take you anyplace you want to go."

"You ain't leaving me out," Ed said.

"Me, either," agreed Leon.

"That goes for me, too," Rachel added.

Logan looked at Rachel's stubborn face and sighed. "Like I said, you've grown into a remarkable woman."

Warmth coursed through her. "Thank you."

"Can any of you tell me what Jake values more than himself?" Logan said.

"His new fishing boat and his Caddy. He brags about them as much as he brags about his long winning streak at the horse races and gambling casinos in Louisiana." Gunther shook his head. "There ain't no justice in the world if slime like Jake can win thousands of dollars."

Logan grinned. "Maybe there is. Won't it be a shame with so much time on his hands, he won't be able to enjoy either."

"I can't believe I let you talk me into this," Logan said, as he closed Gunther's truck door. He had to pitch his voice to be heard over the loud music of Big Al's. Jake's blue truck was parked two spaces over.

"You're too good to stoop to Jake's level," Rachel said. "You couldn't have damaged his Cadillac and boat without regretting it later on. You've been through enough because of me. I didn't want there to be any more regrets."

"The only regret I have is that I didn't come back sooner." Logan saw the shocked but pleased expression on Rachel's face and vowed he was going to keep her that way. He started for the honky-tonk. Gunther, Ed, and Leon were close behind him.

Entering the smoke-filled place, Logan went directly to the bartender, gave him a fifty, and whispered something in his ear. The barrel-chested man nodded. Logan skirted the tables until he reached the jukebox and pulled the plug. The music ground to a halt. Protests littered the club. The brawny bartender banged the business end of a baseball bat on the counter and the voices quieted.

Logan stepped forward to make sure he was in Jake's line of vision. "Sorry for the interruption, folks, but I wanted to make sure everyone heard I'm offering a two-thousand-dollar reward for information leading to the arrest and conviction of the person or persons responsible for damaging my car." Out of the corner of his eye, Logan saw the two men standing with Jake at the far end of the bar cut him a sharp glance. Rachel was right. Jake inspired fear, not loyalty.

"I'm offering an additional two thousand for the arrest and conviction of the person or persons responsible for damaging the trucks of Ed Adams and Leon Green."

"Cut the music back on," Jake bellowed.

"The music stays off until the man's through," the bartender said, his right hand sliding up and down the length of the bat.

"I came here to have a good time, not hear some mama's boy cry because someone messed up his fancy car," Jake snarled.

Jake gave Logan the opening he was waiting for. "I wonder if you would say the same if someone decided to sneak out to your place and make scrap metal out of *your* car and boat?"

Jake banged his glass of beer so hard on the counter, it splashed over the side. Shoving people out of the way, he crossed to Logan. He looked mean and ugly. "No one better touch what's mine."

"Then perhaps you had better hurry home. Who can tell where this crazy person is going to strike next?" Logan said calmly.

Jake's face hardened. "If you bothered my boat or my car, I'm going to tear you apart."

"Why would I bother your boat or car?"

In the face of Logan's simple question, Jake faltered. Logan's smile taunted him.

Jake's fist shot out without warning. Logan dodged the blow and sent his own fist straight to Jake's large nose. Logan followed with a sharp slice of his hand to the side of Jake's thick neck. He dropped to his knees. Logan leaned over and grabbed him by the shirt front.

"If you cause Ms. Malone or her men any more grief,

I'm coming back looking for you. Not your boat or your car, *you*. I don't plan to fight fair. When I'm finished with you this time, *you're* the one who's going to need to see a doctor." Logan opened his hand and Jake slumped to the floor.

Straightening, Logan glanced around the silent room. "Four thousand dollars for information, and the identity of the person will remain a secret. Just call the police."

He plugged the jukebox in, nodded to the bartender, and left. He wasn't surprised to see Rachel waiting for him just outside the door.

"Are you all right?"

His arm curved around her waist. "Couldn't be better."

"You should have seen him, Ms. Malone," Gunther enthused. "I've never seen anyone fight like that except on TV. Jake's never been beat in a fight, but tonight he never knew what hit him."

"He won't think he's so big now." Ed slapped Logan on the back. "Did you see how Clyde's eyes bugged when you offered the two-thousand-dollar reward? Then when you mentioned the additional two thousand dollars, I thought he was going to pass out from pure greed."

Rachel knew how Clyde felt. When she'd suggested offering a reward to Logan, she'd had no idea he'd set such a large amount. Where was she going to get two thousand dollars? "Of course I'll pay half."

"No need. My auto club will foot the bill," Logan said easily. "Come on, men, it's after midnight and past time for Ms. Malone to be in bed."

"Sure thing," Ed said, as he climbed into the back of the cab. "Thanks for everything, Mr. Prescott. You'll make me sleep much better. If you don't have any plans, I'd like to invite you over to my house tomorrow for a little get-together with some of the men from work."

"Call me Logan." He opened the door of the truck for Rachel. "I'd like that, but since I don't have a car, it depends on whether someone will take pity on me and pick me up."

"I could pick you up," Rachel quickly offered. Too quickly, from the way her men were grinning at her. She hastened to add, "Ed has already invited me. It's the least I can do after causing you so much trouble."

"You're sure? I don't want to put you out."

Rachel smiled into Logan's mischievous face. "If so, I can handle it."

The men shouted with laughter. Logan shook his head and slid into the seat beside Rachel. She sure had changed, and he was thoroughly enjoying getting to know the new Rachel. He just hoped time didn't run out on them.

Chapter 11

Rachel had never been so nervous in her life. Taking a deep breath, she got out of the truck in front of Logan's house, then brushed her hands over the flared skirt of her gauzy magenta-colored dress. She had wanted to look seductive and feminine for him. She wanted the magic, the special closeness they'd shared last night to continue in the broad light of day.

Ed's phone call and the subsequent events had prevented them from having any time alone to talk after they'd made love. At least she knew he didn't regret their intimacy. Each time she remembered him saying the only thing he regretted was staying away so long, joy burst within her.

She almost smiled at another memory, that of Logan's stunned face when Gunther had asked where he lived so Gunther could drop him off first. Nothing Logan said swayed the determined Gunther, who obviously was awed by Logan's fighting skills. Her smile faded as she recalled her sense of loneliness when Logan got out of the truck. Things between them had to work out this time. She didn't know if she could go through losing him a second time.

"Beautiful women should never be sad."

Her head came up. Logan stood on the porch, his thumb hooked in the front pocket of his denims. And she couldn't tell a blasted thing from his unreadable expression. "Good morning, Logan."

"I don't think so," he said, and stepped off the porch.

"Did Jake come out here last night? Are you all right?" She met him halfway, her eyes wide with worry.

"I haven't seen Jake, and as for being all right, I will be when you tell me you don't regret last night," Logan said.

"Do you?" Rachel asked, her voice a hushed whisper.

Long fingers touched the smoothness of her cheek. "Only that we didn't have the entire night together."

Relief and longing made her voice quiver. "Me, too."

He pulled her into his arms, his lips finding hers. His warm hands palmed her breast, slid over the four buttons. Gently, he set her away. "All those buttons could get you in a lot of trouble."

"One can only hope." She glanced up through a dark sweep of lashes.

Logan laughed and hugged her to him. "Oh, Rae, you're something else."

"Glad you think so. Now, we'd better hurry to Ed's house before he and Gunther come looking for me."

He studied her face. "Is everything all right?"

"It's fine. I only meant they've probably spread your praises far and wide and everyone will be anxious to see you."

It had taken Logan a lot of soul-searching years for him to discover that what people thought of him didn't matter as much as what he thought of himself. At the moment he wasn't high on his list of people he liked. Deceiving Rachel was becoming harder by the second. But he'd protect her at any cost. "I hope they know enough to leave your name out of it."

Rachel was touched by Logan's concern. "They probably will, but if they don't, it won't bother me." She grabbed his hand on seeing the lines of worry hadn't disappeared from his handsome face and started for her truck. "I'm not going to let Jake spoil the day for either of us. Stop worrying about me."

"On one condition."

"Name it," Rachel said, as she paused at the driver's side of the vehicle.

Strong arms pulled her against a wide chest. Ebony eyes beckoned. "That we leave early and come back here."

Desire rushed through her like a fierce, hot wind. "I might be persuaded."

"Name it."

Instead of answering, she wound her arms around his neck and pressed her lips against his. The kiss was long and hot and deep. Finally, she lifted her head. "I thought kissing you would make the wait easier, but…" Her voice trailed off, her gaze fastened on his lips.

This time, it was Logan who was the aggressor. His mouth took hers in a kiss so consuming and hot that it left both of them breathless. "Do you really think they'd come looking for us?"

"Yes," Rachel said on a moan, as sharp teeth nipped her lower lip. She pressed closer, trying to shape her body to the hard length of his.

Logan enjoyed the sensual feel of the woman in his arms for a few moments before sanity returned. His head lifted. She looked so bereft, he was almost tempted to pull her back into his arms. But this time, he wanted no unexpected interruptions. "If we don't stop, we aren't going anyplace but my bed. I wouldn't feel too kindly toward anyone who came knocking on my door."

"Neither would I."

The annoyance in Rachel's face caused Logan's mustache to twitch. He tilted his dark head to one side to study her closer, his thumb grazed across her lower lip. "Come on while I still have some willpower left."

A sense of power swept through her. This was the man she loved, the man she once thought reviled her. For so long she wanted the opportunity to touch and taste him freely.

The tip of her tongue flicked out to graze his roughened thumb. Logan inhaled sharply. She sent him a brilliant, seductive smile. "That's so you won't forget your promise."

"Not in this lifetime," Logan said. "Now let's get to this party before the search party comes looking for us."

Even as Logan helped Rachel into the truck, he wondered if he would have a lifetime with her or if they were always destined to part. They still had a major hurdle to get over. He only hoped she'd listen. The thought of losing her again twisted his gut.

A fierce determination swept through him as he climbed in on the passenger side. Not again. Nothing was ever going to separate them. He ignored the small voice that reminded him he had thought the same thing the night of their honeymoon.

"Times have changed," Logan commented, as he looked from the large white frame house in front of him to the city park across the street. "Black families didn't live in this part of town when I left. Heck, like most small towns, the railroad tracks were an unspoken dividing line."

"Stanton is a progressive city. As more and more black businesses prospered and black men and women got into politics, they made things happen and change. Mayor Davis's election speaks for itself. Things have certainly improved since 1855, when John Mercer Langston became the first black to hold elective office as township clerk in Brownhelm, Ohio," Rachel said. "People of all colors in Stanton worked together to promote unity. Before his last heart attack, Daddy attended every planning session to see that everyone was treated fairly."

Logan's fingers on the curve of Rachel's waist flexed. J. T. Malone didn't care about anything or anyone except himself and appearances. "I hope the food is ready. I didn't eat any breakfast."

Aware that he had purposely changed the subject, Rachel touched Logan's stiff shoulder. "I'm sorry he hurt you," she said quietly, her face shadowed. "He may be hard sometimes, but he's a good man."

"How can you defend him after the way he treated you at the hospital?" Logan asked through gritted teeth. "He probably tore you up one side then down the other yesterday for firing Jake."

Rachel flinched. "He's been under a lot of strain lately, but that's all going to change very soon. Things are going to be like they used to."

No, they aren't, Logan thought, because after speaking with Mayor Davis yesterday morning Logan gathered it was going to take a miracle for Malone to get the contract. And Old Man Malone was going to lay the blame squarely on Rachel's already overburdened shoulders. It would crush her. Because no matter what, she loved her father. And she wasn't going to want to be within a mile of anyone who had caused the apparent rift between them to widen.

"Ms. Malone, Logan. I was just going to look for you two," Gunther spoke from the front porch.

"Hello, Gunther." His hand on Rachel's waist, Logan climbed the wooden steps. "Sorry we're late."

"No problem. The men have been waiting to meet you."

"I hope you didn't involve Ms. Malone in this." Logan's voice took on a sharp edge.

Gunther sensed the change and hastened to reassure him. "No way, man. We only told people you were trying to help us locate the maggot who cut up the tires because the same thing had happened to you. Ms. Malone's been through enough because of us."

Something clicked in Logan's brain and he remembered Ed's comment last night that they should have stood up for themselves. "So there's more to this with Jake than I was told."

Gunther's eyes widened. He looked to Rachel for help.

"Hunger must make you suspicious, Logan." Rachel gave him a smile.

Black eyes narrowed. "You wouldn't try to keep something from me, would you?"

"Why would I do that?"

"Because you have this crazy idea you need to protect me."

"A man who can fight like you can take care of himself," Gunther said, then added, "We told everyone Ms. Malone was going to pick you up since you helped us and you didn't have a car."

"You and the men seem to have thought of everything, Gunther. I told you not to worry, Logan."

"Why doesn't that reassure me?" Logan said dryly.

Gunther opened the screen door. "Come on in. Everyone is in back."

"Everyone" was about twenty people scattered around the huge backyard playing cards, sitting at the two redwood tables under the shade of the elm tree, or playing volleyball. The instant Ed spotted them, he waved them over to the smoking grill with a pair of tongs.

"Glad you finally made it." Ed lifted a slab of ribs from the rack. "My ribs are always the first to go."

"That's because of my sauce," said a soft, feminine voice from behind them.

The small group turned to see a pretty black woman in the obvious last stages of pregnancy with a little girl by her side. On seeing Rachel, the dark-haired child squealed with delight and ran straight for her.

Knowing what was coming, Rachel bent to scoop up the tiny dynamo. With a smile, she hugged the soft body to hers. She would always regret the loss of her own child, but the ache was no longer unbearable.

At least Rachel thought so until she saw Logan watching her with an indefinable emotion in narrowed black eyes. He had always wanted children. Fate had taken his first child from him and he had yet to grieve for his loss. The thought of him going through the gut-wrenching misery she experienced shook her to her very being. Her legs trembled so badly, she wasn't sure she could stand. She didn't try. She sank to her knees.

"I missed you, Rachel," Lauren said, her hands on either side of Rachel's flushed cheeks.

"I missed you, too, sweetheart," she said, her voice unsteady.

"She's been excited all morning since I told her you were coming." The other woman curved her arm around Ed's waist, then leaned her head against his broad shoulder.

"You're all right, Ishira?" Ed asked anxiously.

"I would be if your son would stop kicking and go to sleep." Smiling, she straightened. "You must be Logan Prescott. It's nice to have you. I'm Ishira Green, Ed's wife. The octopus around Rachel's neck is our youngest and only daughter, Lauren."

Logan shook her extended hand. "Hello, Mrs. Green, and thanks for having me. Please call me Logan."

"I will, if you'll call me Ishira. From what I hear, we owe you our thanks." Ishira looked at Rachel. "Thank you for being on call last night."

"You're welcome." Rachel blew a kiss into Lauren's chubby palm. The child burst into giggles.

"On call?" Logan frowned.

"The baby is due any day now," Ishira explained.

"And that bas…dirty, lowdown snake knew it," Ed said heatedly, his beefy fist clutched around the wooden handle of the meat fork. "I would give anything to have taken him down last night. But seeing you put Jake on his back was almost as good."

"It sure was." Gunther rubbed his hands together. "Maybe Logan can show us some of his moves after we eat."

"No. I'm having a tough enough time with the boys imitating the action scenes on TV and in comic books. We're going to have a nice, quiet day." Ishira looked at Ed, then Gunther, and both men nodded.

"I'll go put the meat on the table. Come on, Logan, I'll introduce you to the other people here." Picking up the pan overflowing with links, ribs, and chicken, Ed headed toward the redwood bench. Logan and Gunther followed closely behind.

Rachel barely smothered her laughter as she watched the men cross the grassy lawn. She had never seen Ed or Gunther so docile. "If you ever need a job, I'd hire you in a New York minute to supervise the men."

Ishira snorted delicately. "The only reason they're being so compliant is because I'm pregnant. Pregnancy is the only time I can get one up on Ed, and believe me, I use it to full advantage."

"He doesn't seem to mind," Rachel pointed out.

"That's because he knows I love him as much as he loves me."

Rachel pulled Lauren into her lap and stared up at the older woman wistfully. "I can't imagine anything more wonderful than what you and Ed have."

"The way Logan is looking at you, you may have the

real thing soon," Ishira predicted, her hand slowly making a circular motion on her stomach.

Rachel felt her face heat. "We're just friends."

"If a 'friend' looked at Ed the way Logan was looking at you, I'd pull her hair out by the roots."

"I thought you didn't condone violence," Rachel teased.

"All bets are off when someone bothers me or mine. If Jake's sneakiness had caused one moment of worry for this baby, I'd string him up by his thumbs," she said fiercely.

Rachel stood with Lauren in her arms. "Everything is all right, isn't it?"

"Yes." She sighed. "I guess you worry about them until you can hold them in your arms and count to make sure they have everything they're supposed to."

"I guess so," Rachel said, her voice again thick and strained. Not once in the short days of her pregnancy had she thought something might go wrong. She had been so sure of herself. And so agonizingly wrong.

"Rachel, are you all right? Rachel?"

Lauren squirming in Rachel's arm, more than the thread of anxiety running through Ishira's voice, pulled Rachel from the past. Her fingers relaxed on the waist and shoulder of the child. "Sorry, what did you say?"

"Is everything all right?"

Rachel forced a smile. "Everything's fine. I guess I didn't get much sleep last night. Do you need any help in the kitchen?"

"No. Everything is on the table. We were just waiting

for Ed to finish barbecuing." Ishira ran her hand lovingly over her daughter's braid-covered head. "I better go help. If you don't mind, keep an eye on Lauren. It's been a long time since I've been able to get down on the floor and play with her the way she likes."

"I can't think of anything I'd like more."

Lauren wiggled to get down. She beamed up at Rachel. "Wanna see my new doll?"

"I sure do." Clasping hands they went inside the house to Lauren's bedroom. Rachel had expected the stuffed animals and toys; she hadn't expected the baby things. Obviously, the new baby was to share the room with his youngest sibling, while the seven- and nine-year-old boys shared the bedroom next door.

"Isn't she pretty?" Lauren brought out the elegantly garbed Nubian dancer in ceremonial attire for Rachel's inspection. "Grandma Green sent it."

"Yes, baby, very pretty." Rachel's chest felt tight. "Let's go back outside now."

Lauren danced away and sat on her twin bed covered in a circus print. "Wanna play with Princess in here?"

At any other time, Rachel might have smiled at the playfulness of the small child. With the memories of her shattered dreams twisting through her, she wanted nothing more than to leave the room, which overwhelmingly reminded her of her loss. Perhaps if Logan hadn't been outside. Perhaps if she had been able to share her loss with him.

Crossing the room, she sat on the bed beside Lauren. With everything within her she wanted to run, and because she did, she pulled Lauren into her lap with hands that shook.

"Should we offer to serve Princess tea?"

"Is he gonna help?"

Rachel glanced up to see Logan poised in the doorway. Once again he looked at her with an expression she couldn't decipher. She shut her eyes. He had a right to know, but how could she tell him?

"Rae, are you all right?"

Slowly, her lids lifted. Logan was kneeling in front of her, his face lined with concern. She looked at the man she loved more than life, and knew her secret could shatter everything between them.

"We don't have to play," Lauren said, her own lower lip trembling. "I don't want you to cry."

"Neither do I." Logan hauled both females into his lap. "Rae, it's all right, honey. Everything is going to be all right."

"Oh, Logan," she sniffed, her throat burning, her eyes stinging.

Warm lips brushed her forehead. "It's all right. Whatever it is, it will be all right. Talk to me. Is this about Jake, or the company?"

She shook her head. "I'm sorry."

"When I cry, Mama always kisses it better," piped up Lauren.

Logan met Rachel's gaze. Without speaking each knew the other was thinking of the night before, when Logan kissing it better had turned into a steamy bout of lovemaking.

"That's an excellent idea, Lauren." Logan's lips gently grazed against Rachel's.

"You did it wrong." The toddler threw her arms around Rachel's neck and gave her a loud, wet kiss on the cheek.

"I stand corrected." Logan did the same to Rachel's other cheek, only he kept on. With a giggle, Lauren joined in on the other cheek. In a short while the three were on the carpeted floor with Rachel in the middle, and receiving the loudest, wettest kisses Logan and Lauren could give. In between the smacking sound was the ringing of laughter from all of them.

"Am I interrupting something?"

Rachel scrambled to sit upright, her task complicated by the thirty-five pounds that refused to release its hold from around her neck. "Ishira."

The older woman smiled indulgently. "I sent Logan to rescue you from playing dolls. It looks like you found another game to play."

Logan grinned. Rachel elbowed him in the side. To her disgust, he didn't even grunt.

"We were kissing Rachel to make her feel better," Lauren told her mother.

"It was your daughter's idea, and it worked." Logan gently yanked one of her braids. "You've got yourself a smart young lady."

"Thanks, but it's past time for her to eat." Mrs. Green held out her hand.

"Wanna stay with Rachel and him."

"His name is Mr. Prescott, and I have your plate fixed."

The child sent Rachel a pleading look. "She can eat with us."

"I may need my partner again." Logan stood and helped Rachel, who was holding Lauren, to her feet. "Kissing and making it better is hard work."

"All right. Don't say I didn't try to rescue you. She isn't overly fond of napkins. You'll both have barbecue sauce everywhere."

"We'll take our chances," Rachel said. "Besides, I've been known to be a little careless myself."

The doorbell rang. "I'll get it," Lauren said, and scrambled down from Rachel's arms. She ran from the room as fast as her legs could go.

"No, you don't, young lady," her mother said, as she started after her daughter.

Logan threw his arm around Rachel's shoulder and whispered in her ear, "I'll be only too happy to lick all the sauce away."

Rachel looked up into his dark, handsome face and knew in his own way he was trying to make it better with words. "Only if I can return the pleasure."

He grinned. "You're on. Now let's go—" He stopped as Ishira reappeared in the door, her hand clamped with her daughter's, her face devoid of its usual smile. "What is it?"

"It's the police. Jake's disappeared."

Chapter 12

"What do you mean, disappeared?" asked Rachel.

"I don't know." Ishira's arm circled her stomach. "The policeman wants to speak with Leon and Ed. Our oldest was in the front yard playing, so I sent him to get them."

"If Ed doesn't mind, I'd like to be there to hear what the police have to say," Logan requested.

Mrs. Green gave a sigh of relief. "I'm sure he wouldn't." The back door slammed. "That's probably them. Both of you, please come." Turning away, she went down the wide hallway and met Ed, Leon, and Gunther just as they were entering the living room where the deputy waited.

The blue-uniformed policeman stood and bowed his sandy-brown head as soon as the group entered the room. "Evening, folks. I'm Officer Peabody. Seeing you all here makes my job a lot easier. I had planned on seeing Mr. Prescott next."

"Would you mind telling us what this is all about?" Logan asked.

"Yes, sir. I was going to give you a report on the progress of our investigation. Mayor Davis has taken a personal interest in the case," Officer Peabody explained, then smiled. "Can't have our important visitors thinking the city's not safe."

Rachel glanced at Logan. "How important are you?"

"Probably the car," Logan said evasively. He had met twice with the mayor since his return to Stanton and once in a private meeting with the entire city council.

"How did the mayor find out?" Rachel queried.

"We fax a daily report to the mayor of all major crimes in the city." The slender officer nodded toward Logan. "Because of the extent of the damages to Mr. Prescott's expensive sports car, his police report was included in the report sent to Mayor Davis."

"In other words, Leon's and my tires don't matter," Ed said tightly.

"I didn't mean to imply anything of the kind, Mr. Green. We take *all* crime seriously in Stanton," consoled the slender black policeman. "I'm over here now to let you know how the investigation is going."

"You told me Jake disappeared," Ishira said, and

touched Ed's arm. "Do...do you think something happened to him?"

"No, ma'am. Sorry if I gave you that impression. We received two anonymous calls last night, asking if the reward was real, and when we told them yes, both callers implicated Jake." Officer Peabody gripped the rim of his Stetson. "We've been out to Jake's place at least four times to question him since last night, and he's disappeared."

"What do you mean disappeared?" Rachel asked.

"Just that." The policeman shrugged his slim shoulders. "No one will admit to seeing him once he left Big Al's last night. His house is locked tighter than Dick's hatband."

"What about his Cadillac and boat?"

"Both gone, Mr. Prescott, just like Jake. I figure he's gone into hiding."

Logan clenched his fists. "Not for long. He'll be back."

"Yes, reckon he will. But he'll have to answer a few questions when he does." The officer slapped his gray Stetson back on his head. "Guess I better be going."

Ishira closed the door behind the policeman. "I thought he was coming to arrest someone. I'm sorry, I overreacted."

"I probably would have thought the same thing," Rachel said, then smiled. "Jake's gone and now we have another reason to celebrate besides the Fourth."

The men followed the women outside. Their steps slowed until a good fifteen feet separated them. "Jake's disappearance makes me uneasy," Logan said.

"Me, too." Gunther rubbed his neck. "It's easier to chop off the head of a snake when you can see him than when he's hiding in the bushes."

"Exactly." Logan looked at all of the men long and hard. "You'll have to keep a lookout for him."

"We will, but what about Ms. Malone?" Ed asked.

"I'll take care of her, and if Jake knows what's good for him, he'll stay beneath whatever rock he's hiding under." The menace in Logan's voice caused each man to be thankful he wasn't Jake.

Something was wrong.

Logan stood in a small circle of people listening to the conversation going on around him with only half his attention. The other half was on Rachel, who stood by his side. The tears hadn't returned, but her eyes still hadn't lost the shadows he'd seen earlier. She was putting up a great front, but it was just that, a front.

The last thing he had expected on going to get her and Lauren for lunch was for her to look so stricken when she saw him. His first thought was that somehow she had learned he was part-owner of Bridgeway. But her eyes held an almost palpable sadness, not anger or hate. Her tears had twisted his insides. In the short days since he'd returned, he had learned Rachel was a fighter. She wasn't a woman who cried easily.

She hadn't cried when she'd hurt her shoulder or when Dr. Perry had cleaned and sewn it up. The only time she had cried was at his house, when she was holding his family picture. He'd thought her tears were the result of their brush with death, now he wasn't so sure.

For her to start crying again made no sense, but as soon as they were alone, they were going to have a long talk and he was going to find out what had upset her. At least her mood had lightened since she'd learned Jake had left town. He only wished he didn't have this nagging feeling that Jake was going to disrupt their lives even more when he finally slunk back into town.

"Logan, you're awfully quiet," Ed said.

Ishira laughed. "I think Lauren wore him out. Too bad he can't take a nap, the way she is now. I'm sorry about your shirt."

Logan didn't even glance down at the barbecue stains on his white polo shirt. "Please don't worry. I'm used to children."

"I've got a little boy from my first marriage," Gunther said proudly. "You have any?"

"No. My best friend and his wife have two sons," Logan said. "I get to share them every now and then."

"Why share when you can have kids of your own?" Ed took a swig of beer. "What are you waiting on?"

"The right woman, I guess," Logan answered, his gaze unerringly going to Rachel.

All eyes in the small circle followed. Rachel shifted uneasily under their regard. "I think I'll go inside and get a glass of water."

"You can get it on our way out." Logan casually draped his arm around her tense shoulder. "It's time we were leaving, anyway."

Protests abounded, but he was adamant. It was past time for them to talk. However, before they left, Ishira had insisted on preparing two sturdy paper plates overflowing with food.

Logan chuckled as he climbed into the truck. "I'd forgotten how hospitable and friendly people were in small towns. No one is ever allowed to leave hungry."

"They're good people." Rachel pulled away from the curb. "I'm glad you had a chance to get to know them."

"Me, too. Ed has a great wife and wonderful kids. He's a lucky man."

Rachel gripped the steering wheel. "Yes."

Logan was no good with small talk, so he didn't even try. "You want to talk about what made you unhappy?"

"Stress, I guess. Most women cry."

"You aren't most women," Logan pointed out, and watched Rachel's back become stiff and inflexible. "If it's anything I can help with, you know I would. Just tell me."

The cellular phone rang and Rachel grabbed it. "Hello." She briefly glanced at Logan. "Hello, Mother." He looked out the window.

On the other end, Martha Malone gently chided her daughter. "Where have you been? I've been trying to reach you for over an hour."

"At a house party. I thought you and Daddy were

going to have some friends over." Rachel stopped for a red light, her emotions in a jumble. She had wanted to distract Logan, but not with her family, not when they had so many other problems.

"We are, but we expected you, too. Since you're already in the truck, why don't you come on over and meet our guests? Three of the city council members are here," Mrs. Malone said. "Your father needs their votes to win the bid and as his general manager, you should be here with him."

At another time, Rachel might have said no, but not with Logan asking questions she wasn't ready to give the answer to, not with the vote so close. "I'll be over as soon as I can."

Logan whipped his head back around. His onyx eyes glittered. "So much for promises."

Rachel flicked the phone off, then drove through the green light. "It's business, Logan."

"Yeah, right." Once again she had chosen her family over him. "You'd think I'd learn. You can pull over at the convenience store up ahead and I'll get out."

"Logan—"

"Pull over, Rae."

Flicking on her signal, she drove into the empty parking lot and stopped. "You also promised something, Logan. You promised your and my father's problems were not going to interfere with us. What happened to that promise?"

"You made the decision."

"A business decision. It has nothing to do with us. These are people I need to see, can't you understand that? I'm sure as general manager of your company you've had to put your personal desires aside for the good of the company. Why do you belittle me when I do the same?"

He remained silent.

Turning from him, she stared straight ahead. "Okay, Logan, have it your way. Just remember, this time it's *you* who's turning your back on *me*. I want you to stay, but I'm not going to beg you."

Logan's fingers curled around the door handle, but he couldn't bring himself to exert the force needed to open the door and leave. "Every time your family needs you, no matter how they've treated you, no matter your promises to me, you go running."

"I was brought up to respect my parents. I love them deeply. They've always been there for me. I can't turn my back on them just because I don't agree with them sometimes." Rachel touched his arm. "Despite everything with your parents, you kept their house, the furnishings, when obviously you could have sold the place and never come back. You must understand a little bit of what I feel for my parents."

He hadn't kept the house intentionally; it had been Ida Mae's idea. However, he had to admit he was glad she hadn't sold the place as he'd asked. Living with his parents in the small frame house almost made him feel as if they might one day become a real family. It hadn't happened, but he had never stopped hoping. He couldn't blame Rachel for trying to win her parents' love; Lord knew, he had tried to gain his.

He released the doorknob. Once he had thought he and Rachel would be a family, that her first loyalty would be to him. It hadn't happened. He was still on the outside looking in. "I understand, but I just wish you were as concerned with pleasing me."

"You think I'm not?"

Silence stretched between them. Turning away from the flat expression on Logan's face, Rachel put the truck into gear and pulled back into the street.

His head whipped around. "Where are we going?"

"To your place, like I promised."

"What about the business meeting?"

"I have something more important to take care of."

Logan should have felt triumphant that Rachel was finally choosing him over her parents, but he didn't. Ultimately, she would be the loser, trapped again between her parents' possessiveness and her lover's jealousy. He had made another promise; not to cause her pain again. "Pull over."

"I'm not stopping this truck until we reach your place."

"Yes, you are," he said. "You're going to go to your parents' house and charm everyone there. I'll be waiting at the house when you finish."

"You don't care?"

"I'll mind being without you, but I can handle it, knowing you'll be coming back." He nodded at the approaching street corner. "Stop at Fourth. Ida Mae doesn't live far from here."

She stopped by the curb and put the truck in park. "You're sure about this?"

His hands cupped her cheeks. "Just hurry back to me."

"I will." Her lips pressed against his palm. In the next instant she was across the seat and in his arms, his mouth hungrily devouring hers.

"Mr. Prescott, I'm so pleased you could come to our July Fourth party," Mayor Davis greeted effusively as Logan entered the den filled with laughing, chattering people. "I apologize for not extending the invitation sooner."

"No apology needed, Mayor. I know what a busy man you are." The smile on Logan's face showed none of his irritation in being there instead of home waiting for Rachel. Yet she was right about business obligations sometimes coming before personal desires. In this case, he'd give it thirty minutes to be polite, and then he was leaving.

A small frown worked its way across the mayor's forehead. "I hope the unfortunate incident with your car didn't make you think any less of our city?"

"No. The city can't be blamed for the vindictiveness of one man." Logan watched the city official's entire body relax. Apparently he had been worried about the image of the city. The last thing the small town needed was a reputation of being unsafe just as its economy was growing. Logan just wished the mayor hadn't picked tonight to seek reassurance. "Bridgeway is just as interested in winning the bid as we ever were."

Mayor Davis grinned. "Good. Let me introduce you to some of my other guests."

"Fine." Logan glanced at his watch. Twenty-five minutes and counting.

Logan accepted a glass of wine from the mayor and allowed himself to be introduced to the other people in the room. From the questioning looks he kept receiving, he knew some of the people remembered him as the young man with the bad reputation. At one time Logan had wanted to rub his success in their judgmental faces, now he couldn't care less.

"Nice meeting you again, Mr. Prescott," Fred Mason said. "You had my vote from the beginning. Malone is a sorry excuse for a construction company."

"Fred, remember you're a city councilman," the mayor chided. "This is not the time or the place to air personal grievances."

"Just because you're friends with the Malones is no need to stick up for them," Fred said with feeling.

"When it comes to what's best for this city, I don't have any friends," Mayor Davis pointed out. "Rachel has done a fine job managing the company."

"She sure has," agreed Jim Anderson, another city council member.

"You're all swayed by that pretty face of hers," Fred snorted.

"Actually, Ms. Malone has a beautiful face, as well

as integrity, honesty, pride in her work and a courage that I've seen in few men," Logan defended.

Fred puffed up like a bullfrog. "I call them as I see them. I paid their worthless behinds ten thousand dollars over budget to build my apartment complex. They're lucky I didn't sue."

"You're the one who's lucky." Logan ignored Mason's startled expression and set his untouched glass of wine on a table. "Good night, Mayor."

"Mr. Prescott, please don't leave." The mayor threw an angry glance at Mason. "Please, this is not the kind of relationship we need to work in."

"I think it's best I leave." Logan didn't have to look around to know they were the center of attention.

"Then leave," Fred Mason snorted. "Maybe we acted too hastily in awarding his company the contract to build the city hall complex."

Logan's body tightened. He whirled to face Mayor Davis. "We got the contract?"

The mayor pulled Logan away from the interested crowd. Fred Mason followed despite the mayor's glare. "The city council made the decision to accept Bridgeway's bid late last night. The official announcement will be made Monday after I notify the other two companies."

He had beat Malone. He had finally paid him back.

Logan waited for the jubilation, the sense of triumph to hit him. He had destroyed the man who eight years ago had tried to destroy him. Without the contract, Malone wouldn't be able to stay afloat six weeks. He'd be forced to watch everything he had worked so hard to accomplish slip from his grasp. He'd have to stand by and look into the faces of his wife and daughter and know he had failed them, just as Logan had had to stand by and look into Rachel's face and know he had failed her.

Instead of jubilation, Logan's chest felt tight. He was the one seeing Rachel's pain-filled face when she learned she had lost the contract and to whom. She'd feel betrayed and would hate him. She had welcomed him into the loving shelter of her arms and he had repaid her with deceit. Disgust rolled through him.

"You don't look too happy about winning the contract," Fred Mason commented. "Maybe we made a mistake."

"Mason, my company won the bid." Logan nodded to the other men. "Good night, gentlemen."

Logan turned to leave and abruptly halted. Directly in his path was Rachel, her face as stricken as he had imagined. Her parents were with her and so was an unfamiliar man with his arm curved possessively around her waist. Logan wanted to snatch her out of the man's arm even as he realized he might never have the right to touch her again.

"Mason. Sometimes, I could…" The mayor stepped in front of Logan and greeted the Malones. "Martha, J.T., Rachel. I was wondering when my son would get you here. It's always nice to have you."

"Cut the crap, Roger. What's going on here? Why is he here?" J.T. asked, his dark brown eyes on Logan.

"If you'll come into my study, I'll explain everything," the mayor said.

Mayor Davis began speaking to watchful guests, "I'm sorry for this, folks. Please go back to having a good time." He turned to Logan, Rachel and her parents. "This way."

The man holding Rachel's arm released her with only momentary hesitation. Somehow his desertion annoyed Logan. Rachel was going to need someone in the next few minutes. He wouldn't have left her side no matter what anyone said.

But you did.

The condemning truth came out of nowhere, sharp and clear. Eight years ago he had turned his back on her and left her with her parents, left her to deal with a problem he had helped create. Instead of becoming bitter, she had gone on to make a success of her life…until he had returned seeking revenge.

The mayor closed the door of his study and waved everyone toward a seat. Everyone stood where they were.

"Talk, Roger. What's going on here?" J.T. asked, his hand clamped tightly on his cane.

"I can't tell you how sorry I am you had to learn things this way." Mayor Davis looked uncomfortable. "I had planned on telling you and Rachel Monday morning."

"We didn't get the contract, did we?" Rachel asked, her voice strained.

The mayor sadly shook his head. "It went to Mr. Prescott's company."

"I…I thought Bridgeway was the closest competitor," Rachel stuttered.

"They we—"

"Let me," Logan interrupted the mayor and stepped forward. Pain shot through his heart when Rachel flinched and stepped back. "I didn't tell you everything about me. I'm more than just the general manager, I'm part-owner with Charles Dawson. The company's name is Bridgeway."

Chapter 13

"No," the strangled cry erupted from Rachel's lips.

"Rae, I wanted to tell you ever since last night, but the time never seemed right," Logan attempted.

"You mean you continued to see him after the day I saw you at the hospital?" J. T. Malone asked in disbelief.

Rachel made herself turn away from the pleading look in Logan's face to her father, knowing yet dreading what she would see when she answered. "Yes." He looked stunned.

"Daddy, are you all right?" She reached for him, but he waved her away.

"How could you let him anywhere near you after what happened the last time?" her father asked in bewilderment. "Didn't we all pay enough the last time? I can't believe a daughter of mine could be so gullible. He used you just like he did the first time and you let him. You haven't learned anything in eight years."

"J.T., please," Martha pleaded.

He took an unsteady step closer to his daughter. "Now I understand why you fired Jake. It wasn't because he was being insubordinate, it was because *he* didn't like him. I told you the day at the hospital this was our last chance and instead of working hard, you've been wasting time with him."

"I worked hard, Daddy," Rachel defended.

"Not hard enough. It's taken you six months to run a company into the ground that it took four generations to build," he railed.

"You've said enough," Logan said and placed himself between father and daughter.

"Don't you ever try to come between me and my daughter again." J.T. shook his cane and lost his balance. Logan reached for him, but Martha was the one who steadied her husband.

"Everyone calm down," the mayor pleaded.

J.T. turned on him. "Easy enough for you to say. Your only child didn't turn her back on you and ruin your business, your reputation." He looked at his daughter again. "We lost the contract because of you."

"That's a lie, and you know it," Logan denied heatedly. "Malone has been in trou—"

"I don't need you defending me," Rachel quickly said.

"Rae, I didn't mean—"

"Haven't you done enough?" she said, her voice thin and strained.

"Tell him, Mayor. Tell Mr. Malone why you chose Bridgeway over Malone." Logan ordered, his gaze still on Rachel. "Tell him Rachel isn't the reason they lost the contract."

Before the mayor could say anything, Rachel was speaking. "The reason doesn't matter any longer. The bottom line is we lost. I know you're supposed to congratulate the winner, but I'm not feeling that magnanimous."

"Rae—"

"Goodbye, Mr. Prescott," she cut him off again, then turned to the mayor. "Good night, Mayor. Thanks for inviting us, but we're leaving." Unsteady hands reached for her father's arm.

He jerked away. "I don't need your help."

She flinched. Misery shone in her eyes. "Daddy, please."

"Stop treating her like that," Logan yelled. "You know it wasn't her fault you lost the contract."

Martha Malone looked at Logan with tears shimmering in her eyes. "Why did you have to come back? You tore my family apart once. Wasn't that enough?" Trembling fingers wiped the telltale moisture away. "J.T., give our daughter your arm. We're the Malones and we have a position to uphold. More importantly we're family. We're going to leave as a family. Mayor Davis, will you see us to the door?"

"Of course." The mayor moved to Martha's side.

Logan couldn't let her leave thinking the worst. "Rae, please, I care about you. Try to understand, I never meant to…" His voice trailed off as he realized this was exactly what he meant to happen, but that time seemed so long ago.

As if she had read his mind, her chin lifted. "Thank you at least for not continuing the lies. If you care as you really say, just stay away from me. Just stay away."

The mayor opened his study door and there was nothing Logan could think of to do or to say to get Rachel to stay and listen to him. Heads erect, she and her parents left with the mayor. The unmistakable, soulful voice of Patti LaBelle that greeted them was unexpected and appreciated.

Remembering some of the accusations J. T. Malone had made against his daughter, Logan was glad someone had turned up the music's volume. She didn't deserve his condemnation. None of it was her fault. If Mason hadn't opened his mouth…

If you hadn't wanted revenge…

By seeking revenge, Logan had hurt the woman who meant more to him than anything. He had also let his partner down. Charles wasn't going to be pleased with what Logan had let happen in Stanton. Instead of Logan helping his fellow black brother on the climb upward as he and Charles had always done, Logan had not only turned his back, he had initially reveled in the other man's coming fall.

Revenge wasn't sweet as someone had said, it was as bitter as bile. Yet it probably didn't compare to the hurt Rachel felt. It didn't take much to remember the absolute desolation he'd felt when he'd thought she didn't love him.

She didn't just think he didn't love her, she thought he had intentionally set out to avenge himself and ruin her father's company. Knowing at one time she might have been right made his misery increase tenfold. Somehow he had to get her to listen and understand. He had to. Because if he didn't, his life wasn't going to be worth living. Silently he slipped through the French doors in the mayor's study.

"Rachel, you're sure you don't want me to come in for a little while?" asked Lamar Davis, his handsome brown face creased with lines of concern.

The mayor's son had been a friend since his family had moved to Stanton seven years before. Within the last three months, Lamar had made it no secret that he wanted their friendship to grow into something deeper. Although she had never given him any hope of that happening, he refused to stop trying to change her mind. One man had always stood between them. And he had just betrayed her in the cruelest way possible. Her insides clenched.

"I—I'm sure. Thank you for following me home. Now, if you don't mind, I'd like to get some rest."

"I'm sorry about tonight. Fred Mason had—"

"Lamar, please," she said, her voice as unsteady as her hand trying to unlock the door. "I really don't want to discuss it anymore. Good night."

Aiming for her lips, he lowered his head. She turned her face. He kissed her cheek instead. "I'll be in town for the weekend. I'll call you in the morning."

Without another word, Rachel entered her house, closed the door, then leaned against it. What a fool she had been. She had let her love for Logan blind her to everything else. She had trusted him and believed every lie…hook, line, and sinker. Worse, his duplicity had helped widen the gulf between her and her father. His harsh words still resounded in her brain.

This time, she didn't blame her father. The loss of the bid to build the city hall complex was like a slap in the face to the man who had been an integral part of the town's growth. Not only was his pride hurt, Malone Construction badly needed the revenue to continue. She wasn't sure how much longer the company could stay solvent if another large project didn't come through.

Yet once word got out that they'd been passed over again, and by their hometown city council, she didn't hold out much hope for future contracts. Logan couldn't have planned his revenge any better. And she had been so glassy-eyed, she hadn't suspected a thing.

Pushing away from the door, she started for the bedroom. The peal of the doorbell stopped her halfway across the room. She didn't want to talk to anyone. The summons came again. Why couldn't Lamar understand she wanted to be alone? The last thing she wanted was to see another man who professed he cared about her. She yanked the door open and froze. The person she never wanted to see again in her lifetime stood on her tiny porch.

"Can I come in?" Logan asked.

She tried to slam the door in his face. The flat of his palm prevented her from accomplishing her goal. "Leave, before I call the police."

"Won't you please listen?"

"For what? To hear more lies?" Again she pushed against the door to no avail. His strength mocked hers and infuriated her further. "You got what you came after. So leave."

"I got more than I came after, Rae."

She gasped. Humiliation swept through her. "Leave."

"Damn it. I didn't mean it that way, and if you'd stop being angry long enough and think, you'd know it," he told her tightly, his temper starting to rise. "I meant being with you, getting the chance to start all over again."

"Logan, stop the lies. If I hadn't saved your life, you'd be someplace toasting your success. Guilt brought you here and nothing else." Moisture glittered in her brown eyes, but she refused to let the tears fall.

"Tonight you got the revenge you always wanted against the Malones in triplicate. Not only will the town have a field day discussing my father's poor opinion of me, after tonight, no one would hire us to build a chicken coop. So take your guilty conscience someplace else. I would have done the same for anyone even if, like you, he didn't deserve it." This time the door slammed shut.

Rachel was trembling with anger, with fear—anger at herself, and fear for what she was feeling. She wanted to believe him. Something inside her wanted to believe that perhaps he hadn't meant things to turn out so badly for them. With fingers that shook, she threw the locks on the door. She was keeping herself in as much as she was keeping him out.

Logan stood on the dark porch, his fists clenched in anger and fear. Anger at himself for ever conceiving the idea of revenge, and fear that he had lost Rachel forever. Spinning on his heels, he went to Ida Mae's car.

Instead of getting in, he leaned against the fender of the car and stared at Rachel's house. He would be doing a lot of that before the night was over. Jake still posed a potential threat to Rachel, and until Logan could hire someone to watch her, he was going to do it himself.

Suddenly her front door opened and Rachel marched across her postage stamp yard toward him. Logan straightened. He was well aware of what she was going to say.

She didn't disappoint him. "Get off my property."

Before speaking, he glanced down. "The street is considered city property." For a moment she looked so furious he thought she might take a swing at him. Good. At least fury was better than the tears he had seen in her eyes earlier.

"Do you want to gloat, Logan, is that it?"

"There's nothing to gloat about. We both lost tonight, and we're going to continue to lose until you and I can talk."

"You just won a multimillion-dollar contract. What could you have possibly lost to compare with that?" she asked coldly.

"You."

His simple reply stunned her. Her mouth opened, but nothing came out.

Calloused hands reached for her. Spinning on her heels, Rachel ran back into the house. Logan was on her walk before he realized his intention of going after her. He wanted her and needed her, and despite her anger, she felt the same way.

The light in the bedroom came on. Memories of last night when he'd made love to Rachel assaulted him. No woman had ever made him lose control so easily or incite his passion so quickly or inspire such tenderness. He gritted his teeth against his growing terror of losing her. Unlike eight years ago, he wasn't going to leave town. This time he was going to stay and fight for her. Rachel might have won the battle tonight, but his time was yet to come.

Monday morning. Rachel both welcomed and dreaded her alarm going off. Work was what she needed to get her mind off Logan, but that meant she finally had to face the townspeople. Logan had probably caused her family to be a hot topic of gossip.

Leaning against his car in front of her house Saturday night he had made her so enraged she wanted to hit him. After she had calmed down, she was well aware that he was probably watching her house because of Jake. Guilty conscience again. She hoped he got a crook in his neck from sleeping in his car. She had enough to worry about without adding a guilt-ridden, lying, treacherous guardian angel who had betrayed her.

All day Sunday she had stayed inside the house, going from tears to despair to rage. The answering machine had monitored calls from the mayor, his son, three city councilmen, some of her crew, and Logan. She took perverse pleasure in cutting him off.

The only person she talked with was her mother. By tacit agreement, neither mentioned her father. As always, her mother didn't condemn, didn't lecture. She just wanted her family to be close again. But that closeness was shattered eight years before and after Saturday night, it would take a miracle to heal the wounds and bring them all together again.

Grabbing her keys, she went out to the garage and backed her truck out. The brightness of the day caused her to shut red, swollen eyes. Fumbling fingers pulled her sunshade from atop her head. At 7:30 a.m. it was already sunny. She let the garage door down and started down her street.

Everything looked the same. Mr. Wilson was out walking his poodle, the Gabriels' oldest was washing her car, Mrs. Nelson was weeding in her yard. Everything looked normal, but Rachel didn't think she would ever know what normal felt like again.

A short time later, she pulled into a one-story medical building's parking lot and got out. A laughing young couple passed in front of her. The man had his arm around the woman, hers were around a baby. Unexpectedly, moisture gathered in Rachel's eyes. She had lost so much, and was still losing. In an instant, she remembered Logan saying the same words. She refused to listen then, just as she did now.

Blinking rapidly, she fought the stinging in her eyes. Never again. All her tears had accomplished were a headache and puffy red eyes. She certainly didn't feel any better, and all her problems remained. If there was any chance of salvaging Malone Construction, she had to be in control, not sniffing and crying over a man who had betrayed her.

First she was going to have her sutures removed, then she was going to check in at her office and the sites. All the employees had probably heard Malone had lost the bid, but if they hadn't, they deserved to hear the news from her.

Her chin lifted in determination, she entered Dr. Perry's office building. Behind the L-shaped counter, the two receptionists smiled and spoke. Rachel relaxed a little. Neither of them looked at her any differently than the last time she was there.

While she was waiting in line to sign in, the door to the offices and exam rooms opened. Dr. Perry's nurse, Donna Hall, came out.

"Good morning, Ms. Malone. Don't bother about signing in. Dr. Perry can see you now."

Again, the same friendly smile. The tension in Rachel's body eased a little more as she followed the nurse. Perhaps Lamar hadn't been trying to make her feel better when he'd assured her that he had turned the music up so loud, the guests couldn't hear anything but the finger-snapping voice of Patti LaBelle belting out one of her fast songs.

The statuesque nurse stopped and opened the door of the last exam room at the end of the hall. "Just slip off everything from the waist up and put on the gown on the table. It opens in the back."

"Thank you." Rachel smiled and entered the room. Her steps faltered on seeing the suture removal set and a package of gloves on a small stainless steel tray by the exam table. She hadn't expected this.

The only way she had been able to make it through the dressing changes was because Nurse Hall had always taken her into the lounge. She looked back at the door, then took a deep breath. Small children probably did this without a moment's hesitation. She had faced worse than this and gotten through. Unbuttoning her blouse, she did as the nurse instructed. However, she refused to sit on the table until it was necessary.

The door behind her opened and she turned to see Logan. "Get out of here."

"I promised to be here with you," Logan told her calmly, his face expressionless.

"How could you possibly think I'd want you anywhere near me after what you did?" Rachel said caustically.

"The entire office is going to know it if you don't keep your voice down," Logan said. "I told the nurse you were expecting me."

She glared her hostility at Logan. "You're very good at twisting truths into lies. Either you leave or I do."

"The sutures need to come out today. I know why you don't like hospitals or doctors. I wasn't there for you then, but I want to be with you now."

She refused to be swayed by the sadness in his face and voice. "I don't want you here."

"You need someone here with you, if not me then who?"

Her chin lifted. They both knew her choices were limited. "I'll call Lamar Davis, the mayor's son."

"I'll call him for you. What's his number?"

His calm acceptance threw her off balance. For some reason she had been so sure that he would be jealous, that he wouldn't want another man near her. But why should he be? To be jealous required some kind of emotional attachment toward the person. Logan felt nothing for her except guilt.

Her chin lifted a little higher. "On second thought, I won't call him. Unlike you, he wouldn't enjoy seeing me hurt."

The flare of anger she had expected earlier flashed in his black eyes. "Lie down, Rae."

Jerking her gown tighter in the back, she sat on the table. Logan wasn't leaving. If she asked the nurse to put him out, she wasn't sure what his reactions would be. She wouldn't put it past him to create a scene and give people another juicy bit of gossip. And she couldn't very well get dressed in front of him or leave in a gown. She was trapped. But he wasn't going to win on this. She planned on acting as if he wasn't there.

The exam room's door opened and Dr. Perry entered. "Good morning, Logan, Rachel. I see you're all ready for me." He lifted the leg rest. "Scoot back some, Rachel, and lie on your stomach. That's my girl. I'll cover you up with this sheet. Now let's take a look at my handiwork."

The moment his hand began to lift the bandage, she jerked. Her eyes shut, her hands fisted.

"Looks fine." He snapped on his gloves. "You'll be out of here in no time."

Her left shoulder lifted. She couldn't take this. A warm hand settled on her naked flesh. She jerked again. This time for a different reason. She'd know that touch in her sleep. Why shouldn't she? It had alternately created and banished her worst nightmares.

"Easy, Rae."

She wanted to tell him not to touch her, to leave, but she couldn't. Even as she hated herself for her weakness, she concentrated on the slow, sweeping motion of Logan's soothing hand, not the time she had called for him and he hadn't come.

"All finished. Once the discoloration from your bruises

goes away, you'll only have a few tiny scars to remind you of your accident," Dr. Perry said with confidence.

Rachel disagreed, but she said nothing. She was more concerned with getting Logan's hand off her. Quickly, she rolled over and sat up. Surprise widened her eyes as she saw him leave the exam room.

"I guess he didn't have as much fun as he thought," she quipped.

Dr. Perry looked at his patient over the top of his wirerimmed bifocals. "Me thinks you protest too much."

She flushed and hopped off the exam table. "I don't want him anywhere near me again."

"Yes, you do. That's what's got you all upset. I was at the mayor's house Saturday night." Dr. Perry held up his hands when she started to speak. "That's all I'm going to say on the matter. I wouldn't want to jeopardize getting my chocolate cake."

She didn't care about Logan and she wasn't going to give credence to Dr. Perry's mistaken assumption with an argument. "I'll bring the cake by Thursday morning."

"Good. Now I'll let you get dressed." Whistling, he left the room.

She jerked off the paper gown and snatched up her bra as soon as the door closed. Logan meant nothing to her. She was still fuming when she left the building. Seeing Logan, arms folded, leaning against her truck intensified her anger.

She halted by the tailgate. "What does it take for you to understand, I don't want you anywhere near me?"

He pushed upright. "I'm not going anyplace this time until we talk and I make you understand."

"Oh, I understand all right." She took a step closer. "I understand how you lied and made a fool out of me."

"I never lied to you. I am general manager of Bridgeway, and we are trying to get a share of the Texas market. You asked me who I worked for and I gave you my partner's name, C. Dawson. Charles works for me as much as I work for him."

"Lying by omission is just as bad," she flared. "I must have mentioned Bridgeway half-a-dozen times in talking with you and you never said a word. You let me go on while you had a good laugh."

"I never laughed at you. If you'll just listen. I didn't even know my partner had bid on the city hall complex until a couple of weeks ago." His jaw tightened. "I never planned on coming back here. Charles is the one who handled the restoration of the Victorian House for me."

Surprise widened her eyes. "For you?"

"I own the place. Ida Mae had the idea of turning the house into a multicultural shopping center. I listened to her and bought the condemned mansion for her."

"At least you can be nice to someone."

"Maybe because she was nice to me. Ida Mae was the only one in this stinking town who cared if I lived or died. She was the only one who never believed the worst. She gave me what money couldn't buy."

"I believed in you once," Rachel said, before she had time to think.

"Yeah, that's why you turned your back on me at the hospital," Logan reminded her, his voice clipped. "You believed I was nothing, just like your father said. You weren't even willing to admit we were married."

"I couldn't," she cried.

He took a step closer. "Why, Rae?"

The desperation in his voice tore at her heart. She couldn't get the words out. She shook her head. How had she become the one on the defensive? "It doesn't matter anymore. Just get away from my truck."

"Yes, it does. This time we're going to talk. There'll be no more running for either of us." In two swift strides he clasped her upper forearm.

Brown eyes flared. "Take your hands off me."

"I will as soon as we get in my truck." He opened the door to the black vehicle next to hers and helped her inside. "I advise you to stay put. Police Chief Stone may once have threatened to lock me up for daring to breathe the same air as you and your family, but that was a long time ago. This time I have the mayor on my side."

"That's right, everyone just loves you," she said snidely.

He looked at her with eyes that burned. "No, they don't. Few people in my life have loved me." Switching on the engine, he drove out of the parking lot.

Rachel was so stunned by the bleakness in his voice and what he had said she didn't try to get out of his truck when Logan stopped to merge onto the main highway. "Your parents—"

"Loved each other to the exclusion of everything else,

including their unwanted child," he interrupted. "They tolerated me. I learned early to care for myself because they had lives of their own that didn't include me."

"But...but you couldn't have taken care of yourself."

He stopped at a signal light. "Couldn't I? By the time I was five, I could pull up a chair to the stove and fix myself something to eat, make my bed, set my alarm clock to get up in the morning for school." He laughed a cold, hollow sound. "My mother did wash and iron my clothes for me because she had to do her and my father's anyway. From the time I was six, they thought nothing of leaving me in the house and going off to have a good time. Nothing my parents loved more than partying and gambling with their friends. There were a lot of hot spots in Chicago and they knew them all."

Horror washed across her face. She felt sick. "How could they neglect their own child?"

"They didn't see it as neglect. I was clothed and fed and had a place to sleep. For a long time I wondered why they didn't include me in the closeness they shared, then I realized it didn't matter."

The silence grew as she waited for him to continue. When he didn't she asked, "Why didn't it matter?"

He looked straight at her. "Because I promised myself that one day I was going to have a family of my own and we'd love each other so much my parents not loving me wouldn't matter."

A broken cry tumbled from Rachel's lips.

She clutched her stomach on remembering the day

of the construction accident when she held the picture of his family. *No child of mine will ever doubt that I love him.* His words replayed in her mind. How could you survive emotionally if you thought no one loved you? Despite everything that had happened between her and her father, she knew with absolute conviction at one time her father would have walked through fire for her. Her mother still would.

She had told Logan many times she loved him and she'd never leave him. But she had. He didn't know she had been trying to protect him; he only knew that the wife who promised to love him forever didn't stick around longer than a day. "I'm sorry."

"I don't need your pity." He turned off the blacktop into his driveway.

Rachel stared at the unyielding line of his jaw. No, he had needed her love and she had walked away just like his parents had.

He pulled in front of his house and got out. "Come on, it's cooler in the house."

Getting out of the truck, Rachel followed Logan inside. He closed the door as soon as she walked over the threshold. The closing of the door seemed unusually loud. For some reason she felt trapped. She wrapped her arms around her.

"Don't look like that. You know I've never hurt you."

"Physical pain isn't the only way to hurt someone."

"No one knows that better than I do," Logan told her "When I walked out of the hospital eight years ago I had four cracked ribs, yet having a bride who refused to acknowledge me hurt worse. You were everything to me and you treated me like something that had crawled from under a rock. I want to know why, Rae, and we're not leaving here until I have the answer."

Chapter 14

She didn't want to discuss the past. "It's over, Logan. Talking can't change the past."

"I know it won't change, but I need to understand it. I need to know what went wrong between us." Gentle hands settled on her tense shoulders. "Talk to me, Rae."

She bit her lips. Her gaze fell to the middle of his wide, blue-shirted chest. "I have to go to work."

"Neither one of us is leaving until I have answers to the questions that have been plaguing me for eight years." His hands slid from her shoulders. "You know where the phone is if you need to call someone."

"You can't keep me here against my will."

"Some part of you wants this as much as I do. I can

see it in your eyes," Logan told her. "I made a mistake, a terrible one, because I thought you were too selfish and too weak to stand up against your parents. But since I've been back I've learned nothing could be further from the truth. You're loyal, compassionate, honest, and hardworking. So, I have to ask myself again what went wrong. The only way I can understand is for you to tell me."

"If your need to understand was so great, why didn't you say something sooner?" She didn't wait for him to answer. "I'll tell you why, it's because the only reason you're asking now is because your conscience is bothering you. You want to rehash the past so you can feel justified in ruining my parents' and my life. You keep saying how I turned my back on you, but you did the same to me. I needed you and you weren't there for me."

"I told you how sorry I was for not being with you after your accident," he said solemnly. "I'll always regret not being with you."

"No more than I will. If you'd loved me enough you would have stayed," she accused, her gaze defiant.

Ignoring the glint in her brown eyes, Logan again caught her rigid shoulders. "The only reason I left was because I thought you didn't want me to stay. That morning at the hospital when I saw Jake whisper something to you, then touch you… I almost lost it. You wouldn't even look at me. Yet, you let that scum touch you. You let him comfort you."

Some of the anger went out of her. "I hardly knew he was there. All I could think of was how badly things turned out for all those I loved, how horribly I had hurt all of you because I had made the wrong choices. I know you didn't cause Daddy's heart attack, but if he hadn't stormed out of the house to confront you, he would have been five minutes away from the hospital instead of forty." She looked at him with haunted eyes. "You were injured so badly you could barely stand. We should have told my parents we were dating like you always wanted. It would have prevented so much misery and pain. I was just so afraid they wouldn't let me see you again."

"You were seventeen almost eighteen. They couldn't dictate to you forever."

She glanced away. "No. I guess not."

"Were you ashamed of me?"

Her head jerked up. "Never. How could you think such a thing?"

The pressure on her shoulder lessened. "Then why didn't you tell Sheriff Stone we were married?"

She swallowed. "It would only have caused more trouble."

"How?"

Rachel shied from the whole truth. She didn't like feeling vulnerable toward a man she couldn't trust. "Knowing we were married would have given him a reason for you and my father to fight and could have put you in jail."

"It would have also given me the right to stay with you," Logan said softly.

She shook her head. "My mother was too upset for that. It was best for everyone that you leave the hospital."

Logan released her shoulder. "How many times have I heard that?"

"What?" The desolation in his voice pricked her.

"Whenever I used to ask my parents why I couldn't go with them or why they dumped me on their friends, they always said it was best for everyone. What they were really saying was that it was best for them and what I wanted didn't mean a rat's behind."

"I didn't mean it like that. You've got to believe me," she pleaded.

He laughed harshly. "At least they stuck around longer than twenty-four hours and they didn't feed me lies about loving me."

She recoiled as if she had been struck.

"Well, I guess I have my answers. Sorry I troubled you. I'll take you back to your truck now," he said, his face as emotionless as his voice.

Rachel felt the sting of tears behind her eyes and in her throat. He thought she hadn't loved him. In some ways, he was still that little boy desperately seeking and needing to be loved.

I promised myself that one day I was going to have a family of my own and we'd love each other so much my parents not loving me wouldn't matter.

She couldn't let him leave thinking he wasn't capable of being loved. Nothing was worth that. "I never lied when I said I loved you. But…but I didn't tell you the truth about something else."

His entire body tautened. "Go on."

Where to begin? She looked at the unrelenting lines of his face and forced herself to continue, "From the moment I saw you leaning against your old truck eating your lunch away from the other men in my father's work crew something inside me protested. When our gaze met your expression remained indifferent, then you looked away, completely dismissing me as something unworthy of your attention. Yet somehow I sensed you were rejecting me before I had a chance to reject you. A self-defense technique the callousness of the townspeople had probably forced you to acquire." She took a steadying breath before continuing.

"Never before had I felt so strongly the need to reach out and touch another person, to be there for them, to let them know I cared. I couldn't get you out of my mind. You were the most magnificent man I had ever seen, light years ahead of the boys I had dated, and forbidden enough to make my heart pound every time I saw you. At first I thought I'd never get you to notice me, then when you did I was afraid of losing you."

The stern line in his face softened. "You're the one who was forbidden. I couldn't believe I was interested in a high school senior and the boss's daughter at that. You set me in a tailspin every time I saw you. That's why I tried to act as if you didn't exist. I fought long and hard against taking you up on those shy signals you were sending me.

"Your innocence drew me to you as much as it kept me away. I never wanted to do anything to take the smile from your face, the laughter from your lips. Then you came out to the house, tripped, and I ended up almost kissing you. I tried to frighten you off and then you hugged me with complete trust. I wasn't strong enough to push you away. From that moment on you were my woman. You wouldn't have lost me."

"Yes, I would." She took a deep breath and plunged ahead. "I lied to you from the first day we met and I kept on lying." She shrugged. "A small lie, I told myself. The ends would justify the means. You wouldn't have given me a second look if I hadn't and I knew there were a lot of women in town who wanted you."

He frowned. "What could you have possibly lied about?"

"My age. I was sixteen, not seventeen, when we started dating. That's the real reason I didn't want you to meet my parents," she admitted in a rush of words.

"Sixteen!" Disbelief washed across Logan's dark features. "How could you lie about something like that?"

Rachel barely kept from recoiling at the whiplash in his voice. "At the time, I only knew I wanted to be your girlfriend. I didn't know you could get into trouble because of my age until Daddy told me the morning after we were married."

Logan raked his hand across his hair. "No wonder he

went ballistic at the construction site. With my reputation, he probably thought I seduced you before we got married."

"I told him we'd waited," Rachel said. "He was so angry he wouldn't listen. He left the house vowing to have you arrested. Instead, he ended up in ICU and you ended up in the emergency room. Everything went wrong and I knew it was my fault. I thought if I told Sheriff Stone we were married he would have taken you to jail."

"Thought?" he snapped heatedly.

"A—A couple of years later I got up enough courage to call the district attorney's office about a 'paper' I was doing for a family counseling course I was supposedly taking in college. I learned the police wouldn't have arrested the man because they needed proof he had been intimate with the young girl. For that they needed a witness. Since, as the lawyer in the district attorney's office put it, there's usually only two in the room, the father could make a lot of noise but that was all. In the end he'd probably end up only hurting his daughter's reputation. I knew then that Daddy either didn't know the law or he had been bluffing. Either way he wouldn't have put Mother through something like that. I learned too late I had caused you a lot of misery for nothing."

Logan muttered a heated expletive. "What else did you lie about? Is there something else you're not telling me?"

She flinched. She opened her mouth to tell him about the loss of their baby, but the words wouldn't come out. Not with the fury in his face already condemning her.

"You'll never know how sorry I am for being so selfish. I'm ready to leave, or would you prefer I called a taxi?"

Logan didn't say anything but simply looked at Rachel, tense and shaken before him. For eight long years he had hated J. T. Malone for almost destroying his life. Logan didn't agree with his methods, yet he certainly understood his reasons better. "All you can say is I'm sorry?"

"I've paid for my mistake in ways you'll never imagine. There is nothing you can say that I haven't said to myself. If you haven't, my father has."

Her last words brought Logan up short. After seeing Rachel and her father together, Logan didn't doubt that Old Man Malone had never forgiven his daughter for marrying down, and after losing the bid to Bridgeway, he wasn't likely to. It must have been hell for her these past years, trying to redeem herself.

What must it have been like for someone who had always been her father's little princess to be turned against? Was it easier never to have been loved, or to have been loved and suddenly have it taken away?

"I'll call a taxi." Rachel went into the kitchen and picked up the phone.

Logan followed. "Hang up."

She continued dialing. "The taxi is fine."

"Hang up or I'll do it for you," he warned.

With trembling fingers, she did as he'd requested. Slowly she faced him. "Please, can we leave now?"

The raspy sound of her barely audible voice cut

through him like a jagged knife. She was hurting. He clenched his hands to keep from taking her into his arms. She had almost ruined his life. *Because she wanted to be with you. You ruined her life because you wanted revenge. Who is more at fault?*

"Come on, if you're so anxious to leave." He whirled and left. By the time he reached his truck, Rachel was still a good ten feet behind. He stared straight ahead. He didn't want to see her slow, measured progress as if she had to concentrate on each step. Most of all he didn't want to see her take another swipe at her cheek.

The passenger door opened. She climbed inside and closed the door.

But instead of starting the engine, Logan found it impossible not to look at Rachel. Hands clamped in her lap, she sat stiff-backed and rigid. Sunshades prevented him from seeing her eyes, but the stream of tears gliding down her cheeks were clearly visible. Gritting his teeth, he started the engine and spun out of his driveway. Neither said a word during the drive to the doctor's office.

As soon as Logan stopped in the parking lot, Rachel yanked open the door and got out. Head down she didn't see the car driving too fast as she passed in front of Logan's truck to reach hers. Logan did.

Heart pounding, he jumped out of his truck. By the time he reached her, he was at a dead run. He locked his arm around her waist, pulling her out of the way of the speeding late-model sedan. In a squeal of brakes the vehicle came to a halt several feet away. A door slammed.

"I-Is she all right?" queried an anxious male voice. "My little girl is sick and I was rushing to get her here."

Logan didn't look at the man. Although he knew it had been as much Rachel's fault as the driver's, he wasn't sure about his reaction. His arms tightened around her trembling body. He didn't know which one of them was shaking the most. "She's not hurt."

"I'm sorry. If—"

"Hadn't you better get your little girl inside?" Logan asked.

"All right. Please tell her I'm sorry." In a matter of seconds, a car door slammed shut.

Logan picked up Rachel and carried her to his truck. His hands shook as he put the truck into gear and pulled into a parking space. Picking her up again, he settled her in his lap. One hand curved around her shoulder, the other swept up and down her arm.

"It's all right, honey. You're fine." After a minute and no response, Logan began to worry. Sitting her up, he stared into her face. He expected fear and shock, he didn't expect the resigned look on her face. "I'm taking you inside for Dr. Perry to look at."

"I'm fine, Logan." She slipped off his lap and out of his arms.

"I'm shaking like a leaf. How can you be fine?" he asked, incredulous.

"Because now we're even."

"Even?"

Her mouth curved into the saddest smile he had ever

seen. "I saved your life; you saved mine. We're even, and now you can leave town without feeling guilty. Goodbye, Logan." The door closed behind her.

This time, Rachel made it to her truck without any mishap and drove away. Logan watched her leave. She had done it again. She had walked away from him when he had intended *to walk* away from her. Either way, he didn't like it. In fact, he felt worse than he had eight years ago.

"Morning, Ms. Malone. I'm so glad you're here," said Teresa Hernandez, the receptionist/secretary at the Malone office.

Rachel tensed. "Hello, Teresa. Problems already?"

"No, ma'am," Teresa assured her with a grin. "Mayor Davis called and wants to meet you for lunch. Mr. Anderson wants to see you as soon as you can schedule him in to discuss another project. The president of the junior college and two members on the college's board of trustees called to tell you they thought you were doing a fine job. You also had a call from a Mr. Donaldson, who said it was very important that he speak with you today." She held up several slips of yellow paper in her manicured hand. "I've been answering the phone since I came in."

As if to prove her point, the phone rang again. The secretary picked up the receiver. "Malone Construction." Her hazel eyes widened. "Just a minute, Mr. Dawson, I'll see if Ms. Malone is in." A bright red nail pushed the hold button.

Teresa's accented voice dropped to an unnecessary whisper. "It's Charles Dawson, co-owner of Bridgeway. Do you want to talk to him?"

"No." Rachel's reply was curt and final. There wasn't one thing she could think of that they had to talk about. She certainly wasn't up to chitchat or hearing him wish her luck in the future. "The same goes if his partner, Logan Prescott, calls. Please call the mayor back and accept lunch at twelve. He can name the place. Set up Mr. Anderson at two and the other man at four. I'll return all the other calls in between." Rachel was turning to leave before the last words were spoken.

"Ms. Malone?"

Her hand curled around the doorknob, Rachel glanced over her shoulder. "Yes?"

"I just wanted you to know that I think you're doing a great job and I'm behind you. Those city council men and women will regret this come election time. One in particular."

Genuinely touched, all Rachel could get around the lump in her throat was, "Thank you."

She left the office at a fast clip, a new purpose in her step. All the long hours and hard work had paid off. Most important, Malone had a chance, a slim one, but a chance nevertheless of surviving if the dorm stayed on schedule and Jim Anderson's project was large enough and they could go to contract quickly. She couldn't wait to tell the crew.

Once again, she was in for a surprise. At each of the

three sites, the men reassured her instead of the other way around. They were behind her one hundred percent. She had always been fair with the men, always respected them. More than one person offered to pay Fred Mason a little visit. No one knew what transpired in Mayor Davis's study, but what happened in his den was common knowledge. Her men were upset at Mason's unprofessional behavior. None more so than her four, self-appointed guardians at the dormitory site.

"The best way to handle someone like Mason is to ignore him," Rachel told the men crowded around her.

"Just because he's rich, he thinks he can say anything. I'd like to plant my fist in his face." Leon spat a wad of brown tobacco juice on the ground.

Four pair of eycs stared at him. That was the longest speech he had ever made.

"I would, too, but Logan has first dibs," Gunther said.

Every nerve in Rachel's body went on alert. "What did you say?"

"Now you've done it," Ed accused.

"Someone had better start talking and fast." Rachel looked from one man to the next.

Typically, it was Jimmy who spoke up first. "Ed and them drove by Sunday night to check on you and saw Logan outside. As it happened, I had the same idea. We talked."

"And," Rachel prompted.

"He said he had made a mistake by not telling you about Bridgeway, but he was working on fixing things.

But he didn't want us to say anything to you. He was afraid you might become upset if you thought we were discussing you." The young man's gaze narrowed on his boss's tense features. "Guess he was right, huh?"

Instead of answering the question, she posed one of her own. "Gunther, why did you say Logan wanted first dibs on Fred Mason?"

Gunther swallowed. The Adam's apple in his massive neck bobbed up and down. "I…er…"

"Spit it out, Gunther!"

"He said Mason was going to regret the day he hurt his woman."

They took a tiny step back as Rachel clenched her fists, closed her eyes, and leaned back her head. Her guardians acted as if they might need guarding.

"Ms. Malone, we didn't mean to cause you any more problems."

Inhaling deeply, Rachel slowly opened her eyes and looked at Leon, his craggy face filled with concern. Then her gaze moved to the other men standing in a semicircle, all good men. She wasn't angry with them so much as she was with herself. Despite everything that had happened between her and Logan, she was unable to suppress a tiny thrill of pleasure at him calling her his woman. But he had thought that before this morning.

She forced her hands to relax. "I know you meant well. You'd better get back to work." She went a few feet over the uneven terrain before she glanced back and said, "Thanks for caring enough to watch out for me."

With determined steps, she proceeded to her truck and drove away. She had to stop thinking about Logan and get on with her life. He was not going to haunt her next eight years as he had the last eight. She had a business to run. Things were looking up. Malone just might make it.

"Logan, you're wearing me out pacing," Ida Mae said.

"I could shake her. First she spouts off some nonsense about us being even, and now she won't take Charles's call," Logan said, his irritation obvious as he continued to pace in front of Ida Mae's desk. "He told me her secretary said she couldn't be reached. I know differently. She would never be out of contact with her office. For all she knows Charles could be calling to offer her company some subcontracting work on the city hall complex. She's being stubborn and her company is barely hanging on."

The slender amber-skinned woman behind the desk lifted a perfectly arched black brow. "Why would she think one partner wants to save her after the other one tried to ruin her?"

Logan spun around. Dark eyes glinted.

"Isn't this what you wanted to happen?"

"Don't remind me of what a fool I was."

Ida Mae smiled devilishly. "Well, I'll be. Never thought I would live to see the day a man admitted he was wrong."

Logan threw his partner a lethal look. Her grin widened. "This is serious, Ida Mae."

"Honey, I'm sorry. I tried to warn you this could blow up in your face, but if you're worried about Rachel, from what I heard at church yesterday, more people than ever are pulling for her after the stunt Fred Mason pulled."

He halted. A muscle jumped in his jaw. "It was all I could do to keep from ramming my fist down his throat. I may still do it if he doesn't apologize to her."

"You're not alone. I told you a lot of people took notice of the way Rachel worked alongside her men. She doesn't mind getting dirty or sweaty if she has to. Never once have I heard she acted like she was better than them because she grew up with money. She's gained the respect of a lot of people. Her mother's no slouch, either." Ida Mae shook her head. "She was at church yesterday, chin so high she probably couldn't see where she was walking. You should have seen Mayor Davis and his family making room for her in the pew. People respect courage, and they both have a lot."

"Courage won't pay the bills."

"No, I guess not. But that's not your problem any longer, is it? You tried, Charles tried." She twirled a gold pen. "Guess you can go back to Little Rock with a clear conscience. You said yourself, the girl lied to you. Then she had the nerve to give you some hogwash that she did it because she loved you. The fact that she was sixteen and just a kid doesn't excuse her. You're thirty and you wouldn't have lied to her because you were afraid of losing her. Real men always tell the truth."

With each of Ida Mae's words, Logan had grown

stiller and stiller. Each telling truth dug deeper and deeper, cutting through pride and anger until nothing was left except the startling realization that he had no right to judge anyone.

"Promise me you'll give me a kick in the pants if I need it again."

"I think I'll let Rachel have the pleasure."

"First I need to make a couple of phone calls and then I'm going to give her the chance."

Fifteen minutes later, Logan parked beside Rachel's truck in the parking lot of the Wagon Wheel restaurant. As Logan expected, Jimmy had been easier to gain information from than Rachel's secretary.

Inside, he tipped his Stetson to the smiling hostess. "I'm looking for Mayor Davis and Ms. Malone."

"Right this way, sir."

Logan followed. People nodded as they did in a small town, but no one seemed to pay him any undue attention. He suspected that would change once he reached his destination.

Mayor Davis saw him first. His green-bean-laden fork paused inches from his mouth. Immediately, his gaze flickered to Rachel, sitting across from him at a small table. What Logan was about to do was chancy, especially in the middle of a crowded restaurant. But for his purpose, the setting was ideal. He only hoped Rachel wasn't as upset with him as Jimmy thought.

"Good afternoon, Ms. Malone, Mayor Davis."

At the sound of the unmistakable deep voice, Rachel's fingers tightened on her fork. Her heart pounding, she lifted her eyes from the little pile of carrots on her plate to Logan. The sensual, hungry look on his dark, handsome face caused her breath to lodge in her throat. Unsettled, she quickly dropped her gaze.

"I hope I'm not interrupting."

"Not at all, Mr. Prescott," the mayor finally managed to say, and held out his hand.

Reluctantly, Logan switched his attention from the top of Rachel's bowed head to the mayor, "I thought your son might be having lunch with you. I haven't had a chance to meet him yet."

"Lamar left yesterday afternoon. He's a junior partner in an investment firm in Austin." The elderly man beamed with fatherly pride. "We're very proud of him."

"I can certainly understand why," Logan mused. "I don't know why I thought he lived in Stanton. Do you, Ms. Malone?"

Rachel lifted her head and glared at Logan. "Don't let us keep you from getting a table."

Logan almost smiled. *That's my woman. Never back down from anyone.* "Actually, you're the reason I'm here. My partner has been unable to locate you all day, so I told him I'd see what I could do. We'd like to discuss the possibility of Malone doing subcontracting work for us when we build the city hall complex. After seeing the outstanding job you and your crew have done on the dorm and in other buildings, I can't think of another company we'd like more." He made sure the people sitting around him heard his last sentence. They would do the rest.

"We don't need cha—"

"No need to make a decision now," Logan interrupted. He didn't like the glint in her brown eyes. "Why don't I drop by your office later on today, so we can discuss things?" A lean brown finger touched the rim of his hat. "Pardon the interruption. Good day." He walked away feeling a definite itch between his shoulder blades.

Reluctantly, Rachel pulled her gaze from Logan's retreating back. If he thought she was going to have anything to do with Bridgeway, he had been in the sun too long. She picked up her glass of iced tea. She was going to take great pride in showing Logan that Malone didn't need his help.

"More is going on here than meets the eye, isn't it?" the mayor asked.

Her hand clenched. She slowly set the glass down. "There's always more going on than meets the eye. Thanks for lunch, but I have to get back to the office."

"Lamar doesn't stand a chance, does he?"

She paused in getting up. This question she had no difficulty answering. "I never led him to believe otherwise."

He nodded, then looked pensive. "Something tells me Mr. Prescott is not so easily dissuaded from what he wants."

"Neither am I." She stood. "Good day, Mayor."

Chapter 15

Logan was in a good mood. He didn't even mind Rachel's secretary glaring at him every time she looked up from her computer or her telling him that Rachel wasn't in. Her truck was parked out front and he planned to wait. It was almost four-thirty and sooner or later she had to come out of her office.

Leg crossed over his knee, he stopped flipping through *Architectural Digest* and winked at the secretary. To his surprise, she blushed, ducked her head, and went back to her typing. Too bad a look couldn't get Rachel as easily flustered. If their meeting at lunch was any indication, she would be more likely to give him a swift kick, just as Ida Mae had said.

The door to Rachel's office burst open. Instead of Rachel, a man in an ill-fitting navy blue suit swiftly crossed the room to the secretary's desk. "I—I think Ms. Malone needs a glass of water."

Logan came to his feet. In a matter of seconds he had rounded Rachel's desk and knelt by her chair. Body rigid, back straight, she stared straight ahead. "Rae, honey. What is it? Baby, talk to me."

"Here's some water."

Logan took the glass from the secretary and pressed the rim against Rachel's tightly compressed lips. She averted her head and the water ran down her chin. Hand clenched around the glass, he stood, his accusing glare locked on the tall stranger. "What did you do to her?" he asked, his voice hard and forbidding.

The man blanched and backed up. Manicured fingers shook as they fidgeted with the knot in his print tie. 'Nothing."

A loud "thunk" sounded as the glass hit the desk. 'I'm not going to ask you again!"

The man swallowed. The wall stopped his retreat. "I—I was only doing my job. My name is Peter Donaldson. Th… The bank has been very lenient with Malone's deficient payments."

Logan cursed under his breath. "Where are the papers?"

The obviously frightened man pointed toward Rachel and swallowed again. "She…she has them."

Turning away from the cowering man, Logan knelt beside Rachel. For the first time he noticed the papers clutched in her hand. There was no way he was going to be able to get them away from her. "Whatever it is, I'll fix it, Rae. I promise."

She finally looked at him. He wished she hadn't. The challenge he had seen earlier in her eyes was gone; now they were desolate. She looked like a woman without dreams, without hope. "Come to gloat again?"

He felt like a fist had slammed into his chest. "A man doesn't gloat when the woman he cares about is in trouble."

Logan heard a sound behind him. Briefcase clutched to his thin chest, the banker was trying to slip away. Logan came to his feet and caught him in the outer office. "You're not going anywhere."

"Please, I was only doing my job," he pleaded, trying and failing to free his arm.

"I don't give a damn about you doing your job, but you hurt a woman who had been hanging on to her family's company with guts and determination for six hard months. I'm about two seconds from losing it, so I suggest you tell me everything the first time. Talk and talk fast," Logan warned, his voice razor sharp.

Eyes bugged, Donaldson talked like a tape recorded on fast-forward. The Malones were three months past due on the payments for their heavy equipment and they had until August first to pay up or everything would be confiscated. There was also the matter of a personal loan of Mr. Malone's that was delinquent. He had wanted both loans kept quiet, but after Malone Construction had lost the bid, the bank president had felt the person in charge should be made aware of the loans. With Mr. Malone's heart condition, they hadn't wanted to put him under any more stress.

"So the bank decided to dump everything in his daughter's lap for her to take care of," Logan said tightly.

"The bank only wants its money, as promised."

"You'll get your money, every cent. If it wouldn't cause the Malone family more unpleasantness, I'd make sure the entire town knows how the bank operates." The little remaining color in the man's face vanished. "Get out of here, and if I ever hear of you causing Ms. Malone any problems, one of us will be in the hospital and the other one will probably be in jail. You guess which."

Briefcase still clutched to his chest, Peter Donaldson hit the door running.

Logan went back to Rachel's office. The secretary stood with a protective arm around her boss's hunched shoulders. "Thank you, but I'll take care of Ms. Malone now."

This time, instead of glaring, the secretary nodded her approval. "If you need anything, holler."

Logan waited until the door closed before he crossed the room, knelt by Rachel, and took her cold hands in his. He said a little prayer of thanks when she didn't pull away, but she didn't look at him.

"I promise you're not going to lose your company. I meant what I said about the subcontracting work. The papers can be drawn up tomorrow and I can give you a check to cover all the past due payments at the bank. Rae, honey, can you hear me? Let me help you."

"You knew this would happen." Her voice was raspy thin. "Everyone knew except me."

"You're wrong. My partner knew because we've always made it a point to know who we're competing against. He told me only because it looked like we were going to win the bid. We like winning, but we don't want to cause another company to go under because of it."

"So you offer them scraps to ease your conscience." She tugged her hands free. "We don't need charity."

"I'm not offering you any. Yours won't be the first black-owned company Bridgeway has helped. Other companies helped us in the beginning. If I hadn't been so blinded by wanting revenge, I would have offered you help the first day I hit town."

Her head lifted. "What changed your mind? A guilty conscience again?"

"Sleepless nights and restless days changed my mind. I had a lot of time to think. I can't deny my feelings for you any longer. I don't hate anymore. I changed my mind because I don't want to go through a day without seeing you smile or hearing you laugh. Because it hurts too damn much and you're the only one who can make the hurting stop."

She looked into his eyes and saw the truth staring unflinchingly back at her. Unending pain she understood. "But I'm also the one who caused the problems."

"So did I. Can't we put the past behind us and start over?"

There wasn't anything she wanted more and dreaded

at the same time. Before they had a chance for a future, Logan had to know about the loss of their child. She glanced out the window. "I don't ever want to look in your eyes and see hate staring back at me."

Calloused hands palmed her cheeks and turned her to him. "I was angry, but I never hated you. Believe me, I tried. I'd catch myself thinking about you at the oddest times, wanting you, needing you. I'd try to shut you out of my mind, but you'd always come back."

"The past can't be forgotten."

"Maybe we can't forget the past, but we can learn from it." His voice rang with conviction. "I won't make the same mistakes again. If you want me to, I'll swe—"

Her shaky fingers pressed against his lips to stop the flow of words. "Please. Don't swear. Not until you know everything."

His hand captured hers. He kissed her fingertips, his heated gaze never leaving hers. "I only want to know two things: can you forgive me, and will you give me another chance to make things right?"

"There is something you have to know first."

"Later. Just answer my questions."

"Yes, but—"

His lips took gentle possession of hers. The kiss wasn't so much passionate as it was one of tender promise. A long moment later, he lifted his head. "I was afraid I'd never get to do that again."

"So was I," she confessed softly.

He kissed her again. "We'll just have to make up for lost time."

The word "lost" made her remember they had one final hurdle to overcome. Her face became shadowed. "Logan, there's something I need to tell you."

"I can have the contracts and the check on your desk by ten in the morning."

She shook her head, her hands clamped around his. "It's…it's about something that happened after you left town eight years ago."

"If it's going to upset you that much just thinking about it, we can just forget it."

"No. Please." Her voice sounded as frantic as she looked.

He pulled her back into his arms. "All right, honey, you can tell me, but can it wait until I come back for the weekend?" His hand swept reassuringly up and down her back. "If I'm not in Little Rock by nine in the morning, Charles has threatened to send a search party out for me. I won't leave if you're upset."

"You neglected your job to be here with me?" She pushed out of his arms.

He kissed the frown from her face. "Let's just say I'm grateful to whoever invented the fax and the mobile phone. So can our talk wait until Friday? I should be back no later than nine that night, and I'll come straight to your house."

She didn't want to wait. Now that she had gathered enough courage to finally tell him, the need was almost consuming. She needed to share the loss.

What's more she needed to know if he could forgive her her final betrayal.

"Honey?"

She looked into his face, saw the concern and knew she couldn't tell him and expect him to leave as planned. Her burden might be lifted, but she would put a heavier one on him. Somehow she managed to smile. "Friday is fine."

He kissed her on the lips, then pulled them both to their feet. "Now that that's settled, how about having dinner with me tonight?"

"I'd like that."

"Good. I'll pick you up at eight. Be sure to wear the wrap dress Ida Mae sent over the day of the accident." With a wicked smile and a wink, he left.

Bemused, Rachel sat down. The look vanished on seeing a copy of the loan agreement. Her father had some explaining to do.

"Is it true?" Hand clenched around his cane, J. T. Malone barked the question from the front porch of his house as soon as Rachel got out of her truck.

Immediately, she knew he referred to the subcontracting work for Bridgeway. The meeting at the restaurant with Logan had probably traveled faster than the speed of sound through the small town. As usual, her father's gaze was somewhere over her left shoulder. For the first time, she didn't blame herself or feel as if she had failed him. "Let's go inside, Daddy."

"I don't want you to have anything to do with him."

Rachel paused on the bottom step, surprised to hear more fear than anger in his voice. "You left me in charge and I'm signing the papers tomorrow."

"Somehow, it's a trick. He wouldn't help either of us after what happened."

Finally she understood the reason for his agitation. "I've already told him that I lied about my age."

"If only that was all."

Her father had whispered the words, but Rachel heard them. She fought against the uncertainty she felt. "He'll understand about the accident."

"No, he won't. He'll leave and this time…" His gaze locked on her. Desperation shone back at her. Shoulders slumped, he turned to go back into the house.

Rachel bounded up the steps after him. "Why shouldn't he understand it was an accident?"

"I don't want to talk about it. It's too late anyhow."

She didn't know if he meant too late for her and Logan, or too late for their company. "It's because of Logan that Malone Construction has a chance. But why didn't you tell me you weren't repaying the loans, and in fact, had taken out a new one?"

His shoulders jerked. The glass door he opened swung shut. After a long moment, he turned slightly toward her. "How did you find out?"

Her voice softened on seeing her father's haggard, defeated expression. "The bank sent someone today. Was it the doctor bills? Is that what you needed all the money for?"

Bleak eyes scanned the front yard. "Two things I never doubted, that I could cover the ground I stood on and that I could protect my family. I find I can't do either."

"Daddy, everything is going to be all right. With the check we'll receive on signing, I can catch up the payments and we're back in business."

"Nothing will ever be all right again." Opening the door, he went inside.

The bleakness of her father's voice stayed with Rachel long after she arrived home. She had expected him to be indignant over the loans and angry over her accepting Logan's offer. The defeated look on his gaunt face haunted her all the while she got ready for her date with Logan. Her father was a proud man who couldn't take care of his family or his business. It was a heavy blow to his pride. The chime of the doorbell intruded on her thoughts.

She opened the door expecting to see Logan. She did, but he wasn't alone. He and Ed were grinning and shaking hands.

"Ed is a new father," Logan said.

"I never would have guessed," Rachel teased. "Come in. Is it a boy, like Ishira expected?"

Ed's grin widened as he stepped inside. "A beautiful little girl. Weighed in at seven pounds, eight ounces, twenty-one inches long. Ishira called just after you left."

"How is Ishira?" Rachel asked, and waved him to a seat.

"Just fine. She was asleep, so I thought I'd leave for a little while, check on the kids, and spread the word." He sat down, then sprang up and pulled two cigars from his shirt pocket and handed one each to Logan and Rachel. "I almost forgot."

"You're entitled." Logan propped his arm on the headrest of Rachel's chair. "Being a father has got to be the scariest and proudest feeling in the world."

"It is." Ed glanced at Rachel. "I hope you find out for yourself real soon."

"I hope you're right."

Rachel felt her cheeks heat, but the pain of remembered loss didn't come. She looked up at Logan and saw her dreams staring back at her. A family in a circle of love. Unconsciously, her hand lifted to him. His hand closed around her.

"Well, I guess I'd better get going." Ed went to the door.

"Thanks for coming by. Please give Ishira our best," Rachel said. "I'll let Randy work the crane until you get back."

Ed looked incensed. "He's not touching my crane. I'll be there tomorrow. Ishira's parents are with the kids and I'll just be underfoot at the hospital. Anyway, from what I heard, we need to get through with the dorm because we might be having more work to do."

"There is that possibility," Rachel said, as they stepped outside.

Logan's arm slid around her slim shoulder. "Definitely a possibility."

Ed smiled, tugged on his baseball cap, and headed down the walkway.

Logan's arm around her shoulder, they went back inside. "His new daughter is probably going to be as spoiled as Lauren. They're both lucky little girls."

"Once I would have agreed, but..."

Logan stopped. He lifted Rachel's chin and stared into her troubled face. "Go on."

"What happens if one day you aren't Daddy's little girl anymore? What happens when the man you've always looked up to and admired no longer feels the same way about you?"

"You go on and live your life. Your father will come around, Rae," Logan told her. "He's just angry because he can't control you anymore."

She shook her head. "Something else is bothering him, I know it."

"Of course there is." At Rachel's puzzled look, Logan continued, "You. He doesn't want to share you. He isn't the only man in your life anymore and he resents it. Just like I resented his influence over you when we were dating. Each time you left, I'd wonder if I'd ever see you again."

She palmed his cheeks. "I'd wonder if you'd want to see me again. I was so afraid of losing you."

"You were the only one I wanted then, the only one I want now." His mouth found hers. His tongue swept inside the dark interior of hers. She whimpered and pressed closer. What had begun as a reassuring kiss turned into one of need and hunger. Logan lifted his head. "How hungry are you?" he muttered thickly.

Dark lashes slowly lifted. The one unquenchable desire in her life that had remained constant, no matter how she tried to deny it, was to be wrapped in the secure warmth of Logan's arms, feel the unleashed power of his body pressed to hers, taste the wild, hot sweetness of his mouth. "For you, always."

Her words ripped through his waning control. Swinging her into his arms, he quickly went into the bedroom. His mouth took hers as he followed her down on the bed. Wild, untamed hunger ripped through him. His hand swept beneath her skirt, then cupped her hip. With a whimper of need, she pressed closer to the rigid fullness of his lower body. He gritted his teeth against the exquisite torture. Only this woman made him fight for control.

His seeking hand glided to her waist, then upward to close over the swell of her breast. The turgid fullness lured him to touch bare skin. He quickly divested them of the unwanted barriers between them.

His lips closed around her nipple. Her moan of pleasure drove him on. His lips sought hers again. They were moist, trembling, waiting. He couldn't wait any longer. He joined them in one sure thrust. Her arms closed around his back, her hips lifted in an ageless welcome. Gathering her closer, he took them on a soaring ride filled with undeniable passion and aching tenderness.

* * *

A sound tried to draw her from her sensual cocoon. Rachel resisted and snuggled closer to…nothing. Her eyelids swept upward and she sat up in bed. The sound came again and this time she recognized it as the doorbell. *Logan.*

She faintly recalled his good-natured grumble earlier about no milk in her kitchen to make waffles from scratch and said he was going to the grocery store. After a night of almost nonstop lovemaking, she had sent him off with a kiss of appreciation and gone back to sleep.

Throwing back the covers, she was halfway across the room before she remembered she was naked and the last time she opened the door expecting only Logan, he hadn't been alone.

"I'm coming," she yelled. Putting on her baggy sweatpants and top, she started for the door again. If she wasn't presentable, at least she was covered.

She flung open the door with a smile on her face. Rage took it away. For a stunned moment she couldn't believe Jake had had the nerve to show up on her doorstep. Then she remembered his malice. She tried to shut the door, but it was too late. He easily pushed his way inside and slammed the door behind him. For some reason, she recalled the night she and Logan had dueled with the door. Now she knew he had let her win. Just thinking about him made her stop backing up. He was probably already on his way back.

"Get out of my house."

Jake's lips curled. "Still trying to give me orders. I'm the one giving the orders, now that your guard dog has finally left."

"You've been watching my house." A chill went through her.

"You owe me, and you're gonna pay." His unshaven face hardened. "I've lost everything because of you and Prescott. The police are watching my house and my friends are too scared to help me."

"You never had any friends. You bullied people, and when that wouldn't get them to do what you wanted, you used your fists. You deserve everything that's happened to you, so don't come whining to me. Leave the same way you came in."

He took a menacing step toward her. "I'm tired of you giving orders."

"Get out of here."

He laughed, a cold, evil sound. "Talk big all you want, but when I get ready to have you nothing you or Logan Prescott can do will stop me."

"You must have forgotten the beating Logan gave you at Big Al's," she said, trying to keep her voice from shaking and Jake's mind off trying to make his threat a reality. "I'm sure he won't mind jogging your memory. He should be back from the store any moment now."

Jake's wary gaze darted from Rachel to the window. "Prescott is welcome to you. I'd rather have money. Five thousand dollars should be enough for now."

She laughed in his face. "I wouldn't give you a wooden nickel."

"You will if you don't want your father facing charges when the dorm collapses." She gasped. Jake grinned. "You were right about the switches, but it was your daddy that started it."

"You're lying. Daddy wouldn't do anything like that."

He sneered again. "You don't know anything about your old man. He's the one who ordered me and the boys to beat up your lover boy the morning after you two ran off. Sissy that Prescott was, he didn't even try to defend himself when J.T. took the first swing at him. Just dodged the fist and said he was taking you with him and you were never coming back. Made your daddy so mad he lunged at Prescott and they both fell on the floor in the trailer. Took me awhile to figure out J.T. had had a heart attack."

"*You* made up the lie about Logan attacking my father," Rachel said with certainty.

"I thought J.T. was going to die, and with Prescott out of the way, I'd be left to run the construction company," he reasoned.

"And to steal with little disregard for whose life you endangered."

Bleary eyes flared. "Your daddy's just as guilty. He's been paying to keep me quiet for the past year, but now he says he can't pay no more. I liked not having to live from paycheck to paycheck, having a nice fishing boat, having money to gamble with in Louisiana. I'm not giving it up," he warned. "After what I heard about you teaming up with Bridgeway and since Prescott is sleeping with you, you can get me plenty. If you don't, I'm going to make a few anonymous phone calls and your father will be in jail and the dorm will be bulldozed to the ground."

So Jake's streak of luck had been blackmail money from her father. Rachel looked at the coldness of the man staring at her with hatred and made her decision. "Help yourself. I'm not endangering one person's life. Daddy will have to answer for what he did, but so will you."

Surprise widened his eyes on hearing the determination in her voice. "You think you're so uppity, just like your old man. Well, maybe you'll change your mind when you hear he paid me off for more than keeping quiet about the substandard building material. He hated the idea of you having Prescott's brat. Turned his stomach. We had a beer and a good laugh the night you got rid of the baby."

"You're lying!" With a cry of rage, Rachel hit Jake in the face with a balled fist. She didn't flinch when he raised his hand to hit her. The blow never landed.

Logan jerked Jake around and slammed his fist into his stomach, followed by another and another to his face until Jake dropped to his knees. Blood dripped from his nose and mouth.

"Logan, stop!" Rachel cried, trying to catch his arm.

Shaking her off, he wrapped his hands around Jake's neck. "You'll never laugh again."

Oh, God, Rachel thought, he had heard everything. She grabbed his arm again and this time she held on. "He's lying about me and Daddy. I lost our baby in the car accident I told you about. Logan, please. You're killing him."

Hands grabbed her shoulders and pulled her upright. She glanced around to see the room filled with policemen. Three of them were attempting to pull Logan from Jake's inert body. Finally, they succeeded in separating the two men.

Tears streamed down her cheek. "Logan, please stop before they hurt you. Jake isn't worth it."

Logan didn't stop struggling against the officers until Jake was out of sight. Only then did he slowly turn his head and scan the room.

Rachel sucked in her breath when their eyes met. She had never seen such naked pain or barely leashed rage before. On trembling legs she went to him. "He lied about me and Daddy. I packed a bag the morning after I found out I was pregnant, left my parents a note, and started for Oklahoma. I was in Amarillo when a woman ran a stop sign and hit my car broadside. I...I lost our baby. My father might not have said much, but he seldom left my mother's side and she refused to leave mine during my three-day hospital stay."

Nothing moved on him, not even when the policemen holding him released his arms and left the house.

"Maybe you should talk to him later," suggested the

officer who had pulled her from Logan. He was the same one she had met at Ed's house July Fourth.

"Later may be too late. He needs to understand now."

The officer looked sympathetic but steadfast. "I don't think he's in any mood to listen. You'll have to come down to the station and sign a complaint, and by the time that's done, he'll probably be ready to talk." He turned to Logan. "Mr. Prescott, we appreciate the call on your mobile phone telling us Jake was at Ms. Malone's house. We'll handle things from here. Now, if you'll just move your truck to one side of the street so traffic can get through. Or if you want, I can do it since you left the door open, the engine running and the key in the ignition."

After an endless moment of staring at Rachel, he started for the front door.

"Logan. I love you," Rachel cried. He never slowed.

"He's dealing with a heavy load right now," the officer said. "It'll be all right."

She remembered what her father had said and now knew what he had meant. Nothing would ever be all right again.

Feeling more desolate and more alone than she ever thought possible, Rachel stopped her truck in front of her parents' house. Not even after the loss of her baby had she felt such emptiness. If Logan hadn't been there, at least her parents had. Now she would be without either. She hadn't seen or heard from Logan since he'd walked out of her house. And there was no way she could continue working with her father if the accusations Jake had made against him earlier were true.

Since Jake had regained consciousness, he had been raging against Logan and demanding his release. He hadn't mentioned her father; he probably wouldn't. If he did, he'd only implicate himself and open the way for blackmail and theft charges. As it was, he was being held on vandalism, breaking and entering, and assault.

Now, she needed to talk with her father to see if Jake had told the truth. Because thus far, Tom hadn't been able to find any cash receipts made out to Jake except the one for the cable. She also wanted to know how Jake had known about her miscarriage.

Going around the side of the house, she opened the glass door and walked inside. Her mother rushed into the room. On seeing Rachel, the hope shining in her eyes dimmed.

"Mother, what's the matter?"

"Your father's gone."

"Maybe he just went into town for something."

"You know he never leaves without telling me where he's going and when he plans to be back." Twisting her hands, she bit her lip. "I didn't even know he was leaving until I heard a car outside and looked out the window. He must have been waiting for the cab on the porch."

Dread swept through Rachel. "Don't worry, Mother. I'll find him."

"I'm going with you."

"All right." Her arm around her mother's frail shoulder, Rachel led her to her truck. *Please be okay, Daddy. Just be all right,* she prayed.

His guts twisted in knots, Logan turned into his driveway. His mood was as foul and as bitter as the taste in his mouth. A part of him had died before it had a chance to live, before its father knew of its existence. His vision blurred, the knot tightened.

Jake's taunting words of sharing a beer and a laugh tore through Logan. His hands clenched on the steering wheel and he knew he'd gladly give twenty years of his life to have his hands around Jake's worthless neck for twenty seconds.

That's why he had to get away. He was too close to losing control, too close to ignoring the police and anything else to get to Jake. The only reason he hadn't was because of the pleading note in Rachel's voice and the pain in her eyes that mirrored his own. She had had to endure so much because of him. Yet she still loved him.

He had carried her words with him all during his high-speed drive through the back roads surrounding Stanton. He loved her, too. Just as soon as he changed out of his blood-smeared shirt, he was going to find her and tell her.

He stopped the truck in front of his house and got out. Head down, he almost walked over the man sitting on his bottom step. Rage he had been trying to control flared hot and high. He reached for J. T. Malone's shirt collar with every intention of dragging the man who'd ruined his life, Rachel's, and their unborn child's, off his property. Malone's ragged words stopped him.

"I cried the night she lost the baby. She was in such pain and she kept asking me to make it stop. In the next breath, she'd ask for you. I hated you for putting her through that, and I hated being so helpless. I knew then if she ever found out I ordered Jake to beat you up, that I was bluffing about having you arrested for seduction of a minor, she'd never forgive me. Too late, I realized she might be barely seventeen, but she loved you with a woman's devotion. She needed you that night, and I was the cause of you not being there. So instead of going to find you, I told her you had moved and left no forwarding address." He brushed an unsteady hand across his gaunt cheek.

"From that moment on I waited for the day she'd find out how my lies had taken you away from her, for her to start hating me. I'm not trying to defend myself, but I wanted only the best for her. A welder barely making enough money to get by wasn't what I wanted for her. Besides, she was just a child and I figured you only wanted one thing from her. You were a grown man with desires and a reputation for satisfying those desires with a string of women. That wasn't going to happen to Rachel. You weren't going to use her for her money and leave her with a broken heart. I was willing to use any means necessary to make sure you never bothered her again. In trying to protect her, I ended up hurting her much worse. I dreaded and waited for the day for her to find out what I had done."

He glanced up at Logan. "That's why I pushed her so hard sometimes. I thought if I could push her away, sort of prepare myself, her leaving wouldn't hurt so bad. It was worse. She just kept trying to please me, not understanding why, but loving me anyway. She became an architect instead of a fashion designer to help me out in the business. All her life she had talked of being a designer, but she gave up her dream and never once complained. That kind of blind love, when it's undeserving, will kill a man."

J. T. Malone looked at Logan with tears sparkling in his eyes. "She loves you the same way, only more. Martha worried about Rachel not dating, but I always knew you were the reason. One night about a year ago I tried to drown my guilty conscience with alcohol and made the mistake of doing it while I was with Jake. I told him everything. Since then I've been paying him to keep quiet, but I ran out of money. Paying him is the reason why I took out another loan from the bank and why Fred Mason's apartment building went over budget. The bad economy didn't help. Jake called this morning and threatened to lie and tell Rachel I cheated on building materials unless I gave him more money. I never used substandard building materials in my life. I hung up. Telling her will finally end things between us.

"She'll leave the company and town. Jake said he plans to call the building inspector. Once Fred Mason hears, the Malone name won't be worth spit. She has to be gone before that happens."

He sniffed. "I knew if you'd ever come back, I'd lose her to you. Two weeks after I was released from the hospital I learned from Sheriff Stone how you stood up to him at the hospital, how you ignored his orders to leave town and went to see Rachel. Listening to him I knew in my gut you weren't lying when you told me that day in the trailer you only wanted one thing from me, and that was for Rachel's sake, was my approval of your marriage. You left before because you thought she didn't want you. I'm betting by now you know you were wrong."

Sadly, he shook his graying head. "Instead of avoiding her, I should have given her hugs and stored up memories. It's too late now. With you two talking everything is going to come out about what I did to you, how I lied, how I manipulated her. She'll hate me. Once Jake gets through spreading lies, the whole town will, too. Only she'll be included. I couldn't stand that."

With excruciating slowness, Mr. Malone used his cane and the front door facing to push upright. He met Logan's steady gaze without faltering. "She has to be gone by then. I know you must still love her because you wouldn't lift a finger to save Malone Construction or me. So…so I'm asking when you leave that you take Rachel with you. I know it's asking a lot, but do you think you can take Martha as well?"

Logan looked away from the pleading in the man's eyes, a man he had set out to ruin, a man he had accused of ruining his life. Logan knew in that moment, all the hurt and anger he had carried in his heart for eight long years for J. T. Malone were gone. Looking back was a waste of time. He had too much to look forward to.

He reached for Malone's arm. "Come on, Mr. Malone. Let's go inside where I can change this shirt, then I'll take you home."

"You'll take my baby, won't you?"

"Forever and always."

Logan never got a chance to take his unexpected guest anywhere. He was pulling on his shirt when there was a frantic knock on his door. Opening it he discovered Mrs. Malone standing hesitantly in the doorway. Rachel stood behind her.

"Mr. Malone, looks like your family found you first."

Martha Malone rushed to her husband. By the time she reached him, he was standing. "J.T. You had us worried. If Rachel hadn't thought to call the cab company we might still be looking for you."

"I'm sorry for worrying you, Martha," he told her. "I had to come and apologize to Logan and ask him to do me a favor."

"What are you talking about?" Martha queried. "He's the cause of all our problems."

His bent shoulders slowly straightened. "No. I'm the one who caused the problems and it's past time for me to admit it." His gaze swept from his wife's puzzled frown to his daughter in the doorway. Hers was locked on Logan as his was on hers.

Rachel wanted to say so much, yet the words stuck in her throat.

"It still hurts, doesn't it?" he asked tenderly.

She nodded. "Sometimes I don't think it will ever stop. I wanted the baby so much. I felt so guilty afterwards. If I hadn't lied, things might have been different."

Strong arms pulled her into the comforting shelter of his body. "Don't, Rae. Don't blame yourself."

"I wanted to tell you…but you were so angry at first." She burrowed closer. "Then, when I finally got up enough courage, you asked me to wait."

His arms tightened. "I figured that out while driving around after I left the police at your place."

"When you walked out without saying anything, I almost died. I thought you hated me."

He kissed the top of her head in reassurance. "It was that or go through the police for Jake." He leaned away and lifted her chin with his finger. "By the way, he lied about your father. Jake was angry because your father had run out of blackmail money."

"Jake told me."

"What Jake told you is probably a lie. Why don't you let your father tell you himself."

"Daddy has a lot to answer for."

"My guess is he already has," Logan said.

"Rachel, what are you doing?" Mrs. Malone asked, her voice rising.

"Leave them alone, Martha," J.T. said. "This is the way it should have been a long time ago."

Martha Malone looked at the three occupants in the room as if in a daze. "I don't understand."

Logan took pity on her. "Mrs. Malone, why don't you and I get to know each other better while Rachel and her daddy have a little talk?"

J. T.'s eyes rounded. He gripped his cane. "You said you'd take her."

"I am, but we aren't going anywhere. First, you and I will figure out the best way to repay Fred Mason after he makes a public apology to Rachel, then Jake's next on the list. If he wants to make trouble, the Prescotts and the Malones will face it head on, together. I figure that's what families do."

Rachel gasped softly.

Martha Malone looked at Rachel and Logan staring at each other as if all their happiness depended on the other and bowed to the undeniable truth. J.T. was right. They were destined to be together. "If that was a proposal, it was a pitiful one," Martha told Logan. "And you can just forget about eloping. This time our daughter is having a formal wedding."

"He hasn't asked and I haven't said yes," Rachel said.

"Yes, I did, every time I looked at you. And you said yes every time you looked back. I love you, Rae. I always have and I always will."

With a cry of pure joy, she flung herself into his arms, then looked around his shoulder at her watchful parents. Reluctantly, she pulled away. "Come on, Daddy. Why don't we go for a drive and you can buy me an ice-cream cone, the way you used to."

"I can't think of anything I'd like better."

Logan turned at the sound of an approaching car. "Looks like Charles got tired of waiting."

The late-model luxury sedan had barely stopped before Charles got out of the passenger side. Although he was on crutches, his wife barely caught up with him by the time he reached Logan. "You better have a good reason for still being here."

Logan's grin widened as his arm circled Rachel's slim waist. "Rae, meet my best man, Charles Dawson, and his wife, Helen."

Charles blinked, then his smile almost matched Logan's. "You just saved yourself from a good tongue-lashing." He pumped Rachel's hand. "You're getting a good man."

"I know and this time I'm keeping him," Rachel said and looked at Logan with an undeniable commitment of love. He returned the look full measure.

That night in each other's arms, they mourned the loss of their unborn child and reaffirmed their love. He was hers and she was Logan's woman. They had finally completed their circle of love that would expand to include their children and children's children, but could never be broken. A love that was undeniable and strong enough to last a lifetime and beyond.

Torn between her past and present...

After Dark

DONNA HILL

ESSENCE BESTSELLING AUTHOR

Elizabeth swore off men after her husband left her for a younger woman...until sexy contractor Ron Powers charmed his way into her life. But just as Elizabeth is embarking on a journey of sensual self-discovery with Ron, her ex tells her he wants her back. And with Ron's radical past threatening their future, she's not sure what to do! So she turns to her "girlz"—Stephanie, Barbara, Anne Marie and Terri—for advice.

Pause for Men: Five fabulously fortysomething divas rewrite the book on romance.

Available the first week of July, wherever books are sold.

KIMANI
ROMANCE

www.kimanipress.com   KPDH0240707

He's determined to become the
comeback kid...

THE
VERY
THOUGHT
of
YOU

ANGELA
WEAVER

Drafted to hide a witness's daughter in a high-profile
murder case, Department of Justice operative
Miranda Tyler seeks the help of Caleb Blackfox,
who once betrayed her. Now Caleb is willing to do
whatever it takes to win back the girl who got away.

Available the first week of July,
wherever books are sold.

KIMANI
ROMANCE
™

Almost paradise...

one gentle
KNIGHT

Part of The Knight Family Trilogy

WAYNE JORDAN

Barbados sugar plantation owner Shayne Knight fulfills
his fantasies in the arms of beautiful Carla Thompson.
Then he's called away, leaving Carla feeling abandoned.
But Carla goes home with more than memories...and
must return to paradise to find the father of her baby.

*Available the first week of July,
wherever books are sold.*

KIMANI™
ROMANCE

www.kimanipress.com

Forgiveness takes courage...

A MEASURE OF
Faith

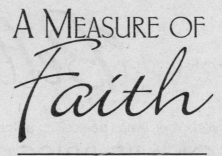

MAXINE BILLINGS

With her loving husband, a beautiful home and two wonderful children, Lynnette Montgomery feels very blessed. But a sudden car accident starts a chain of events that tests her faith, and pulls to the forefront memories of a very painful childhood. At forty years of age, Lynnette comes to see that it takes a measure of faith to help one through the pains of life.

"An enlightening read with an endearing family theme."
—*Romantic Times BOOKreviews*
on *The Breaking Point*

Available the first week of July wherever books are sold.

Celebrating life every step of the way.

YOU ONLY GET *Better*

New York Times bestselling author
CONNIE BRISCOE
and
Essence bestselling authors
LOLITA FILES
ANITA BUNKLEY

Three fortysomething women discover that life, men and
everything else get better with age in this entertaining
three-in-one anthology from three award-winning authors!

Available the first week of March wherever books are sold.

KIMANI PRESS™
www.kimanipress.com KPYOGB0590307